DESPERATE SOLUTION

Lucas shook his head. "I don't know what the hell's happened to Neilson. Maybe he's had a breakdown or something, but we can't count on him anymore. He's become a liability."

"Maybe this is it," said Andre. "Maybe this is what Dr. Darkness meant. Maybe something has happened to Scott and he forgot who he really was and somehow disrupted temporal continuity."

Lucas sat very still, staring at her for a long moment.

"It's possible, isn't it?"

Lucas nodded slowly. "Yes. It's possible. The question is, what are we supposed to do about it?"

"No," said Andre. "That's not the question. The question is, what is it that we're *going* to do—or not do—that we're going to have to do differently to save the future?"

"Jesus," Lucas said. "How the hell are we supposed to know?"

"Darkness said he's going to tell us."

"Yeah. At the last possible moment. Only *why*? Why wait till the last minute?"

"Maybe to make sure that we don't have a chance to think about it," she said. "Lucas . . . it's possible that we may have to kill Scott."

12 TIMEWARS

THE SIX-GUN SOLUTION

SIMON HAWKE

ACE BOOKS, NEW YORK

This book is an Ace original edition,
and has never been previously published.

THE SIX-GUN SOLUTION

An Ace Book / published by arrangement with
the author

PRINTING HISTORY
Ace edition / June 1991

ISBN: 0-441-76851-2

Ace Books are published by The Berkley Publishing Group,
200 Madison Avenue, New York, New York 10016.
The name "ACE" and the "A" logo
are trademarks belonging to Charter Communications, Inc.

PRINTED IN THE UNITED STATES OF AMERICA

10 9 8 7 6 5 4 3 2 1

To all the fans
who have faithfully followed theTime Wars
series through the years, and especially to
those who have written letters of comment,
encouragement and criticism, this, the final
novel in the series, is for you, with gratitude
and fond appreciation.

A CHRONOLOGICAL HISTORY OF THE TIME WARS

April 1, 2425:   Dr. Wolfgang Mensinger invents the chronoplate at the age of 115, discovering time travel. Later, he would construct a small-scale working prototype for use in laboratory experiments specifically designed to avoid any possible creation of a temporal paradox. He is hailed as the "Father of Temporal Physics."

July 14, 2430:   Mensinger publishes "There is No Future," in which he redefines relativity, proving there is no such thing as *the* future, but an infinite number of potential scenarios, which are absolute relative only to their present. He also announces the discovery of "nonspecific time," or temporal limbo, later known as "the dead zone."

October 21, 2440:   Wolfgang Mensinger dies. His son, Albrecht, perfects the chronoplate and carries on the work, but loses control of the discovery to political interests.

June 15, 2460:   Formation of the international Committee for Temporal Intelligence, with Albrecht Mensinger as director. Specially trained and conditioned "agents" of the committee begin to travel back through time in order to conduct research and field test the chronoplate apparatus. Many become lost in transition, trapped in the limbo of nonspecific time known as "the dead zone." Those who return from successful temporal voyages often bring back startling information necessitating the revision of historical records.

March 22, 2461:	*The Consorti Affair*—Cardinal Ludovico Consorti is excommunicated from the Roman Catholic Church for proposing that agents travel back through time to obtain empirical evidence that Christ arose following his crucifixion. The Consorti Affair sparks extensive international negotiations amidst a volatile climate of public opinion concerning the proper uses for the new technology. Temporal excursions are severely curtailed. Concurrently, espionage operatives of several nations infiltrate the Committee for Temporal Intelligence.
May 1, 2461:	Dr. Albrecht Mensinger appears before a special international conference in Geneva, composed of political leaders and members of the scientific community. He attempts to alleviate fears about the possible misuses of time travel. He further refuses to cooperate with any attempts to militarize his father's discovery.
February 3, 2485:	The research facilities of the Committee for Temporal Intelligence are seized by troops of the TransAtlantic Treaty Organization.
January 25, 2492:	The Council of Nations meets in Buenos Aires, capital of the United Socialist States of South America, to discuss increasing international tensions and economic instability. A proposal for "an end to war in our time" is put forth by the chairman of the Nippon Conglomerate Empire. Dr. Albrecht Mensinger, appearing before the body as the nominal director of the Committee for Temporal Intelligence, argues

passionately against using temporal technology to resolve international conflicts, but cannot present proof that the past can be affected by temporal voyagers. Prevailing scientific testimony reinforces the conventional wisdom that the past is an immutable absolute.

December 24, 2492: Formation of the Referee Corps, brought into being by the Council of Nations as an extranational arbitrating body with sole control over temporal technology and authority to stage temporal conflicts as "limited warfare" to resolve international disputes.

April 21, 2493: On the recommendation of the Referee Corps, a subordinate body named the Observer Corps is formed, taking over most of the functions of the Committee for Temporal Intelligence, which is redesignated as the Temporal Intelligence Agency. Under the aegis of the Council of Nations and the Referee Corps, the T.I.A. absorbs the intelligence agencies of the world's governments and is made solely answerable to the Referee Corps. Dr. Mensinger resigns his post to found the Temporal Preservation League, a group dedicated to the abolition of temporal conflict.

June, 2497—
March, 2502: Referee Corps presides over initial temporal confrontation campaigns, accepting "grievances" from disputing nations, selecting historical conflicts of the past as "staging grounds" and supervising the infiltration of modern troops into the so-called "cannon fodder" ranks of ancient warring armies. Initial numbers of temporal combatants are kept small, with infiltration facilitated by cosmetic surgery and implant conditioning of soldiers.

The results are calculated based upon successful return rate and a complicated "point spread." Soldiers are monitored via cerebral implants, enabling Search and Retrieve teams to follow their movements and monitor mortality rate. The media dubs temporal conflicts the "Time Wars."

2500–2510:

Extremely rapid growth of massive support industry catering to the exacting art and science of temporal conflict. Rapid improvement in the international economic climate follows, with significant growth in productivity and rapid decline in unemployment and inflation rate. There is a gradual escalation of the Time Wars, with a majority of the world's armed services converting to temporal duty status.

Growth of the Temporal Preservation League as a peace movement with an intensive lobby effort and mass demonstrations against the Time Wars. Mensinger cautions against an imbalance in temporal continuity due to the increasing activity of the Time Wars.

September 2, 2514:

Mensinger publishes his "Theories of Temporal Relativity," incorporating his solution to the Grandfather Paradox and calling once again for a ceasefire in the Time Wars. The result is an upheaval in the scientific community and a hastily reconvened Council of Nations to discuss his findings, leading to the Temporal Strategic Arms Limitations Talks of 2515.

March 15, 2515—
June 1, 2515:

T-SALT held in New York City. Mensinger appears before the representatives at the sessions and petitions for an end to the Time Wars. A ceasefire resolution is framed, but tabled due to lack of agreement among the members of the Council of Nations. Mensinger leaves the T-SALT a broken man.

November 18, 2516:   Dr. Albrecht Mensinger experiences total nervous collapse shortly after being awarded the Benford Prize.

December 25, 2516:   Dr. Albrecht Mensinger commits suicide. Violent demonstrations by members of the Temporal Preservation League.

January 1, 2517:   Militant members of the Temporal Preservation League band together to form the Timekeepers, a terrorist offshoot of the League, dedicated to the complete destruction of the war machine. They announce their presence to the world by assassinating three members of the Referee Corps and bombing the Council of Nations meeting in Buenos Aires, killing several heads of state and injuring many others.

September 17, 2613:   Formation of the First Division of the U.S. Army Temporal Corps as a crack commando unit following the successful completion of a "temporal adjustment" involving the first serious threat of a timestream split. The First Division, assigned exclusively to deal with threats to temporal continuity, is designated as "the Time Commandos."

October 10, 2615:   Temporal physicist Dr. Robert Darkness disappears without a trace shortly after turning over to the army his new invention, the "warp grenade," a combination time machine and nuclear device. Establishing a secret research installation somewhere off Earth, Darkness experiments with temporal translocation based on the transmutation principle. He experiments upon himself and succeeds in translating his own body into tachyons, but an error in his calculations causes an irreversible change in his subatomic structure, rendering it unstable. Darkness becomes "the man who is faster than light."

November 3, 2620: The chronoplate is superseded by the temporal transponder. Dubbed the "warp disc," the temporal transponder was developed from work begun by Dr. Darkness and it drew on power tapped by Einstein-Rosen Generators (developed by Bell Laboratories in 2545) bridging to neutron stars.

March 15, 2625: *The Temporal Crisis:* The discovery of an alternate universe following an unsuccessful invasion by troops of the Special Operations Group, counterparts of the time commandos. Whether as a result of chronophysical instability caused by clocking tremendous amounts of energy through Einstein-Rosen Bridges or the cumulative effect of temporal disruptions, an alternate universe comes into congruence with our own, causing an instability in the timeflow of both universes and resulting in a "confluence effect," wherein the timestreams of both universes ripple and occasionally intersect, creating "confluence points" where crossover from one universe to another becomes possible.

Massive amounts of energy clocked through Einstein-Rosen Bridges has resulted in unintentional "warp bombardment" of the alternate universe, causing untold destruction. The Time Wars escalate into a temporal war between two universes.

May 13, 2626: Gen. Moses Forrester, director of the Temporal Intelligence Agency (which has absorbed the First Division), becomes aware of a super secret organization within the T.I.A. known as "The Network." Comprised of corrupt T.I.A. section chiefs and renegade deep cover agents, the Network has formed a vast trans-temporal economic empire, entailing extensive involvement in both legitimate businesses and organized crime. Forrester vows to break the Network and becomes a marked man.

PROLOGUE ═══════════

It was said that the town of Tombstone in the Arizona Territory was hell on Earth and Scott Neilson believed it. It was certainly hot enough. He would have welcomed air conditioning, but such conveniences did not exist in 1881. He would have felt more comfortable in a pair of khaki slacks, boat shoes and a polo shirt, but such attire would have made him a decided oddity in the Oriental Saloon.

All around him, men were dressed in high-heeled boots and jeans and long-sleeved, loose cotton shirts in solid colors and prints. Some wore leather or cloth vests. Some even wore overcoats or trail dusters. Most wore kerchiefs and high-crowned Stetsons, while others wore black bowlers. The men in bowlers were more elegantly dressed, in long, black frock coats and pinstripe, stovepipe trousers, white shirts and silk cravats with stickpins, silk vests with gold watch chains dangling from them. Many of them also carried walking sticks. And beneath that, they wore union suits. They had to be sweating like pigs, thought Neilson. He knew he was. None of them openly wore guns, though Neilson knew there were bound to be some Remington derringers and the occasional six-gun concealed here and there.

The law in Tombstone was clear on the subject of firearms. Only officers of the law or men with special permits issued by those officers were allowed to carry guns. On entering Tombstone, one was supposed to check his guns at one of the corrals or leave them in a hotel. The practice of going armed on the streets of Tombstone was definitely frowned on and could result in arrest and a fine of twenty-five dollars. Nevertheless, many people disregarded the law and wore concealed weapons beneath their coats, often tucked into their belts or waistbands. Tombstone, it was said, had a man for breakfast every morning, which was a wry way of saying that there was at least one killing every night.

The town did not exist when prospector Ed Schieffelin arrived in 1877, looking to make a strike. Thirty years old and a seasoned miner, Schieffelin was a wild-looking character with long, dark red hair and a matted beard, his clothing patched with animal skin. The country he had come to prospect was desolate and ruled by the Apaches. After he arrived at the Army post at Camp Huachuca, he did some prospecting in the area and then accompanied an Army detachment as a scout through the Sonoita Valley and the Patagonia Mountains, near the Mexican border, then back along the San Pedro River. Upon returning, he announced his intention to go back and do some prospecting in the area. He had taken a fancy to the hills he saw along the San Pedro.

"All you'll find out there is your tombstone," he was told. "The Apaches will see to that."

Nevertheless, Schieffelin went and made a silver strike that was the richest in the territory. Remembering the warning he'd been given, he showed his sense of humor by naming his claims Tombstone and Graveyard. News of the strike soon had settlers flocking to the area and the town that grew up on Goose Flats also came to bear the name of Tombstone, as did the hills around it. It soon became the largest mining boomtown in the country, rivaled only by Colorado's Leadville, nestled in a Rocky Mountain valley at an elevation of ten thousand feet. At least it was cool up there, Neilson thought, wistfully.

He had arrived in Tombstone early that afternoon and checked into the Grand Hotel. He had come in by stage from Benson, which was as far as the Southern Pacific railroad went. However, he had not arrived in Benson on the train. He had used a considerably more advanced form of transportation and he had come a long, long way. Over eight hundred years, in fact. He had made the trip in the blink of an eye, using his warp disc, which he wore camouflaged as a heavy silver Indian bracelet on his left wrist. The large, blue-green turquoise stone was actually a cleverly hinged cover, hiding the chronocircuitry controls.

Sergeant Scott Neilson was a temporal agent, a soldier in the First Division of the United States Army Temporal Corps, an elite commando unit tasked to adjust temporal disruptions. With the advent of the Temporal Crisis, the First Division had been merged with the Temporal Intelligence Agency under the directorship of Brigadier General Moses Forrester, commander of the First Division. Neilson had come to Tombstone to investigate a situation involving Observer Outpost G-6898. The three Temporal Observers assigned to this sector had failed to make their last two scheduled reports.

Given the hazardous nature of their duty, any of a number of things could have happened to them. The Arizona Territory could be highly dangerous. If something had happened to them as a result of the normal dangers of this time sector, Neilson's job was to ascertain precisely what it was and arrange for their replacement. But if something had happened to them that was *not* a result of the normal hazards of this period, it could mean serious trouble. It could mean an infiltration by soldiers of the Special Operations Group, the undercover commando strike force from the parallel universe. And Tombstone could become another battlefield in the Time Wars.

Neilson had been selected for this assignment for a number of reasons. One was that he had already proven himself on a significant temporal adjustment mission in 19th-century London, when the insane, crosstime terrorist named Nikolai Drakov had brought about a temporal disruption by using his genetic engineering skills to release a plague of vampires and werewolves upon the unsuspecting city. That mission had been one of the most complex and dangerous assignments the T.I.A. had ever faced and Drakov was their most dangerous antagonist. Half of the adjustment team in that assignment had been killed. Neilson had been one of the survivors, which had netted him both a promotion and a decoration. Another reason he was chosen was that his file showed him to be a student of the frontier era, as well as a collector of antique firearms and an expert in their use.

He had grown up in Tucson, Arizona, though the Tucson of the 27th century was a far cry from the town of Tombstone in the 1800s. In his own time, Tucson was a sprawling, multileveled metropolis with skyscrapers over a hundred stories tall. Yet even so, many of its residents still clung fondly to the tradition of its wild West beginnings and even in the 27th century, some of them still wore western boots and Stetsons. Neilson's father had been a university history professor whose hobby was studying the Old West. Over the years, at considerable expense and time involving extensive computer searches of collector lists and estate auctions, he had accumulated a collection of antique western firearms that was worth a fortune. It included old black powder pistols such as Patterson, Walker and Navy Colts, Remingtons and Colt Single Action Armys, Winchester carbines and shotguns and Sharps buffalo rifles. Most of these weapons were in poor condition and would have been dangerous to fire. Shooting them would also have diminished their collector value. However, Scott's father had also obtained a number of late-20th-century reproductions and he had a number of them duplicated by skilled Japanese artisans so that they were identical to the authentic western guns down to the last detail. And those could be safely fired.

Ammunition for them was, of course, no longer available and had to be made from scratch. It had been necessary to make the brass cases and melt the lead to be poured into antique bullet molds. Lead projectile weapons had not been in general use for several hundred years and the smokeless powder for them that had been used in the 20th and 21st centuries was no longer commercially available. It had been necessary to duplicate the old black powder of the frontier era, but this was more easily accomplished and had appealed to Scott's purist father. The most difficult thing about the process had been manufacturing the primers, but Scott's father had been determined to pursue authenticity at all costs.

The result was that, as a child, Scott had learned to shoot just like the gunfighters of the Old West had and, since the weapons were hopelessly outdated reproductions, they had not required special permits to own. His natural hand-eye coordination was excellent to begin with and by the time he was in his late teens, Scott had become an astonishingly proficient marksman. He had picked up an interest in the Old West from his father at a very early age and, in addition to becoming an expert in its history, incessant practice in trick shooting had given him an almost supernatural level of skill. His fast draw had been clocked at 25/100 of a second and he had mastered the technique of "point shooting" (firing from the hip without using the sights) to such a degree that he could split cards edgeways at ten paces. It had pleased his father, and Scott had gotten a great deal of enjoyment out of it. However, he had always believed it was a completely useless skill . . . until he enlisted in the Temporal Corps.

Now, at the age of twenty-five, Neilson's skill had already saved his life and the lives of fellow agents on several occasions during missions to the past. Life as a temporal agent was hazardous in the extreme and the mortality rate was very high, but for Neilson, as for most other temporal agents, the adventure was well worth the risk. It was a chance to literally see history in the making. And, at the same time, to preserve it from disruption. Added to that, one of Neilson's great joys on becoming a temporal agent was the opportunity to augment his collection.

It was, of course, illegal to bring anything back from the past, but General Forrester had a tendency to wink at the practice and look the other way. Forrester, himself, possessed perhaps the most priceless collection of artifacts in the entire world, many of them presented to him by the people under his command as they returned from missions to the past. It was considered a singular honor to obtain something worthy of being included in the Old Man's collection, which he kept housed in a room behind a hidden panel in his quarters at TAC-HQ. Among his prized collection were the sword of El Cid, a .45 Colt semiautomatic that had once belonged to General Patton, the mask of Zorro, the helm of Ghengis Khan, and the original manuscript of *20,000 Leagues Under the Sea*—the actual original, not the one which the author had painstakingly copied by hand and submitted to the publisher. This one, unknown to history, had been specially inscribed by the author himself—"To my very dear friend, Moses Forrester, who allowed me to glimpse the wonders of the future. With undying gratitude, Jules Verne."

Scott Neilson's own collection was nothing compared to that. He had inherited the collection of his father, which he kept stored in a vault, yet he delighted in adding to it at a cost to him that was a mere fraction of what his father had paid for the pieces he acquired. And the weapons Scott obtained in Minus Time were in spanking new condition.

The first thing he had done on his arrival in Benson was to

outfit himself with a brand-new Colt Single Action Army in .45 caliber, nickel-plated, with a four-and-three-quarter-inch barrel and gutta-percha grips. He paid a total of thirty dollars. In his own time, even in condition that was less than pristine, the pistol would be worth several thousand times that sum, even after it had been fired. Unfired, it would have been nearly priceless. However, on this assignment, Neilson knew that he could easily find himself in a situation where he would have to fire the piece, so he had purchased several boxes of cartridges and gone outside the town limits, to fire his new weapon and see how close the bullets struck to point of aim. The pistol's sights were fixed and not adjustable, meaning that there was only a front sight blade on the end of the barrel and a groove along the top, but it shot close enough to point of aim to satisfy him. Within twenty-five rounds, he was capable of hip-shooting it with unerring accuracy.

He had also purchased a Winchester carbine and a floral-carved holster for his Colt, made by the Lawrence Company, along with a money belt that was looped for cartridges. Other supplies, such as a horse and saddle, he could either purchase or rent in Tombstone. He had arrived already suitably attired for the time period in black, pinstripe trousers; high-heeled boots; a dark green calico shirt, a black cloth vest with a silk back; a black frock coat and a black, flat-crowned Stetson. His light blond hair was long, down to his shoulders, and he was clean-shaven, largely because he'd never been able to grow a decent beard or moustache. With the antiagathic drugs used in the 27th century, he would retain his youthful appearance long past the normal human lifespan and in this time period, at the age of twenty-five, he looked no more than seventeen.

It was common practice for temporal agents to go unshaven and not to get their hair cut unless it was demanded by a mission, in case long hair or a beard proved a requirement for an assignment in the past. If necessary, wigs could be woven into their own hair, and beards cosmetically applied in such a manner that they could only be removed with special solvents. However, such procedures were uncomfortable and, if possible, agents liked to rely on their own hair. This unofficially sanctioned practice was initially frowned upon by many senior officers in the regular Corps. Shaggy hair and stubble looked decidedly unmilitary in the 27th century, but Forrester had made it clear that any officer harrassing the people under his command would have to contend with him, personally. That quickly brought an end to questions regarding hirsute temporal agents.

Before he left the 27th century, Neilson had gone in for mission programming, which entailed a computer download via the biochip implanted in his cerebral cortex. The program data was designed to give him all the knowledge he would need to function in this time sector, but for Neilson, most of it was redundant. This time sector, in particular, had long held a fascination for him. One of the most famous incidents in the history of the frontier would soon occur right here in Tombstone. And events which would lead up to it had already begun by the time Neilson arrived.

His assignment would probably be brief. He figured it would take a day or two, perhaps a week, at most, if he could not immediately locate the Observers or ascertain what happened to them. At any rate, he would no longer be in Tombstone by the time October 26th rolled around, which was a bitter disappointment to him. He would not have the opportunity to witness the gunfight at the O.K. Corral. However, while he was in Tombstone, there was a good chance that he would see some of the participants and the thought filled him with an almost childish excitement.

He had a job to do and he could not afford to waste any time in doing it, but he fervently hoped that he'd be able to go back to the 27th century and tell his friends that he shook hands with Wyatt Earp.

The Oriental Saloon was a place that Wyatt Earp was known to frequent. He had a financial interest in the saloon and did a lot of gambling here. As Neilson walked in through the doors, he could barely restrain a gleeful grin. It was all just as he'd imagined it would be. A raucous place, with a high ceiling and an ornate, mirrored bar valued at over one hundred thousand dollars. There were, of course, no stools in front of the bar. One stood. There were tables to sit down at and, at many of these, men were playing cards. The room was filled with smoke and the smells of sweat and kerosene. An upright piano was being played in one corner. He looked around the room and received not a few curious glances in return. He walked over to the bar.

The bartender, in a white shirt, vest, and bow tie, with short, neatly combed dark hair, a handlebar moustache and large, striking eyes, came over and wiped down the bar in front of him.

"Howdy, stranger," he said. "What'll it be?"

Neilson immediately recognized him from old photographs he'd seen in countless books on western history. It was none other than Buckskin Frank Leslie, the famous scout and buffalo hunter, a man who often entertained himself by shooting flies off the ceiling and the occasional cigar out of someone's mouth. A good friend of Wyatt Earp's.

"Whiskey," Neilson said.

"Comin' right up," Leslie replied, setting a glass in front of him. "New in town?" he asked, as he poured.

"Yep," said Neilson, paying for his drink.

Leslie was sizing him up. "Where you hail from, son?"

"Montana," he replied, taking a drink. He knew that a lot of these characters had drifted all over the west, from Dodge City to San Francisco, but the Montana Territory was still fairly wild and sparsely populated. There wasn't much happening in Montana yet except for cattle ranching and farming in the western part of the territory, along the Bitterroot. And Indian trouble. Especially Indian trouble.

"Is that right?" said Leslie, with some surprise. "Montana Territory, eh? Where ole George Custer met his Maker?"

"Yep."

"Ever meet 'im?"

"Nope. Heard all about him, though."

"He was one hell of a man," said Leslie.

"One hell of a stupid man, if you ask me," said Neilson.

Leslie raised his eyebrows. "How old are you, son?"

"Old enough," said Neilson.

Leslie grinned as he wiped out a glass, amused by the arrogance of youth. "What brings you to Tombstone?"

Neilson shrugged. "Heard some friends of mine might be here, prospectin'."

"That right? What are their names? Could be I know 'em."

"Ben Summers, Josh Billings and Joe McEnery."

Leslie's grin faded. "Hell, I know 'em, all right. Or knew 'em, I should say. I'm right sorry to tell you, son, they're dead. All three of 'em."

Neilson put down his glass and stared at him. It was what he'd feared. Only how did they die?

Before he could ask Leslie, shouting broke out behind him and he heard a chair crash to the floor.

"You goddamn, cheatin', tinhorn, son of a bitch!"

Neilson turned around. Out of the corner of his eye, he saw Leslie's hand go down below the bar.

"Step aside, son," Leslie said, softly, his eyes on the table where the altercation was taking place.

There were five men seated at the table. One of them, a cowboy, had jumped up, sending his chair crashing to the floor. He had pulled a six-gun from beneath his coat and cocked it. The others were still sitting at the table, staring at him nervously. All except one man, who sat very still with his hands flat on the table.

He had his back to Neilson, but he was dressed like a gambler, in a dark, dandy's suit. The cowboy with his gun out was standing at a right angle to Neilson, his left side toward him, about a dozen feet away. Neilson quietly stepped aside, knowing that Leslie had a gun beneath the bar. The entire room became suddenly, completely silent.

"Come on now, take it easy, Slim," said one of the other men at the table.

"That damn deck's marked!" the cowboy named Slim furiously accused the man with his back to Neilson.

"I can assure you, sir, that it is not," the gambler replied, in a calm and steady voice. "You are welcome to examine it. Any man here is welcome to examine it. I won that hand fair and square."

"You lyin' bastard, you did not! You pulled some cheap, tinhorn trick!"

Men were quickly edging away from the vicinity of the table. Leslie waited until his field of fire was clear, then pulled a sawed-off shotgun from beneath the bar.

"Put up that pistol, friend, *right now*," said Leslie.

Neilson suddenly heard the ominous sound of a revolver being cocked.

"I don't believe he will, barkeep," another cowboy at the far end of the bar said. He had a gun aimed right at Leslie. "Now you put down that scattergun. Just rest it on the bar there, nice and easy, and step away."

Leslie hesitated for a second. "You don't want to do this, friend."

"You shut your damn mouth and do as I said!"

Leslie complied.

Slim turned toward the bar, moving so that he could clearly see both the gambler and Leslie. "You tell him, Jack! We'll show these cheatin' sons of bitches! That pot is mine by rights!"

Nobody moved.

"You, boy," said the man named Jack, talking to Neilson. He came around the end of the bar slowly. He aimed his gun at Neilson.

"Leave him out of this," said Leslie.

"I said, shut your damn mouth! Boy, take that scattergun and slide it down the bar to me, real careful like."

"Everybody just stay right where you are," said Slim, "and keep your hands where I can see 'em."

"Be smart, cowboy," said the gambler, sitting perfectly still. "You shoot anyone in here and you'll never make it out of town."

"Yeah? Well, you won't be around to find out, one way or the other."

Neilson hadn't moved. The situation was getting ugly and he didn't want to chance being shot by a stray bullet. His mission was too important. Not to mention his life. If he slid that shotgun down the bar, Jack would have a better weapon with which to cover their escape after Slim had shot the gambler. And God only knew who else.

"*You, boy!*" shouted Jack. "You tired of livin'? I said, slide that scatter gun down here!"

"Leave him alone," said Leslie. "He's just a kid."

"You opened your damn mouth once too often!" Jack responded, moving his gun to fire at Leslie. And in that moment, Neilson moved.

His hand snaked down inside his coat as he drew and cocked the pistol in one smooth motion and fired at Jack, hitting him in the chest. Without pausing, he recocked the Colt as it rolled with the recoil, brought his arm around and fired at Slim, dropping him before Jack even hit the floor. It happened so fast that no one had a chance to react.

There was a moment's stunned silence, then somebody exclaimed, "Jesus, Mary and Joseph! Did you *see* that?"

"By God, I ain't *never* seen anyone that fast!"

The saloon erupted into activity as Neilson stood there, still holding his smoking gun. Great, he thought. *Now* what do I do?

"Right through the heart!" said someone, bending over Slim. "Dead center!"

"I'll be hog-tied!" said someone else, examining Jack's body. "This one, too!"

"Hold it right there!" said a steely voice, cutting through the commotion. "Put down that pistol, kid, or I'll shoot you where you stand!"

Fuck, thought Neilson, unable to see the speaker behind him. Whoever he was, he had the drop on him. He released his grip on the Colt, allowing it to dangle from his index finger in the trigger guard, then slowly brought it down on the bar and raised his hands.

"It's all right, Virgil," Leslie said. "The kid's okay. He just stopped some killin'."

"Appears to me like he just did some killin'," said the tall, strapping man with the dark, reddish blond hair and bushy moustache who came around from behind Neilson. He was dressed in a dark suit, with a badge pinned to his vest. Virgil, thought Neilson. He recognized him from photographs he'd seen. It was Virgil Earp, eldest of the three "fighting Earp" brothers.

"It was killin' that needed to be done," Leslie replied. "The kid did the right thing."

"I'll say he did," said the gambler, getting up from the table. "The kid just saved my bacon."

"Is that so?" said Virgil. "What happened?"

Neilson stared as the good-looking gambler with the neatly trimmed black moustache came toward him.

"Cowboy over there called me a cheat and threw down on me. The other one got the drop on Frank. And me without my guns."

"Those boys meant business, Virgil," Leslie added. "I would have been shot dead, if it wasn't for this here Montana kid."

"I owe you a debt of gratitude," the gambler said. "I'd like to shake your hand and stand you to a drink. The name's Bat Masterson."

Feeling rather numb, Neilson shook his hand.

"What's your name, Montana kid?" asked Virgil.

"Neilson," Scott replied instinctively, not thinking to give an alias. "Scott Neilson."

"I like Montana Kid," said Masterson, with an easy, charming smile. "Drinks all around, Frank. And a bottle for me and the Kid, here. Virgil, you'll join us, won't you?"

Virgil Earp looked Neilson over. "Well, if Frank and Bat vouch it was a necessary shooting, then I guess that's okay with me. But I'll need to take your gun, Kid, just the same. Those boys were part of Clanton's bunch. Mean customers. You're lucky you came out of it okay."

"Hell, luck had nothin' to do with it," said Leslie, pouring the drinks. "You should've seen it, Virgil. The Kid's greased lightnin' with a gun."

"You don't say," said Virgil.

"Shot 'em both right through the heart, dead center!" said one of the other men around them. "Fastest draw I ever seen in all my born days! If you'd a blinked your eye, you would've missed it!"

The others in the bar quickly agreed with this assessment.

"Sounds right impressive," Virgil said.

"Impressive doesn't do it justice," responded Leslie.

"Is he really that fast, Frank?" Virgil said, with some surprise, apparently expecting exaggeration from the others, but not from Frank Leslie.

"I wouldn't have a prayer against him, that's for damn sure," Leslie said. "And here I thought he was some green kid, fresh off the wagon. Shoot! I'll bet he could beat Wyatt."

"Faster than Wyatt?" said Virgil, raising his eyebrows.

"God's my witness," Leslie replied. "You put him up against Wild Bill, I'd give you even money and it would be a coin toss."

"Hell, Frank, I never heard of anyone as fast as Hickok," Virgil said.

"You're lookin' right at him," Leslie replied, flatly.

"Was he really that fast, Bat?" Virgil asked.

"Well, to tell you the truth, I didn't see it," Masterson replied, "but I heard both shots come so close together, I would have sworn they had been fired from different guns."

Virgil looked at Neilson with new respect. "Where did you learn to shoot like that, Kid?"

Neilson was still slightly overwhelmed. His hesitance and

confusion were taken as modest embarrassment. He simply shrugged and said, "Practice."

The bodies were still lying on the floor. No one made a move to do anything about them. The doors swung open and two more men came in, both with pistols drawn. One man was tall and slim, with dark blond hair and blue eyes. He had a flowing handlebar moustache that curled up at the ends and, like Virgil, he was dressed in a black suit. He also wore a badge. The family resemblance was strong and unmistakable. The other man was pale, thin and slightly built, perhaps a hundred and twenty pounds, with sandy hair, sharp features, a moustache and intense, slate-gray, spectral-looking eyes.

"Heard there was some shootin', Virgil."

"And right fancy shootin', from what I hear," Virgil replied. "It appears that this young gentleman has saved the lives of Frank and Bat. What's more, they claim he could be even faster than you are. Come on over and say hello to the Montana Kid, just arrived in town. Kid, meet my brother, Wyatt. And the gent with him is Doc Holliday."

The two men put away their pistols and Scott was speechless as he shook their hands.

"I'm much obliged to you for coming to the aid of my good friends," said Wyatt.

"Just arrived in town, eh?" Holliday said. He coughed and glanced at the bodies. "Kid, I'll grant you one thing. You sure do make one hell of an entrance."

They took a bottle and moved to a table.

Wyatt glanced down at the corpses. "Jack Demming and Slim Carter," he said, with a grunt. "Well, that's two less rustlers we need to be concerned with. But I'd watch my back from now on if I were you, Kid. The Clanton bunch won't take too kindly to the service you just performed for this community. You plannin' on stayin' in town?"

"He was askin' after some friends of his," said Frank Leslie. "Summers, Billings and McEnery."

Wyatt frowned. "You told him?"

"I started to," said Frank, "and then things got a little hot around here."

"He told me they were dead," said Scott. "What happened to them?"

"Kin of yours?" asked Wyatt.

"No, just good friends. We all grew up together."

"It's too bad about what happened," Wyatt said, sympathetically. "They were good men, thought highly of around here. They were murdered out at their claim."

"Funny thing, though," Doc said. "I never saw bullet wounds that looked quite like that before. No blood to speak of. Had to be small caliber, one of those little Colt New Line pocket pistols. Whoever shot 'em got up real close. You could see the burn marks on the clothing and even on the wounds."

"We thought at first it might've been the rustlers," Virgil said. "They're not above shootin' down a man that's got a roll. But I don't know of any rustlers armed with pocket pistols. They would have used their rifles or their .45s. A pocket pistol is a gambler's weapon. Not much use 'cept at close range. Only there was no sign of them playing cards out there. We thought it could have been some claim jumpers, but then nobody's been workin' their claim. It's a riddle, all right. We get a lot of strangers comin' through town and, sad to say, those kind of things tend to happen around here. Unless somebody talks, we may never know who killed 'em."

Scott was thinking about what Doc had said. He'd never seen bullet wounds like that before. Small wounds. Burn marks. No blood to speak of. To Doc and the others, it may have looked like the sort of wounds a small-caliber pocket pistol like the Colt New Line could inflict. To Scott, it sounded ominously like a laser.

"They were decent men," said Wyatt. "Never gave anybody any trouble. We gave 'em a proper Christian burial."

"What about their personal effects?" asked Scott.

"Sold 'em off," said Frank. "There really wasn't very much. Their rig and horses, saddles, Winchesters and six-guns . . . most everything got cleaned out by the killers. Don't think those boys were pullin' much out of that claim, anyhow, unless they had it stashed. They were right decent enough fellows, but they don't seem to have worked too hard."

"Were there any bracelets?" Scott asked. "Indian bracelets, like the one I've got?" He held up his arm and pulled back his sleeve to show them. "They're not really worth much, but we all had 'em. They'd have sentimental value to me."

"Come to think of it, I do recall those bracelets," Leslie said. "I tried to buy one off 'em once, but none of 'em would sell. They said the same thing, that the bracelets had sentimental value. They all got 'em together somewhere."

"I don't recall any Indian bracelets among their personal effects," Virgil said. "Do you, Wyatt?"

"Nope, I don't believe I do. The killers must've stolen 'em, along with any money they had. They have any kin?"

"Yeah," said Scott. "I'll have to write to 'em. I'd like to take a look at where it happened, if that's all right with you."

"Sure thing," said Virgil. "But I wouldn't plan on goin' out there tonight. I'd wait till mornin' if I was you."

"I'll rent a rig and run you out tomorrow," said Masterson.

"Thanks. I appreciate that."

"It's the least I can do, after you saved my life."

"What are your plans, Kid?" asked Wyatt.

"I don't know," said Scott. "I'd like to find out what happened to my friends, if I can. Ask around, see what I can learn."

"We've already done that," Virgil said. "You're welcome to ask around, so long as all you do is ask. I don't want any more gunplay in this town, Kid. We've got plenty enough as it is."

"I don't want any trouble," Scott replied.

"The way you handle a gun, it's liable to find you just the same," said Leslie.

"What did you do up in the Montana Territory, Kid?" asked Virgil.

"My folks were farmers in the Bitterroot," said Neilson.

"You don't have the look of a farmer," Virgil replied.

"It didn't suit me, so I left."

"You wear your hair like a plainsman," said Wyatt. "Do much buffalo hunting?"

Scott knew that Wyatt Earp had been a buffalo hunter in his youth, along with Bat Masterson. In fact, much of Masterson's early reputation stemmed from a harrowing Indian attack known as the Battle of Adobe Walls, where a handful of buffalo hunters had stood off about two hundred Indians with their six-guns and Sharps rifles. His fame from that encounter had led to his becoming a lawman in Dodge.

"I hunted some," he answered.

"How do you skin a buffalo?" asked Wyatt, softly.

Scott knew what this was all about and he had to handle it just right. Fortunately, he knew the answer, but he made a long pause before giving it, staring Wyatt Earp right in the eyes. Wyatt met his gaze steadily.

"You cut up the insides of the legs and down the belly, then around the head," said Scott. "Then you tie a rope up to the hide and hitch it on a horse. It peels right back. Only that's work for skinners, not for hunters."

Masterson nodded.

"So he hunted buffalo," said Holliday. "Still doesn't mean he's not a gunfighter. 'Specially if he's as fast as Frank says."

"Practice your fast draw on the farm, did you?" Wyatt asked, softly. Virgil simply looked on quietly, watching him carefully.

"Like I said, Marshal," Scott replied, in a steady voice. "I don't want any trouble. I didn't start what happened here tonight."

"Nobody's sayin' that you did, Kid," Masterson said, quickly. "But like Wyatt said, you wear your hair like a plainsman. Only you dress like a gunfighter. And you damn well shoot like one."

"I hear tell you're a fair hand with a gun yourself," said Scott.

"It's been said," Masterson replied. "A man's reputation gets around. Only you see, none of us have ever heard of you before. Someone shoots the way you do, you'd think there'd be some talk. The reason for all the questions is that Wyatt here tends to be the careful type. Virgil, too. It's their job to keep the law in Tombstone and, as you've seen, it can be quite a job."

"Like I said, I don't want any trouble," Neilson replied. "And you've got my gun."

"We've got stores in town that sell 'em," Wyatt said. "There's no law keeps you from buyin' another one. Just don't let me catch you wearin' it in town."

"What about Mr. Holliday?" asked Scott. "I don't see a badge on him."

"Doc's got special permission," Wyatt said.

"I see," said Scott. "So the idea here is the law-abiding citizen is disarmed, but the outlaw carries a gun, is that it? You'd think it should be the other way around."

"The outlaw is not permitted to carry a gun, either," Wyatt said.

"Yeah, but if he's an outlaw, he'll do it anyway, won't he?"

"Only if I don't catch him at it," Wyatt replied, severely.

"Tell me something, Marshal," Scott said, "do you generally catch him before or after he shoots somebody?"

"Before, if I can manage it," said Wyatt, giving Scott a hard stare.

"And if you can't manage it, I guess that's hard luck for the fellow he just shot." They were pushing him a bit to see how he would handle it. If he didn't push back slightly, they'd be suspicious, but he had to be careful not to push back too hard.

"If you don't care for the law in Tombstone, Kid, you're free to move on," said Virgil, in a neutral tone.

"Oh, now that I've been informed of the law, Mr. Earp, I'll abide by it," said Scott. "But I guess it's a lucky thing for your two friends that I wasn't informed of it before." He pushed back his chair and stood. "Meet you right here in the morning, Mr. Masterson?"

"Right here's fine with me. About eight o'clock suit you?"

"Eight o'clock suits me fine." He touched the brim of his hat. "Gentlemen . . ."

They watched him as he left.

"He asked a bunch of questions," Wyatt said, "but he didn't answer many. The Montana Kid, eh? I've never heard of him before."

"Oh, well, that was just a little joke of mine," said Masterson, with a smile. "Frank called him 'this here Montana kid' and I just sort of stuck it on him. His real name's Scott Nelson."

"Neilson, I think he said," said Virgil.

"Nelson, Neilson, I never heard of either one of 'em, " said Wyatt. "But that kid's a gunfighter, that's for certain. Jack and Slim were sure as hell no greenhorns when it came to shootin'. And he got 'em both right through the heart."

"The Kid also saved my life," said Masterson. "And Frank's. He could have simply stood there and stayed well out of it. He didn't have to chance it."

"Only he did chance it," Wyatt said. "And the result was that he killed two men in a fair fight. By tomorrow, everyone in Tombstone will be talkin' about the Montana Kid. And by next week, they'll be sayin' that he killed three men. And then four. And then half a dozen. Before long, we'll have a man in town who's got himself a reputation as a killer."

"Isn't that how you got yours, Wyatt?" Masterson said, with a smile.

"Maybe, only I'm wearing a badge."

"Perhaps you should pin one on the Kid," said Masterson.

"A shootist like that would be handy to have on your side. Especially since Ike Clanton's already got Sheriff Johnny Behan on his."

"I don't need any help against the likes of Ike Clanton," Wyatt said, drawing on his cigar. Unlike the others, he didn't drink.

"Maybe not now," Masterson replied, "but Johnny Behan's had it in for you ever since you took his girl. He's close to Clanton and so are his deputies. You've got a lot of badges in this town, only not all of them seem to be on the same side. That could develop into a sticky situation."

"You sayin' the Kid could side with Clanton and his bunch?"

"Oh, I doubt that very much," Masterson replied. "Not after he dropped two of them."

Wyatt grunted. "I can't say I think much of the men you choose to gamble with, Bat."

Masterson shrugged slightly. "I didn't know them. You know I haven't been in Tombstone that long, Wyatt. I had no idea they were part of Clanton's bunch. And their money was as good as anybody else's."

"You take much of it?"

Masterson smiled and, with a deft motion, produced a card from up his sleeve. It was an ace of spades. "What do you think?"

1 ⎯⎯⎯⎯⎯⎯⎯⎯⎯⎯⎯⎯⎯⎯⎯⎯⎯⎯

"The Montana Kid, you say?"

The man who was speaking was a striking individual. He was wearing an elegant dark suit with a red brocade vest and an expensive watch and chain. He had a large diamond on his finger, as well as in his stickpin. But it was not his attire that was the most striking thing about him. It was his size and his appearance. He was a large, powerfully built man, incredibly muscular, with arms and a chest that strained the fabric of his clothes. People stared at him with awe when he walked down the street. His thick hair was jet black and curly, giving him a romantic, Byronic aspect, and his handsome features were marred by a knife scar that ran down the side of his face from below his left eye to the corner of his mouth. His voice was deep and resonant and his mouth was cruel, but his eyes were his most striking feature. They were a bright, lambent green, with a gaze so intense it was unsettling.

The pretty young saloon girl standing before him had a hard time meeting his gaze. Not just because of the force of his personality, but because he was her creator.

"It was what the others called him," she said. "I don't know what his real name is. If he gave it, I didn't hear."

"And you say his speed with a gun was almost superhuman?"

"I've never seen anything like it," she replied. "I've seen

Wyatt Earp's draw and even he isn't that fast. He fired off two shots in a fraction of a second, without even aiming, and he hit both men in the heart."

"Interesting," said Nikolai Drakov, with a smile.

"You think he's one of them? The agents from the future?"

"There was a young man whose path I once crossed in London," Drakov said. "He was part of the support team working with Delaney, Cross and Steiger. And he was unusually skillful with lead projectile firearms."

"What was his name?" the girl asked. "What did he look like?"

"We never actually met face to face," Drakov replied. "But his name was Neilson. Scott Neilson."

The girl shook her head. "I don't know," she said. "He looks very young. Just a boy, perhaps sixteen or seventeen—"

"Appearances could be deceptive if he's from the future," Drakov said. "With the antiagathic drugs, he could be anywhere from sixteen or seventeen to twenty-five or thirty. What else can you tell me about him?"

"He has light blond hair. He wears it long, like a plainsman. But he has the look of a gunfighter. Dark suit, vest, green calico shirt, black Stetson . . ."

"How does he wear his gun?"

"In a crossdraw holster on his left side."

"A Colt?"

"Yes, nickel-plated, with a short barrel."

"Good for a fast draw. What about jewelry? Was he wearing any jewelry? A bracelet of some sort, perhaps?"

"Yes. Yes, he did have a bracelet. I saw it briefly. It was one of those silver Indian bracelets, with a large turquoise stone."

"Like these?" asked Drakov, opening a drawer in the end table. There were three matching Indian bracelets inside it. He took one out and held it up so she could see it.

"Yes, exactly like that," she said.

Drakov smiled. "You didn't hear what he and the others, the Earps and Masterson, spoke about?"

She shook her head. "I'm sorry. They were all sitting together at a table and I didn't want to seem as if I was trying to eavesdrop. And it was noisy in the saloon and—"

"That's all right," said Drakov. "You've done well, Jennifer. I want you to cultivate his acquaintance. It would be perfectly logical for you to do so. You saw what happened, you're fascinated by him, you want to get to know him. Find out his real name. Find out anything you can. But try not to arouse his suspicion. Be friendly and curious, but not too curious. Don't push it."

"I'll do what I can."

"Yes, I'm sure you will. Did you find out where he was staying?"

"In the Grand Hotel."

Drakov nodded. "Keep an eye on him. I want to know everything he does." He smiled. "Things are starting to get interesting. The players are almost all assembled."

He toyed with the Indian bracelet and opened the hinged cover, revealing the chronocircuitry controls of the warp disc.

"We will move slowly, and with great care," he said. "I will not underestimate them this time. It should prove to be an interesting little drama. Imagine, the Network, the S.O.G., the Temporal Underground and the T.I.A., all gathered in one place, at one strategic time. It will be like playing chess against a roomful of opponents, simultaneously. Only they'll be playing against each other, little realizing that I control the board."

He snapped shut the cover on the warp disc.

"And so the game begins," he said, softly.

The one-horse rig Masterson had rented pulled up in front of the cabin in the Tombstone Hills. It looked abandoned. It was a small, primitive adobe structure with a dirt floor, similar to many dwellings in the area. It couldn't really be called a house. Building lumber had to be hauled in from the Huachucas and the only local wood was mesquite, of which a quantity had been chopped and piled up outside the cabin. It gave off a pleasant aroma when burned. The Observers had a well dug and there was a makeshift shed about twenty feet away, with a crude corral beside it.

"Well, this is it," said Masterson, as he reigned in.

Neilson looked at the place. There was something rather sad about it. It would have been cramped quarters for three men, but this was how a lot of people lived in this time, in this part of the country. They came out from the Eastern cities, or from farms and ranches in the Midwest, or from cities on the coast like San Francisco, chasing the dream of making a rich strike.

A few of them, like Ed Schieffelin, got lucky. Most didn't. But still, they kept on coming.

This was how it all started, Neilson thought. One man came out to this barren desert territory, populated only by Apaches, scorpions and lizards, struck silver and, as word got out, the boom began. Tombstone grew up on Goose Flats, at first nothing but tents and adobe cabins and a few buildings made of lumber that had to be brought in, then saloons and fancy hotels, the railroad coming in to Benson, stage lines connecting the town to nearby points. Arizona was still a wild territory, its raucous towns peopled by miners and gamblers and cowboys coming through with their herds, "hurrahing" the town with their six-shooters after months on the trail and blowing all their money on cheap whiskey, dance hall girls and at the faro tables. The wild West as it really was, a brief, colorful period of American history, one that shaped the nation's character for years to come.

The men that achieved fame in this period seemed bigger than life. They were men like Wild Bill Hickok, with his brace of Navy Colts tucked butt forward into his belt, and Buffalo Bill Cody, the scout and buffalo hunter who would do more than perhaps any other man to give birth to the legend of the frontier with his traveling Wild West Show. Men like Clay Allison, the rowdy gunfighter and rancher who would contribute the word "shootist" to the language and who once, for lack of anything better to do, hurrahed a town by riding through it stark naked. Men like John Wesley Hardin, one of the fastest guns who ever lived, an outlaw who eventually became a lawyer, and Billy the Kid, whom legend was to paint as a misunderstood, romantic young hero but who was, in fact, a mean spirited psychotic. And here in Tombstone were men such as John Henry "Doc" Holliday, the frail, tubercular dentist from Georgia who, as Bat Masterson would write, was ". . . a weakling who could not have whipped a healthy 15-year-old boy in a go-as-you-please fist fight, and no one knew this better than himself, and the knowledge of this fact was perhaps why he was ready to resort to a weapon of some kind whenever he got himself into difficulty." And his skill with those weapons made him feared throughout the West.

Then there was Masterson himself, the gambler and lawman who shot his six-guns from a crossed wrist position and had been credited with killing thirty-seven men, and Wyatt Earp and his brothers, who within a few short months would stride into frontier legend in their famous shoot-out with the Clantons. Yet, for all those larger-than-life, colorful figures, the real men who had built the West were men who lived like this, in small shacks and adobe dwellings, scratching a livelihood out of the dirt and aging quickly in the merciless desert sun.

The blow dust got into their lungs, their faces became lined and wrinkled prematurely, their backs worn from constant toil. They were, frequently, men who walked on both sides of the law, ranchers or miners by day, rustlers and stage robbers by night. Even Wyatt Earp was once accused of horse stealing and, in later years, he would be accused of being a stagecoach robber and a murderer, as well. In the wild West of legend, the good guys wore white hats and the bad guys wore black. In the real wild West, things were very seldom seen in black or white.

"Not much to look at, is it?" said Masterson, interrupting his thoughts. "A sight different from the kind of country that you're used to in Montana Territory."

"Yes, it is," said Neilson. "I was thinking that it seems like a very lonely place to die."

They got down out of the rig and brushed the dust from their clothes. Masterson had changed into a pair of faded jeans and boots, a pale brown cotton shirt, a red kerchief and a well-worn, sweat-stained, light brown Stetson hat. He wore two six-shooters on his hips, nickel-plated Colt Single Action Army .45s with four-and-three-quarter-inch barrels and gutta-percha, or hard rubber, grips. He had them made specially for him by the Colt factory in Hartford, Connecticut, with slightly taller front sight blades, a bit thicker than usual, and hair triggers. In the rig, he also had a Winchester carbine.

"Dying's always lonely," he said, "no matter where you do it."

Neilson nodded. "Only it's the man who's left alive who thinks about it, not the dead."

"You've been thinking about those two men you killed yesterday," said Masterson.

Neilson nodded.

"First time?" asked Masterson. "Not that it's any of my business."

"No, it wasn't the first time," Scott replied. "I've killed before. Not because I wanted to, because I had to. But it doesn't get any easier. I guess you'd know about that, though."

Masterson nodded, solemnly. "No, it sure doesn't. But don't go thinking I'm some sort of expert on the subject. Oh, I know my reputation, and I haven't done much to disabuse folks of it, but to tell the truth, it's mostly hogwash. They say I've killed thirty-seven men. That's nonsense. When I'm asked about it, I never say yes and I never say no. I just always say I don't count Indians or Mexicans. I've been a lawman and I'm now a gambler and in occupations such as those, it can be useful to have people think you're a killer."

"Doesn't that also invite trouble, though?" asked Scott.

"Sometimes," Masterson replied, "but it prevents trouble more often than not. Those penny-dreadful writers back East have got people believing that if you've got a reputation as a gunfighter, reckless young blades from miles around come looking for you, anxious to make a reputation for themselves by taking you on. But that's nothing like the truth. You'll find that out. Most people would think real long and real hard before tangling with someone who's known to have killed thirty-seven men. As a result of my so-called deadly reputation, there've been times when I've simply been able to stare down trouble. Wyatt, too. I've seen some pretty tough hombres back down at just a look from Wyatt, because it's known he's deadly with a gun. Of course, that doesn't always work, as you saw yesterday. The truth is, not counting any Indians I might've shot at the Battle of Adobe Walls, I've only killed one man. That's why I've got this here limp."

"What happened?" Scott asked.

"His name was Corporal Melvin King, a soldier who liked the wild life and fancied himself a good man with a six-gun. He used to like riding with the cowboys and hurrahing towns and such. It happened in Sweetwater. We both liked the same girl, only she had a preference for me. I was spending some time alone with her in a saloon one night and King heard we were together. He'd had a few drinks and he was fixed for trouble. He busted in on us and jerked his pistol. Molly tried to get between us just as his pistol went off. The bullet went right through her and smashed into my hip. I managed to get my pistol out and shoot King as I fell, but it was no help to Molly. They both died. And me, after I healed up, I had to walk around with a cane for quite a spell. That's where the story started that I got the name Bat from batting people over the head with it." He chuckled. "Amazing how these things get around."

"Where did you get the name Bat?" asked Neilson.

"It's short for Bartholomew, which is my real name. I never cared for it, so I use William Barclay. I like the sound of it better. But most folks know me as Bat Masterson, just like they'll probably know you as the Montana Kid from now on. I guess you have me to blame for that."

Neilson grinned. "I don't mind. I kind of like it."

"You may not always feel that way," said Masterson. "Having a reputation as a gunfighter is a sword that cuts both ways. It gets you plenty of respect, but not the kind you'd like. The way Wyatt reacted was the way any lawman would react on hearing of a gunfighter come to town. You represent a threat. Potential trouble. And it didn't help any to have Frank say you were faster than Wyatt. That sort of thing puts a man on his guard right away."

They entered the adobe house and Neilson started looking around. He didn't expect to find much. Observers were always careful to leave no sign that would indicate they were anything but what their covers made them appear to be. Even if someone hadn't already torn the place apart, he would have found nothing from the future here. But that wasn't what he was looking for.

"Well, it's like I told the marshal," he said, "I don't want any trouble."

"You stay around here, you'll find it sure enough," Masterson replied. "By now, the Clantons will have heard about how you gunned down those two. Now, Wyatt, Virgil and Morg know them a sight better than I do, but from what I've heard about that bunch, you'd do best to steer clear of them. Ike Clanton I've met. He's not so much. A blowhard, mostly. His brother Billy seems a lot more likable, offhand, but I hear he's quite good with a six-gun and he'll back up his brother. Then there's the McLaurys, Frank and Tom. Both gunmen. And Frank's said to be dangerous. Billy Claiborne runs with them, but I wouldn't put him in the same class as Frank and Tom. And then there's Curly Bill and Johnny Ringo."

"I've heard of them," said Scott.

"That's not surprising," Masterson replied. "Curly Bill Brocius has killed his share of men. And Ringo has a big reputation as a gunfighter. There's a good number of others, cattle rustlers and stage robbers, not a good apple in the bunch, but of them all, I'd worry about those two the most."

"And you think I have something to worry about?" asked Scott.

"If you stick around, you do," Masterson replied. "I don't want to seem ungrateful or unfriendly, Kid, but if I were you, I'd waste little time in moving on. You're young, yet. Got your whole life ahead of you. You can be anything you want to be. But if you decide you're going to be a gunfighter, then you've closed off a lot of options. You can find some town that needs a good man with a six-gun to wear a badge. A saloonkeeper who'll cut you in for a small share of the business to hang around and make sure there isn't any trouble. Or you can hunt bounty. There's some money to be made from that. But it's not what I'd call an easy life. Or a very good one. Often, it's a short life, too.

"Oh, maybe your reputation as a pistolero will make some men back down," he continued, "but it will also mark you. Instead of trying to face you down, they'll look to shoot you from behind or get you through a window with a scattergun. And then they'll be able to brag about how they gunned down the Montana Kid. You'll be popular with the saloon girls, but most respectable women will keep shy of you. You'd be a bad bet to settle down with. You'll have men respect you and move aside when you walk down the street, but deep down, they won't like having you around and no one will be sorry when you leave."

"What about if you're a gambler?" Scott asked.

Masterson pulled out a crudely made wooden chair and sat down at the table. "Well, it's more respectable, for one thing," he said, as he took out a pack of cards and absently started to shuffle them. "Lots safer, too."

"Like yesterday, you mean?" asked Scott, with a smile.

Masterson shrugged. "What happened yesterday doesn't really happen very often. And, in a way, it was my own fault. Slim was cheating. And he wasn't very good at it. I decided to cheat back a bit, to teach him a lesson. He wasn't good enough to catch me at it, but he tumbled to it somehow. I read him wrong. I didn't figure that he'd pull a gun. That was foolish of me. Yes, there are risks to being a gambler, but the advantage is that you only have to deal with trouble that comes to you.

You don't have to go out looking for it." He glanced at Scott and smiled. "You play?"

He put the deck down in the center of the table for him to cut. Scott looked at him a moment, then picked it up and cut it twice, one-handed. He shuffled it, quickly shot the deck from one hand to the other, split it, fanned the two equal parts in either hand, put it back together and then started dealing from the top, face down.

"Deuce of hearts," he said, as he put the first card down. "Deuce of spades. Deuce of clubs. King of clubs. King of diamonds."

Masterson stared at him, then slowly turned each card over to reveal the full house. He whistled softly.

"Son, I don't know how you did that, but if you could teach me, I'd be much obliged. That's my own deck and I know it's clean."

"All it takes is practice, Mr. Masterson," said Scott. He reached out and pulled a silver dollar from Masterson's ear, then walked it across his fingers, back and forth, snapped them, and the coin was gone. "Lots and lots of practice."

Masterson shook his head with awe. "There sure is a lot more to you than meets the eye."

Neilson smiled. "You could say that."

"You see about all you want to see here?"

"Yeah, I guess I have," said Scott.

They were so small, they could easily have been missed, but he had known what he was looking for. Three tiny holes in the adobe wall. Burned into it by lasers.

The dining room in the Grand Hotel boasted an elegant menu for a town like Tombstone, but Neilson avoided the dubious French cuisine and ordered a thick steak, instead. He had it with a buttered baked potato and some beans and washed it down with a passable claret. He was about halfway through his meal when a soft, feminine voice behind him said, "You're the Montana Kid, aren't you?"

He turned slightly and saw a lovely young girl of about eighteen or nineteen, with long, silky, ash-blonde hair and large, powder-blue eyes. She was wearing a long, light blue calico dress with lace around the collar and high-buttoned shoes. Her creamy complexion was absolutely flawless, she had a small, turned-up nose, a slightly pointed chin and naturally pouting lips. He thought she was one of the most beautiful girls he'd ever seen.

"I'm sorry, I didn't mean to interrupt your meal," she said, coming around in front of him, "but I saw what you did yesterday and I thought it was about the bravest thing I've ever seen."

"You were *there*?" Scott said, with some surprise. He could hardly believe he had missed seeing her.

"I work there," she said, lowering her eyes slightly. "I . . . I wasn't dressed like this. I'm one of the saloon girls. My name is Jennifer. Jennifer Reilly."

Neilson wiped his mouth and stood up. "Pleased to meet you, Miss Reilly. And no, you're not interrupting me. I'd appreciate the company. Please, sit down."

He pulled out a chair for her.

"Call me Jenny. What do your friends call you—Montana?"

He grinned. "No, not really. My friends call me Scott. Scott Neilson."

"It's nice to meet you, Scott." She watched him as he sat back down. "I see you're not wearing your gun."

"No, Virgil Earp took it from me. Said there was an ordinance against carrying guns in Tombstone."

"That doesn't seem to stop a lot of people," she said.

"No, it doesn't, does it?"

"Aren't you afraid? To be without your gun, I mean. Those cowboys that you shot have some pretty nasty friends."

"Like Curly Bill and Johnny Ringo?"

"And Ike Clanton and the McLaury brothers," she said. "I see you've already heard of them."

"Yes. Bat Masterson warned me about them."

"And you're not worried?"

"Well, yes, I confess I am, a little. But the law's the law, isn't it? And I've only just arrived in town. I don't want to get on the wrong side of a man like Virgil Earp. His brother, Wyatt, already seems to have taken a dislike to me."

"Oh, that sounds like Wyatt, all right," she said. "Wyatt's very protective of his brothers. And to him, any man who wears a gun and uses it the way you do means trouble. And wait till you meet Morgan."

"Oh? What's he like? He a lawman, too?"

"He's a shotgun guard on the Wells Fargo stage. You'll know him when you see him. Those three Earp brothers look as alike as peas in a pod, but they're all really very different. Virgil is the steady one. He's calm-tempered and looks to avoid trouble if he can. Wyatt's steady, too, I guess, only in a different way. If there's trouble, he doesn't waste too many words. He'll buffalo you with his six-shooter just as soon as look at you."

To "buffalo" someone, Neilson remembered, meant to get the better of him in some way, usually by force. What Jenny was referring to was Wyatt Earp's penchant for braining miscreants with the barrel of his gun and knocking them unconscious. In a wild frontier town like Tombstone, it was nothing more than sensible law enforcement. Why give a man a chance to draw his gun if you can crack his skull first and avoid all the unpleasantness?

"And as for Morgan," Jenny continued, "he's real hot tempered and can be quite a handful when he's been drinking. He hangs around with that Doc Holliday a lot. Wyatt and Doc are close friends too, which seems a little strange, I guess, seeing as they're so different. Wyatt doesn't drink at all and Doc drinks quite excessively. When him and Morgan have had a few too many, watch out!"

"I'll try to remember that," said Scott. "May I offer you some wine?"

"Oh, thank you, no." She hesitated. "Well, maybe just a smidgen? It goes to my head so."

Scott smiled and signaled the waiter for another glass.

"Anyway," Jenny went on, "Morgan? He only gets riled when he's had a few too many, but that Doc Holliday, he's got a real short fuse. You wouldn't think it to look at him, him so frail and sickly and coughing all the time—he's got consumption, you know—but he's a real killer. They say he's one of the deadliest men with a six-shooter in the whole Southwest."

"Really? You seem to know a lot about the people in this town."

She blushed and looked down. "You must think I'm an awful gossip."

"No, I don't. Just that I'm new in town and it's useful to hear such things. Might help me stay out of trouble."

"Seems to me like you've already found some. With Slim and Jack, I mean. Not that anybody's going to miss them overmuch. They were rustlers, you know. Real troublemakers."

"I gather there's a lot of rustling going on around here," Neilson said.

"Oh, yes. And there's a lot who don't mind it. They can get their cattle and their horses cheaper when they're rustled up from Mexico. Or from one of the bigger spreads around here. People don't ask a lot of questions when they're getting a bargain. Course, the big ranchers, they don't like it one bit, but they don't have all that much to say about it. The rustlers don't bother the smaller ranches and they usually get a real welcome there. And they never cause much trouble in town, either. At least, they didn't until lately."

"Oh? What changed things?"

"Well, there's a lot of money in this town right now. It's growing bigger every day. And there's a lot of bullion going out on the two stage lines. That can be real tempting for some people who don't have too many scruples."

Jenny downed her "smidgen" of wine in one quick gulp and held her glass out for more as she spoke. Scott refilled it.

"So you're saying the town's attracting a bad element?"

"Oh, there's no doubt about that! Sheriff Johnny Behan? You run into him yet?"

"No, I can't say I have."

"Well, you ask me, he's one of them. He's a real handsome man, though his hair's thin on top, and he goes around like he's God's gift to women. He's good friends with Ike Clanton and his bunch. And his deputy, Billy Breakenridge, he's not much better. Sadie calls him Billy Blab, because he talks so much and is real full of himself."

"Sadie?"

"Oh, that's right, you wouldn't know her. Actually, her name is Josephine, but her middle name is Sarah so her close friends call her Sadie. She used to be Johnny Behan's girl, only now she's with Wyatt and there's been bad blood between the two men ever since. See, her daddy paid for her to build this house in town when she was engaged to Johnny, only now Johnny's on the outs with her and she's with Wyatt, but Johnny owns the lot the house is standing on and one night, he came to try and dispossess her. Only Morg was there and he knocked Johnny clear off the front porch."

"Sounds like things keep jumping around here," Neilson said, with a smile. He refilled Jenny's glass as she held it out again for another smidgen. "I just might stick around a while."

"What brings you to Tombstone, Scott? If you don't mind my asking, that is."

"No, I don't mind. I came looking for some friends of mine. Only I found out they'd been killed. Maybe you knew them. Ben Summers, Josh Billings and Joe McEnery?"

"Oh, my, yes!" she said. "They were friends of yours? It was an awful thing, what happened. They were real gentlemen, all three of them, always so nice and so polite. Never pawing at you like a lot of men do. Ben and Josh were always friendly, but Joe was kind of sweet on me. He used to sneak over sometimes to see me, when the others weren't around. See, they were all supposed to be saving up to buy a ranch together out in Oklahoma and he didn't want the other two to know that he was spending any of it on me."

"I see," said Scott. What he hadn't wanted them to know was that he was going to a hooker. That sort of thing was against regulations, though it was known to happen. Observers were only human, after all, and long-term postings had their hardships.

"You don't approve of me," she said.

"No, I wouldn't say that. A girl has to make a living. I'd say that Joe McEnery had good taste."

She lowered her eyes demurely. "It's sweet of you to say that, Scott."

"Did you see Joe often?"

"Every now and then."

"Did he ever say anything about anyone in town he might be worried about? Someone he had trouble with, perhaps, or someone new in town who looked suspicious to him?"

"Well, he did ask some questions, once or twice," she replied. "He seemed curious about that Mr. Drake and a few others."

"Mr. Drake?"

"Oh, well, he had a room right here in this hotel, but he checked out and left town. Nathan Drake, his name was, a rich man from back East somewhere. He came out here looking to make some investments, like a lot of people do. He wasn't interested in silver, I don't think, just property, only he didn't find anything here that suited him. Then there was that Mr. Stone, from San Francisco. Joe was curious about him, as well. He's a gambler and you can find him most nights in the Oriental or the Alhambra. He's new in town, only came in a few weeks ago. And Zeke Bailey, Joe asked about him, as well. Zeke's a gunsmith, works for Mr. Spangenberg at his shop over on Fourth Street. He came to town about a month or so ago and old George Spangenberg, he says he's just a wonder when it comes to tuning guns and fixing them. Zeke makes knives, too. Beautiful things they are, I've seen some of them in the shop. He has a little place just outside of town, where he's got himself a forge and all. Zeke's kind of quiet and keeps to himself a lot. And there's a few other people that Joe asked about. To tell the truth, I think Joe distrusted just about everyone he didn't know. Most folks around here think those three were greenhorns, nice enough, but city boys who didn't know their business and were slowly going broke out there. Me, I think they made themselves a strike and didn't talk about it, for fear of someone robbing them. I think they were hiding what they found till they were ready to pull out. Only it looks like someone found out about it anyway and killed them for it. I guess Joe was right to worry."

The bottle was empty and Scott had only drunk two glasses.

"Oh, look at me!" said Jenny. "My, here I was rattling on so, I went and drank up all that wine and didn't even notice! Now I'm feeling a bit tipsy. Scott, you naughty boy, I do believe you're trying to get me drunk and take advantage of me!"

"I'd never take advantage of a lady," Scott replied.

"Well, aren't you the proper gentleman. But what must you think of me, talking so and drinking all that wine!"

"I think you must have been thirsty," Neilson replied, with a smile.

"Now you're teasing me!"

"Well, maybe a little. But I have enjoyed talking to you, Jenny. You seem to know a lot about what happens in this town. I'd like to try and find out what happened to my friends. You've been very helpful. Maybe we could talk some more."

"You mean, like in private?" she asked, looking at him.

Neilson had been thinking about that. She did seem like a font of valuable information and information was exactly what he needed now. A friend like Jenny could be very helpful. Yet, if he turned her down, he might offend her. Or was he just rationalizing the fact that he was sexually attracted to her? He'd been rendered immune to most diseases, including those that were sexually transmitted, but he wasn't sure if getting involved with her would be a very smart thing to do. On the other hand, he did need intelligence. . . .

Before he could decide, he heard a loud voice say, "I'm lookin' for the Montana Kid."

"Oh, dear," said Jenny. "It's Ross Demming."

"Demming?" Neilson said, looking over his shoulder.

"The brother of one of the men you killed. And the other man with him is Frank McLaury. Don't say anything. Maybe they won't know who you are."

But Demming's gaze had already settled on him.

"You," he said. "You're the one. You're the polecat who shot my brother."

The room had become completely silent, save for the sound of chairs scraping as people quickly moved out of the way. Neilson turned away from him and remained seated.

"He's not wearing a gun, Ross," Jenny said. "If you shoot an unarmed man, it will be murder."

"You stay out of this, Jenny. It's none of your affair. He murdered Jack."

"It was a fair fight," Jenny said. "I was there. I saw it. Ask anyone in town. Jack jerked his pistol first."

"I said, stay out of it!"

"Frank, you get him out of here before there's trouble," Jenny said, speaking to McLaury. "You have more sense. You get him out of here right now."

"Jack was a friend of mine, Jenny. And Ross has a right to be upset about his brother bein' shot down by some young gunfighter out to make a reputation for himself."

"He's got no right to shoot an unarmed man!"

"The Kid can have one of my guns," said McLaury, pulling one of his Colts out of its holster. He held it out butt first. "Here, Kid. Take it. It'll be a fair fight. They say you're good. Let's see how good you are."

Neilson still sat with his back to them. His heart was beating fast and his stomach felt tight.

"I don't want any trouble," he said. "I've got no quarrel with you, Mr. Demming. Or with you, Mr. McLaury. What I did yesterday, I did because I had no choice."

"What makes you think you've got a choice right now?" asked Ross.

"Take the gun, Kid," said McLaury. "Unless you're yellow."

"All right," said Scott. "I'm yellow."

"You take that gun," said Ross. "You stand up and take it, right *now*, or so help me, I'll let you have it in the back."

There was the sound of soft coughing behind Demming and a voice said, "Two can play at that game."

Demming and McLaury both stood very still.

"This ain't none of your affair, Holliday," said Frank McLaury, without turning around.

"I just made it my affair. Wyatt's on his way and so is Virgil. They heard you just rode into town and forgot to check your guns. Morg just got in on the stage, so I expect he'll be along, as well. And I don't think they'll take too kindly to your actions. Funny thing, though, how the sheriff never seems to be around at times like this. Where do you figure Johnny went?"

"Okay, Holliday," said Frank McLaury. "You win. This time. Come on, Ross. Let's go."

"Before you turn around, Frank, put away that six-gun, nice and easy. I wouldn't want to chance your pulling a border roll on me. Hear Curly Bill's right good with it and he's been teaching you."

Slowly, McLaury put away his gun and turned around, with his hands held out from his sides.

"Okay? Now if you stand aside, Doc, we'll be going. Come on, Ross."

Demming shot a hard look at Neilson. "This isn't over, Kid. Not by a long shot. You hear me, yellowbelly? It isn't over!"

"Right now it is," said Holliday. "Now git!"

The two men went past him and out into the street. Neilson exhaled heavily as Holliday backed over to their table, then holstered his nickel-plated Colt.

"Thanks," said Scott.

"Don't mention it," Holliday replied. "Evenin', Jenny."

"Doc, was I ever glad to see you!" she said.

Holliday smiled thinly. "Always a pleasure to see you too, honey." He looked up as Wyatt Earp came in. "Well, howdy, Wyatt. We almost had us some excitement here just now."

"I know," said Wyatt, grimly. "Virg and Morg just took Frank and Ross to jail for carryin' their guns in town. What happened here?"

"They came in looking for the Kid," said Doc. "I heard Demming threaten to shoot him in the back."

"He's right, Wyatt," Jenny said. "The Kid and I were talking and those two came in, looking for trouble. Ross wanted to kill him. And he would have, if it hadn't been for Doc."

Wyatt Earp gave Neilson a hard look. "I knew you were going to be trouble," he said.

"I was only having dinner, Marshal," Scott said. "I didn't do a thing."

"I want you on the next stage out of town," said Wyatt.

"I haven't broken any laws, Mr. Earp. Unless it's against the law to have men threaten you while you're eating dinner."

"Don't sass me, son. I haven't got the patience for it."

"I'm not carrying a gun, Marshal. I'm obeying the law, just like your brother told me to. I haven't done anything to be run out of town for."

"There's no reason for you to stay around," said Wyatt. "And I can think of lots of reasons for you to leave. Next time, Doc might not be there to protect you."

"I'm obliged to Mr. Holliday," said Scott. "But I've still got some business here in town. And I haven't broken any laws. Those cowboys did. They're the ones you should be running out of town."

"They'll be leavin', soon as they've paid their fines," said Wyatt. "And I don't need you to tell me my job. I know what business you have here and it's trouble."

"Your brother said that I could ask around and try to find out what happened to my friends," said Neilson. "That's all I was doing, Marshal. Asking. I told you, I don't want any trouble. Not with you and not with anybody else, either."

Wyatt stared at him for a long moment. Neilson met his gaze.

"The next stage leaves at noon tomorrow," Wyatt said. "If you're smart, Kid, you'll be on it." He touched the brim of his hat. "Jenny . . ."

He turned around and left.

"If I were you, Kid, I'd do as he said," said Holliday.

"I haven't done anything wrong, Mr. Holliday. Or is that how you people do things here in Tombstone? Fine the outlaws a few dollars, but run law-abiding people out of town?"

Holliday shook his head. "You've got Wyatt wrong. He's only trying to do his job. And he's looking out for you, as well."

"I can look out for myself."

"Is that right? Tell me, what would you have done if I hadn't come along when I did?"

Scott looked up at him, then made a quick movement with his wrists, crossing them and pulling two slim throwing knives from concealed sheaths strapped to his forearms, turning quickly in his chair and hurling them. They stuck in the wall by the entryway, exactly where Frank McLaury and Ross Demming had stood.

Jenny gasped, as did a number of other people in the dining room. Someone invoked the Lord's name, softly, and there was an undertone of excited murmuring.

Holliday stared at the knives. "You seem to be a young man of many talents," he said. "You practice that back on the farm, as well?"

"There a law against carrying knives in Tombstone?" Scott asked him.

"Not to my knowledge," Holliday replied. He walked over and pulled the knives out of the wall. He examined them before he gave them back to Neilson. "Clever-lookin' things. Never seen any like 'em before."

Neilson slipped them back into their sheaths. "I had them made special."

Holliday nodded. "Maybe it's too bad that I came in when I did. I've never seen two men dropped with knives at the same time before. You got any other tricks up your sleeve?"

"If I have to leave town, you might never find out," said Scott.

Holliday coughed several times. "I'll speak with Wyatt. See if I can get him to back off a bit. I have a feeling that having you around might prove to be quite interesting. Quite interesting, indeed. Be seein' you, Kid. You too, Jenny."

" 'Bye, Doc," she said. Her eyes were shining as she looked at Neilson. "I've never seen anything like the way you threw those knives in my whole life!" she said. He felt her foot rubbing up against his leg under the table. "I've never met anyone like you."

Neilson cleared his throat. "Waiter? Check, please."

2 ————————————————

Neilson looked a little green around the gills as he stood in the private quarters of General Moses Forrester in the TAC-HQ building at Pendleton Base, California. Part of his ill feeling was due to what was known as "warp lag," the effects of traveling through time. Some people got used to it, others never did. Even veteran time travelers occasionally puked their guts out after temporal transition. Most everyone at least felt dizzy and queasy in the stomach. Complicating the situation was the fact that Neilson was in the presence of the Old Man himself.

Forrester was a large man, built like a bull, with a massive chest and arms that were as big as Neilson's thighs. Even at his advanced age—and no one knew precisely what his age was—he could still run a marathon, do fifty pull-ups without pausing and curl an eighty-pound dumbbell with one hand. His face looked positively ancient. It was lined and wrinkled and he was completely bald. His bright green eyes, however, looked youthful and alert.

Also present in Forrester's quarters were Colonel Lucas Priest, Captain Andre Cross and Major Finn Delaney. Priest, as usual, looked smartly turned out in his sharply creased black base fatigues and highly polished boots. Dark-haired, slim and very fit, he was a handsome, thoroughly professional looking officer. By contrast, the burly Delaney looked like an unkempt longshoreman. He looked about as military as an old sweat sock. His base fatigues were rumpled, his boots were unshined, his dark red hair was uncombed and his full beard gave him the aspect of a drunken Irish poet. His facial expression, even when neutral, conveyed a wry insolence that had often provoked senior officers throughout his military career. That, together with his insubordinate nature, was one of the reasons why he held the record for the most reductions in grade in the entire Temporal Corps. He also held the record for the most promotions, due to exemplary service in the field. Lucas Priest had often chided him about it, saying that if it wasn't for his temper, he would have surely been a general by now, to which Delaney always responded with an irate scowl. At heart, he was a noncom and had always detested officers. And now he was a major. The rank did not sit well with him. He still felt funny being saluted.

Andre Cross sat between the two men on the couch, looking less like a soldier than a model hired to pose for a recruiting poster. Her straw-blonde hair was long and straight, falling to her shoulders, and her sharp, angular features were more striking than pretty. She had the physique of a bodybuilder, with long legs, a narrow waist, small hips and broad shoulders. Neilson had always thought that there was something catlike about her, in the way she moved and in the way she held herself.

Their presence made him feel somewhat more at ease, as he had served with them once before on a mission in the past, that assignment to Victorian London where half the mission team had died. People who had gone through something like that together achieved a special camaraderie that only other soldiers could fully understand. But the Old Man still had Neilson feeling a bit shaky in the knees. It felt a little strange standing before them, dressed the way he'd been in Tombstone. Almost as if he were a boy playing dress-up in a roomful of adults.

As soon as he'd clocked in and made his report, Forrester's adjutant had decided that "the Old Man should hear about this." And Forrester had summoned the others, the agency's number-one temporal adjustment team. Neilson had just finished briefing them on what he had discovered when he had clocked out to check on Observer Outpost G-6898. And now he stood at parade rest, awaiting their response.

"At ease, Sergeant," said Forrester. "Have a seat, please."

Neilson took one of the living room chairs.

"What do you think?" asked Forrester, addressing the others.

"If Neilson thinks those Observers were killed by laser fire, I'm not inclined to question it," said Delaney. "He doesn't leap to hasty conclusions. Of course, we won't know that for a fact unless we send an S&R team back to exhume the bodies, but under the circumstances, I'm not sure if we should risk that."

"I agree," said Lucas, nodding. "If we've got an infiltration in that time sector, they could be on the watch for that. The Observers blew their cover and the opposition, whoever they are, probably know where they're buried. They could be keeping their graves under surveillance, waiting for a Search & Retrieve team to clock back for them."

"It wouldn't be very hard to keep Tombstone's Boot Hill under surveillance, sir," Neilson added. "A small remote unit concealed nearby would do it."

"I'm a little disturbed about the fact that Scott has become involved in the scenario to the extent that he has," said Andre. "I don't mean that as a criticism. It looks as if the situation just turned out that way. But as a result, he's become highly visible."

"Maybe," said Lucas, "but we could turn that to our advantage. If he's going to attract attention, we can stay in the background and see just what kind of attention he attracts."

"Which is another way of saying we can use him as a Judas goat," said Andre. "I don't like it. It leaves him very vulnerable."

"None of us are paid to play it safe, Andre," said Delaney. "Besides, Scott can take care of himself. And we'll be there to provide backup."

"That's always assuming that we'll have the chance to do that," Andre replied. "We don't know what we're going up against. That particular scenario doesn't seem to have a great deal of temporal significance offhand, but if there's a confluence point somewhere in that sector and agents of the S.O.G. have crossed over from the parallel timeline, it would be an important staging area for them. We'd be at a disadvantage. They'd know where the confluence point was and have control of it. We'd be going in cold, with no idea where it might be located."

"On the other hand, maybe it's not the S.O.G.," said

Delaney. "Maybe those Observers stumbled onto a Network operation. That would seem more likely, considering that Tombstone was a mining boomtown in that period. Scott said there had been some stage robberies with shipments of bullion stolen. That's just the sort of thing the Network would be into. Hijack silver bullion from Arizona in the 1880s, sell it in some future period when it hits its peak market value or trade it for some other commodities and pyramid the profits. Security back then would have been a joke, at least to people with resources like the Network has. It would be a prime scenario for temporal speculation. If it is the Network, then it's all the more reason for Neilson to stay highly visible. They'll be expecting someone to clock back to check on what happened to those Observers. Neilson can help draw their attention away from us."

"And maybe get himself killed while he's at it," Andre said. "I think it's too dangerous. Not only for Scott, but for the temporal continuity in that sector. Look, by his own admission, he's already become involved with people like the Earp brothers and Doc Holliday. And he's managed to get himself caught right between the Clanton faction and the Earps. He could unintentionally wind up causing a disruption in the events leading up to the shoot-out at the O.K. Corral."

"Actually, the shoot-out didn't take place at the O.K. Corral," said Neilson. "It took place in the vacant lot between Fly's Boarding House and the Harwood place. The O.K. Corral was about ninety feet farther down the street, with only its back entrance leading out to Fremont Street, where the gunfight actually ended."

"What difference does it make?" asked Andre, impatiently.

"I think it makes a great deal of difference," said Forrester. "Neilson is the perfect man for this assignment. He's got all the right qualifications. He's well versed in the history of the period and he's an expert with the weapons of the period, as well. His cover as a gunfighter couldn't be more perfect. He's tailor-made for the role. I'm against pulling him out. I'm with Finn and Lucas on this one, Andre. There's a risk, but I think it's justified. I'm leaving Neilson in."

"Thank you, sir," said Scott.

"You sure you're up to this, son?" asked Forrester. "You look a bit worn out."

"I, uh, didn't get much sleep, sir. I'll be fine. I can handle it."

Forrester nodded. "All right. What about this situation with you and Wyatt Earp? Is that going to be a problem?"

"I hope not, sir. I think he's just concerned about keeping order in town and I look like a disruptive influence to him. But Doc Holliday said he'd try to intercede for me and the two of them are very close. Bat Masterson also seems to like me. Of course, he won't be in Tombstone much longer after I get back. He'll be called back to Dodge City to help out his brother. And the Earps are going to have their hands full with other problems before long. I don't think they'll have a lot of time to worry about me. Especially if I keep my nose clean."

"That's just the question," Andre said. "Keeping out of trouble might be hard to do with the rustlers out gunning for you."

"Maybe," Neilson said. "But I'll do what I can to stay out of their way. And I'll try to ingratiate myself with the Earps in any way I can. The way things are developing in Tombstone back in that scenario, they're going to need all the help they can get."

"The only trouble is you may wind up giving them more help than they're supposed to get," said Andre. "And you're also faster with a gun and a much better shot than just about anyone who lived back then. How do we keep you from becoming famous as the Montana Kid, fastest gun in the West?"

"That's the very least of our problems," Forrester said, before Neilson could reply. "It's nothing Archives Section couldn't handle. It would be time consuming, but we could easily assign a team to make sure that the Montana Kid remains unknown to history. Our first priority is to determine the nature of what's happening back there. Is it the Network, engaged in one of their clandestine operations, or is it an infiltration through an undiscovered confluence point by agents of the S.O.G.? If that's the case, we could be faced with a situation similar to what happened in the Khyber Pass in 1897. It could be a prelude to a full-scale invasion from the parallel timeline. Compared to that, any minor disruption Neilson's presence could bring about would be insignificant."

"Let's not forget Drakov," Lucas said, softly, feeling that he had to bring that up, but hating to. Forrester was plagued with guilt and self-recrimination over what his son had become. "He's always the wild card. And we still haven't tracked down all his clones, or the genetically engineered hominoids he's scattered throughout history."

Forrester nodded, grimly. "Yes, we can't afford to overlook him, either." He took a deep breath and let it out in a heavy sigh. "The trouble is, we need to capture him alive, so we can track down all his clones. That won't be easy, but it's the only way we can be certain that we've got the original Nikolai Drakov. Only the original would know where all the copies are."

Forrester never referred to Drakov as his son. Privately, it had to be an agony for him. Years ago, when Forrester had been a rookie serving his first hitch in Minus Time, he'd been injured and separated from his unit. Unable to clock back, he had believed that he was trapped forever in the past. He had been found and nursed back to health by a Russian gypsy girl with whom he fell in love. He was later found and rescued, but by that time, Vanna Drakova was already pregnant with their child.

Forrester had broken all the rules and he had made the situation worse by keeping Vanna's pregnancy a secret. He knew if he reported it, it would have been necessary for the child to be aborted and he had not been able to bring himself to do that to the girl he loved. Or to the child. The result was that he went back to the future, after trying to explain to Vanna as best he could exactly who and what he was and why he had to leave her, and the necessity for her never to reveal that knowledge to anybody else.

But the simple gypsy girl had not been able to grasp the meaning of everything he told her. The concept of temporal physics was beyond her and when young Nikolai became curious about who his father was, the story she had told him was a bizarre mixture of truth and fantasy, richly embroidered with her colorful imagination. The poor boy hadn't understood and was left believing that he was the result of a supernatural union between his mother and some kind of demon. Unknowingly, his mother had traumatized him deeply and the harsh lives that they led as Nikolai grew up had only served to make things worse.

They were taken in by a young Russian officer and they had lived through Napoleon's invasion and his disastrous retreat.

Then Nikolai's adoptive father had been arrested as a Decembrist and exiled to Siberia. They had followed him there and it was in that harsh, forbidding country that Vanna met her death at the hands of a savage rapist, who had given young Nikolai the knife scar on his face when he tried to go to her defense. With her death, Nikolai Drakov had been left all alone in the world, frightened and tormented by the question of his own existence.

He never became sick. He didn't seem to age. He did age, of course, but at a rate that was far slower than normal. He had inherited a strong constitution, with an immunity to all known diseases and a lifespan that was far greater than normal for people in his time. And he did not know why or how. It had unhinged him. Then, when he encountered the notorious Sophia Falco, alias The Falcon, one of the leaders of the crosstime terrorists known as the Timekeepers, she had recognized him for what he was, seduced him and recruited him into the organization. She took him to the future with her, where she had further poisoned his mind against his father and obtained a biochip for him. Drakov was then given the benefits of an implant education through computer downloads directly to his brain. Already born with an amazing intellectual capacity, the implant programming had turned him into a genius. An insane genius. And when he found out the true story of who his father was and how he came to be, the hate he felt for Moses Forrester completely overwhelmed him. He embarked upon a course that not even the Timekeepers would have dared to contemplate.

What Drakov sought was nothing less than the complete destruction of the future, a savage revenge against his father and the world and time he came from. His goal was to bring about a massive temporal disruption that would result in a timestream split, the ultimate temporal disaster.

He had at first allied himself with the Timekeepers and eventually became one of their leaders, but after the Timekeepers were defeated, Drakov managed to escape into the past and continue with his mad plan of revenge. With his own expertise and the assistance of the infamous Dr. Moreau, Drakov had created the hominoids, genetically engineered and biologically modified humans, some appearing normal in every respect, others mutated into frightful creatures, all with an unswerving loyalty toward him, obedient to his every command. His crowning touch had been to replicate himself, to create a series of clones that he had planted throughout time, in the care of devoted hominoid parents, children that at a certain stage of their development would be programmed with his own mental engrams, so that they would all be the same in every last respect. They would all share his memories and his feelings, his experiences and his warped personality. They were surrogates of himself that he could send out against his father's agents.

"Priest is right," said Forrester. "We can't overlook the possibility that Drakov might have been responsible for those Observers' deaths. In which case, your covers will be blown the moment you arrive, because he knows you."

"If I can anticipate you, sir," said Lucas, "I'd be against our going in for any cosmetic surgery on this mission. Either way, if it's Drakov or the Network, our being recognized would help draw them into the open. And Scott shouldn't be the only one to bear the risk."

"All right," said Forrester. "It's your call. I want the three of you to report for mission programming immediately. And then take the rest of tonight to come up with a mission plan. I want you to present it to me by 0900 tomorrow. In the meantime, I'll have Operations select a backup team and I'll alert Colonel Cooper to stand by with a Ranger strike team, just in case you encounter the S.O.G. in force."

He turned to Neilson. "And you get a good night's sleep," he said, "then clock back to Tombstone first thing in the morning. Make sure you arrive soon enough after your departure so that you won't arouse any suspicion."

"Yes, sir."

"That will be all, people. Dismissed."

As Neilson checked into some transient quarters to wash up and get some rest, the others proceeded down to Archives Section and the Mission Programming labs, where they reclined on contoured couches while the technicians pulled the necessary data files, accessed their cerebral implants and programmed them with all the information they would require on their mission, everything that was known about the time sector they would be departing to, as well as the pivotal events and characters in the scenario. They then repaired to the First Division Lounge to discuss their strategy and come up with a mission plan.

It was late, but the First Division Lounge was one place that never closed. It was about the size of a briefing room, with a long bar and round tables with comfortable chairs placed around the room. The entire far wall was one huge floor to ceiling window, looking out over the base from sixty stories up. The lounge did not have the ambience of a bar. There were no hanging ferns or potted plants, no pretentious decor, little in the way of decor at all, in fact. One wall was hung with a large plaque of the division insignia, a number one bisected by the symbol for infinity, which resembled a slightly stretched out, horizontal figure eight. Next to it was another large plaque, solid gold mounted on mahogany, a small replica of the Wall of Honor downstairs in the lobby of the building. It listed the names of all those members of the First Division who had died in action. Another plaque had recently been added. It was the insignia of the Temporal Intelligence Agency, the symbol π. It represented an infinitely repeating number and, as such, it had been an appropriate selection.

The resources of the T.I.A. indeed seemed infinite, as did the number of its personnel. Its budget had been staggering from the days of its inception and the highly classified nature of the work the agency performed was such that section chiefs had never needed to justify their budgetary requisitions or fully document their subsidiary personnel. Section chiefs often recruited from among the locals in their time sectors, none of whom, of course, knew whom they really worked for. And just as journalists zealously protected their sources and police officers carefully guarded their informers, so did the section chiefs of Temporal Intelligence protect their field agents and collaborators.

Until recently, there had been no way to obtain a complete and accurate listing of all the personnel the agency employed. It was impossible. The section chiefs would not cooperate. Even now, there was no way of knowing if they submitted complete lists or only partial ones, or even if the lists that they submitted were genuine or fabricated. Abuses had been flagrant and frequent. Upon assuming the directorship of the agency, Forrester had discovered that it was like an octopus that had lost count of its tentacles and had no real ability to control them.

Past directors had simply allowed the agency to operate in its own way, to run on its own inertia. And they had not overly concerned themselves with regulations. Though he was hardly a stickler for going by the book himself, Forrester did not work that way. He took firm charge of the agency and the section chiefs who ran their sectors like feudal kingdoms. He was determined to streamline the agency and mold it into a tight, well-disciplined, efficient unit, just as he had done when he had organized the First Division. To weed out the corruption, he had organized the agency's own internal police force, the Internal Security Division, which had been headed by senior field agent Colonel Creed Steiger.

Forrester had known there were abuses. He had been aware of the corruption. But he had not been prepared for the incredible conspiracy he had uncovered when he found out about the Network. It was a secret agency within a secret agency. The Network made its own rules and was accountable to no one. Its only imperative was profit. The Network went beyond organized crime. It was like a multinational corporation whose influence transcended time. Forrester had been astonished to discover the extent of the Network's operations. They were involved with organized crime in a large number of temporal sectors and they had extended their influence into politics, as well. The I.S.D. had uncovered Network involvement in large multinational conglomerates of the 20th century, in the 18th-century Moroccan slave trade, in piracy on the Spanish Main during the 1600s, and in diverse smuggling operations throughout the timeline. The potential for profit using time travel was simply staggering, and the resources the Network had amassed were impossible to calculate.

As Forrester had reported to his superiors, it was difficult enough trying to unravel the complicated financial structure of modern, 27th-century corporations. But even using all the considerable investigative resources at his command, it was impossible to trace complex and clandestine financial operations that cross the boundaries of time.

Profits skimmed from the revenues of the Roman Empire could be used to finance bootlegging and gambling operations during America's Prohibition, and the capital that was generated there could be invested on Wall Street in the bear markets of the 20th century, using the knowledge gained from time travel to pull off the ultimate in inside trading. Money skimmed from gambling casinos in Las Vegas, Atlantic City and Monte Carlo could be funneled into arms trade in Brussels and profits realized there could finance drug smuggling and prostitution rings operated under the cover of the Mafia. It was impossible to follow the trail of the money unless one or another of those operations were discovered and shut down, the participants taken into custody and interrogated. Even so, the closed cell system that the Network utilized insured that only small portions of its vast, illegal empire could be exposed. And then the trail simply ran out once again.

Unintimidated, Forrester had set out to bust the Network and, in so doing, had incurred a price upon his head. Steiger, too, had a contract put out on him by the Network and, on his last mission, he had been assassinated, though he had managed to take his killer with him. Forrester's relentless pursuit of the Network had driven them more deeply underground and his only real hope of stopping them was to find their leaders, the people who would possess the records of all the Network branches and their operations. However, so far, only a few of the Network's operations had been uncovered. Its leaders remained hidden and unknown.

As a result, the merging of the T.I.A. and the First Division had gone somewhat less than smoothly. There had been considerable resentment for the time commandos among the agents of Temporal Intelligence and the members of the First Division had reciprocated with distrust. For years, the agency had been a lot like a corrupt police division. Not everyone was on the pad, meaning that not everyone was actively involved with the Network, but many of those who weren't involved had known about it and kept quiet. Indeed, there had been little else that they could do, considering the fact that the former agency director had been a Network man, himself.

Forrester had instituted scanning procedures for all agency personnel in an effort to unmask those with Network connections and all the agents, even those who weren't involved, resented it. Many resigned or transferred out. Others, significantly, simply disappeared. New personnel had been brought in to replace them and, eventually, things began to settle down. But it was significant that none of the old agents from the days before the two units had been merged were present in the First Division Lounge. The newer personnel had no background of camaraderie with the soldiers of the First Division. They, like the older agents, tended to socialize together. Consequently, when Delaney, Cross and Priest entered the lounge, they saw only a few other members of the First Division at the bar and lingering over their drinks at several tables. They nodded greetings to them and took a table of their own, near the back wall.

It was late and the sprawling base below them was all lit up. The glass wall gave a panoramic view of the base and the surrounding countryside. Off in the distance, they could see the lights of traffic on the interstate and, farther off, the distant glow of the city of Los Angeles, a vast metropolis that had seen phenomenal growth over the last few centuries, growth that showed no signs of abating. It had already swallowed up many of the towns and cities to its north and south and, at the rate the growth progressed in San Diego, L.A. and San Francisco, the entire coast of California would soon be one gigantic city. Always assuming that the long-predicted "Big One" didn't strike and cause most of it to collapse into the ocean, which would open up fascinating real estate opportunities in the Mojave Desert.

Over glasses of single malt Scotch whiskey, the three of them discussed their plans.

"All right, the first question is our cover," Lucas said. "I think we should all go in separately. Or at least in such a way that we'll appear not to be connected in any way."

"I second that," said Delaney.

"I'm going to have a problem with that," Andre said. "I'm not about to take a job in Tombstone as a saloon girl and have smelly cowboys breathing cheap whiskey in my face and trying to drag me off to some back room. I'll have to go in as someone's wife. So, who's going to be the lucky guy?"

"Oh, gee, I don't know," said Delany, with mock reluctance. "What do you think, Lucas?"

Lucas sighed. "Hell, why does it always have to be me?"

"Tell you what, I'll flip you for it. Loser gets to be her husband. Call it. Heads or tails?"

He flipped a coin. Andre snatched it out of the air. "Very funny," she said, wryly.

"I don't know, Andre," Finn said, "if you go in as a hooker, you'll be able to pick up a lot of information."

"That's true," said Lucas. "And you're innoculated against all known diseases, so—"

"You want to drink that Scotch, or wear it?" she asked.

"Okay, okay," said Lucas, with a grin. "Lt. Cross, will you do me the honor of becoming my wife?"

"You heard him, Finn," said Andre. "He just proposed."

"That's true, he did," Delaney replied, nodding. "I'm a witness."

"I accept, darling," Andre said, smiling sweetly.

"Hey, wait a minute," Lucas said, with a grin. "That wasn't fair. You tricked me."

"Did you hear me use any coercion?" Andre asked Finn.

"Nope," Delaney said. "Far as I could tell, he proposed of his own free will. And he's still sober. Hasn't even finished his first drink."

"Okay, okay, stop kidding around," said Lucas, smiling.

"What makes you think I'm kidding?" Andre said, raising her eyebrows.

"Very cute," said Lucas. "All right, really, let's get serious here."

"What makes you think I'm not serious?"

"Come on, Andre, that's enough. We've got work to do."

"Hey, you proposed. Finn heard you. He's a witness."

"Okay, you guys have had your joke. . . ."

"I wasn't joking," Andre said, with a look of wide-eyed innocence. "Were you joking, Finn?"

Delaney shook his head. "Not me. Hell, I even offered to flip him for it, but he sat right there and asked you to marry him. I heard it."

Lucas rolled his eyes. "I meant only for the mission. Come on, guys. . . ."

"Did you hear him say anything about it being only for the mission?" Andre asked Delaney.

"Nope. He said, and I quote, 'Lt. Cross, will you do me the honor of becoming my wife?' Granted, he didn't go down on one knee, but I don't think that's required. Not very romantic of you, Lucas. And you didn't even give her an engagement ring. Jesus, how cheap can you get?"

"Are you through?" asked Lucas, with exasperation.

"Now if he doesn't go through with it, I've got grounds for a breach of promise suit, isn't that right?" asked Andre.

Delaney nodded. "I'd say so. I'm a witness. And if I'm called to testify, I'll be under oath to tell the truth. I'm sorry, Lucas, but as an officer and a gentleman, what else can I do?"

"As an officer, you leave rather a great deal to be desired," said a deep, Continental-sounding voice behind them, "and if you're a gentleman, then I'm Queen of the bloody May."

They turned around to see what appeared to be a ghost sitting at the table just behind them. The speaker was a tall, slim man with gaunt, aquiline features; dark, wavy hair; brown eyes and a neatly trimmed moustache. He was dressed in brown wool flannel slacks and custom-made, conservative tan shoes with toe caps; a white button-down Oxford shirt that was open at the neck to display a brown and gold paisley silk ascot, and a brown tweed Norfolk jacket. He wore a brown felt fedora tilted at a rakish angle and carried a blackthorn walking stick with a sharp brass tip. He was sitting in the chair, sideways to the table, turned toward them, with his legs casually crossed and his walking stick held across his lap.

They could see right through him. His form seemed to flicker, appearing almost completely solid one instant, then transparent and insubstantial the next. It was an effect of the process that had permanently tachyonized his body, rendering him trapped forever by the immutable laws of physics which he had sought to tamper with. His name was Dr. Robert Darkness.

He was, in every respect, as flamboyant and eccentric as his name. Little was known about him. For years, he had been a mystery man, first coming to prominence as a research scientist who had stumbled upon the principles that led to the invention of the warp disc and the most devastating weapon ever known to man—the warp grenade.

It was the latter that had led to the current crisis. A portable nuclear device and time machine, the warp grenade was so named because of its resemblance to old 20th-century hand grenades, about the same size and shape as a large egg, easily capable of being held in one hand. Its built-in chronocircuitry enabled pinpoint adjustment of its nuclear explosion. It could be set to destroy an entire city, or just a block within that city, or a building on that block, or a room within that building, or even a small area within that room. It could be adjusted so that whatever surplus energy released by the explosion was not required for the task would be clocked through time and space, to explode harmlessly in the far reaches of the cosmos. At least, the ordnance experts who had constructed it, based on the work that Darkness did, had believed that it would work that way.

In practice, such massive amounts of energy clocked through Einstein-Rosen Bridges, "wormholes" in space and time, had brought about a shift in the chronophysical balance of the universe. At least, that was the theory. It was also possible that the actions of the Time Wars had brought about increased instability in the timestream and contributed to the imbalance. Whatever the cause, a parallel timeline, an alternate universe, had been brought into congruence with our own and the proximity of the two timelines had brought about the Confluence Phenomenon, wherein the timestreams rippled and, at various points in space and time, intersected. At those confluence points, it was possible to cross over from one universe into the other.

For the people in the parallel timeline, the disaster had been magnified because each time a warp grenade had been exploded in our universe, its surplus energy had been clocked into theirs. Most of those explosions had occurred in outer space, yet some of them had caused untold destruction. Several space colonies in the parallel universe had been utterly destroyed, with cataclysmic loss of life. It had brought about a war.

The war was, of necessity, a limited one. Strategic weapons were not used, because the moment the Confluence Phenomenon had been discovered, it quickly became apparent to the people in both timelines that attempts to clock stragetic weapons into the other universe could backfire. With the instability in both timelines, there was no telling exactly where or *when* a detonation could occur. As a result, the conflict had become the ultimate Time War, one timeline against the other, with each seeking to cause temporal disruptions in the opposing timestream.

In the parallel universe, commandos and agents of the strike force known as the Special Operations Group were dispatched through confluence points with missions to interfere with history. Their scientists believed a timestream split would serve to overcome the Confluence Phenomenon and separate the two timelines once and for all. The scientists of the Temporal Corps believed the opposite. They were convinced that a timestream split in either universe could set off a temporal chain reaction that would have disastrous consequences. It could bring about ultimate entropy, an end to all of time. It was therefore necessary to locate as many confluence points as possible and to patrol them for their duration. At the same time, it was imperative to preserve temporal continuity and prevent disruptions caused by infiltrations of the S.O.G. while attempting to bring about minor disruptions in *their* timeline, thereby tying up their manpower and their resources while they attempted to adjust them.

It was a situation with unlimited potential for disaster, with a Sword of Damocles hanging over everyone. What Dr. Darkness thought of all this had not been known. Shortly after the warp grenade had been developed, he had disappeared. He had gone off-planet, to some secret research base he had established somewhere in the far reaches of the galaxy. It was there that he began his experiments with tachyon translocation, temporarily converting the human body into tachyons in order to achieve the ultimate in transportation. Only, in his calculations, he had overlooked a little known principle of physics known as the Law of Baryon Conservation, by which his tachyon translocation process was ultimately restrained.

The result was a permanent alteration in his subatomic structure, rendering it unstable. He became the man who was faster than light. He could move through time and space in less time than it took to blink. Yet, upon arrival at his destination, he could not walk so much as one step. The only way he could achieve anything resembling normal mobility was to "tach," to translocate from one spot to another. It could be highly disconcerting. What was even more disconcerting was what Moses Forrester, Lucas Priest, Finn Delaney and Andre Cross had recently learned about him. And they were the only ones who had that knowledge.

Dr. Darkness was from the future. A future in which, it seemed, some cataclysmic temporal disaster had occurred. He would not reveal what it was, nor would he reveal if he'd been sent out on a mission by people from the future or was simply working on his own. He revealed very little, but it was obvious that he was trying to effect a complex temporal adjustment in an effort to avert whatever disaster had occurred in the time from which he came. And the three of them were somehow a part of the mission he was on.

Delaney groaned and shut his eyes. "Oh, God. Don't tell me. He isn't really here. I'm just having a bad dream."

"I'm equally pleased to see you, too, Delaney," Darkness replied, wryly. "I'd sooner have a case of indigestion. Regrettably, one has to make do with the tools one has at hand. And you, Delaney, are unquestionably a tool."

"Doc, I'm almost afraid to ask," said Lucas, "but the last time we saw you, you said something about one more key mission we'd have to perform."

Darkness nodded. "That's right, Priest. This is it."

"Shit," Delaney said. "I knew it. We're all going to die."

3 ———————————————————

"I sincerely hope that none of you is going to die," said Dr. Darkness, toying with his walking stick. "Otherwise all the work I've done will have been wasted."

Suddenly, there was a drink in his hand. He had tached over to the bar and helped himself, then tached back, faster than the speed of light, so that it seemed as if a glass of Scotch had simply appeared in his hand out of thin air. He took a sip. "Ahh. That hits the spot."

"I'm touched by your concern for our lives," said Lucas, wryly.

"Spare me your sarcasm, Priest," Darkness replied. "You owe your life to my concern, as you may recall."

"I haven't forgotten," Lucas said. "And I'm grateful. However, I'm also apprehensive. It has to do with your irritating habit of not telling us your plans."

"That's unavoidable," said Darkness. "I'm afraid it's necessary for you to function on what you'd call a 'need to know' basis. You have to realize that from my perspective, this is the past and I need to be very careful not to interfere with certain actions you must take. At least, not until the proper time."

"So why bother telling us at all?" asked Andre.

"Because Forrester deduced the truth about me. And, as a result, it's necessary for me to impress upon you the importance of what I have to do," said Darkness. "The fate of the future rests almost entirely in your hands. When the time comes, I cannot afford to have you hesitate. You will have to do exactly what I tell you, exactly *when* I tell you. Without question."

"That's asking us to take an awful lot on faith," Delaney said.

"Yes, it is. However, I had hoped that by now, you would trust my motives."

"Don't get us wrong, Doc," Lucas said. "It's not that we don't trust you. You've saved our bacon in the past, no pun intended. You even brought me back from death. I think. I'm still not entirely sure what happened. But the point is that we've got a job to do and it's hard enough doing it without your doing a job on us."

"What Lucas means is that what we do requires peak concentration," Andre said. "That's hard enough to achieve without knowing that at some point, you're going to show up and yank the rug out from under us. You're asking us to trust you. And we'd like to do that. It doesn't seem unreasonable, under the circumstances, for you to trust us, as well."

"I see your point," Darkness replied. "And I appreciate your position. But I need you to understand mine, as well. When you clock out on one of your temporal adjustment missions, one that involves your interacting with significant historical figures, you can't very well approach them and tell them who you are and what you're doing, can you?"

"Of course not," said Delaney, "but that's different. They wouldn't believe us. They'd think we were insane. This is hardly the same situation. We know about time travel. We know you're from the future. And we know that, somehow, we're involved in something—or we're going to be involved in something—that's going to have a significant impact on what happens in the time you came from. We can understand and accept that. And we'd like to help you. But we could do a better job of it if we knew just what it was we were supposed to do."

"I'm not convinced of that," said Darkness. "In fact, I've already told you a great deal more than I should have, much more than I had planned to. My hand was forced when Forrester realized that I was from the future. The fact that you know that alone could jeopardize what I must do. It could affect your actions in a way that would sabotage my mission."

"So then you *are* on a temporal adjustment mission," Andre said.

"That much is obvious," Darkness replied. "However, that isn't what you're asking, is it? You want to know if I'm your counterpart from the future, if I've been specifically sent back here on a mission or if I'm working on my own. And that's something I'm not in a position to tell you. I can't stop you speculating, of course, but I can assure you that it would be pointless. It really makes no difference, either way."

"Damn it, Doc, you've got to tell us more than that!" exclaimed Delaney, with exasperation. "What happens in the future, where you came from? Does it happen because of something we did, or something we *didn't* do?"

For a moment, Darkness did not reply. He seemed to be considering. Finally, he sighed. "It really was unfortunate that Forrester discovered the truth about me. I should have anticipated that, only I didn't. I underestimated his resourcefulness. As a result, without meaning to, he's endangered my mission. That's why I had to tell him that I would have no further contact with him. It would have been too dangerous. If you hadn't known . . . only you do know. And that knowledge could affect your actions. A moment's doubt or hesitation at the crucial time . . ."

He drained his glass and set it down on the table.

"I can tell you this much," he said. "Nothing that you have done—and I'm speaking from a future perspective, of course—served to bring about what I'm trying to prevent. However, you are going to be in a position where you *will* be able to do something to significantly alter the scheme of events in the future. I have seen to that. You were chosen very carefully. Telling you much more at this stage would be risky. You are approaching a key focal point in time. And when that time comes, you must do exactly as I say. Without even a second's hesitation. I had tried to improve your odds for success with those particle level implants that I gave you, but unfortunately, I was unable to perfect them and they ultimately failed. Perhaps that was my fault, perhaps it was the influence of the Fate Factor. It's like trying to swim against the current. I'm struggling to overcome temporal inertia at almost every turn."

"Like when I was supposed to die back in Afghanistan?" asked Lucas, softly. "What really happened, Doc? *Did* you change history? Was that Ghazi sniper supposed to kill me?"

Darkness gazed at him steadily. "No," he said.

"But then, how—"

"That sniper was not a Ghazi," Darkness said. "And he was not supposed to be there."

"*What?*" said Lucas. "Are you saying that . . ."

But suddenly, the chair was empty. Darkness had simply disappeared. Except for the empty whiskey glass standing on the table, it was as if he'd never been there.

Neilson clocked back into Tombstone shortly before dawn, P.R.T. (Present Relative Time). He had been gone slightly longer than twelve hours, but only three minutes had elapsed in 19th-century Tombstone since he had left. He had "gained" a day, a phenomenon of time travel that was one of the most difficult things for rookie temporal agents to grow accustomed to. They would depart upon a mission to the past, or Minus Time, and could be gone for days or weeks or months or even years, yet when they returned, often no more than several hours had passed. And duty spent in Plus Time, or in the 27th century, was all that counted toward the completion of an enlistment period. This was always made very clear to new recruits, but the consequences of it were often overlooked, since there were two different pay scales in the service—one for duty served in the present and one for time spent in the past, with the latter being far more lucrative. The pay scale for Temporal Observers, for example, was higher than that found in almost any other career, and if one was able to avoid the hazards of the duty and survive to complete his tour of enlistment, he could retire a very wealthy man.

But it was not, by any means, a route to easy street. As Neilson had already discovered. It was an exciting way to make a living, but it was highly dangerous, as well. Most temporal agents found that they had to leave their former, civilian lives completely behind them. After Neilson had returned from his first assignment to the past, he had taken some leave and gone back to Tucson to visit his family and his girl. It had been a shock to them to discover how much he had changed. For them, from the time he had gone off to join the service to the time he returned from his first tour of Observer duty in the past, only a month or so had elapsed. For Scott, it had been four years. Four years in which he had grown immeasurably older and more experienced. He had found it

difficult to connect with them. His girl, whom he had loved
with all the fierce intensity of youth, had suddenly seemed
immature and superficial. And the concerns of his family
seemed suddenly irrelevant to him. He was still his mother's
"little boy," but he had returned a man and found that he
could not make the adjustment. Since then, he had not gone
back home again. It was a different time and place.

As he reappeared inside his room in the Grand Hotel, it
looked no different than when he had left, about twelve hours
earlier. Only minutes had passed here. The outline of Jennifer's
head was still impressed into the pillow. He stared at the
rumpled sheets on the bed and thought about her. He found
those thoughts disturbing.

It was hard to believe she was a prostitute. He was not naive
about the subject. He was in the service, he'd been with
prostitutes before. Only this had been different. He'd only had
a couple of experiences with hookers and, at first, there had
been a sort of illicit thrill to it, but it was a thrill that was very
short-lived. He knew that some men liked going with prostitutes because it was easy, uncomplicated sex, coupled with a
sort of sleazy thrill, but he had found it frustrating and
unsatisfying. He'd heard it said that prostitution victimized
women because it made them into objects, but in another
sense, it also victimized those who patronized them—to the
hookers, they were objects, too. There was really no personal
connection. It was, in many respects, a lot like masturbating.
He had found it even less satisfying, because there was another
human being involved, yet there was no real emotion, no
affection, no genuine desire or intimacy. And when it was
over, he was left with an empty feeling.

Only with Jennifer, it had been different. He had expected a
relatively quick coupling, with little or no foreplay, and with
her making all the obligatory expressions and sounds of sexual
passion, only it had not turned out that way. It had started with
that damn calico dress. It made her look like something out of
Little Women, for God's sake, demure and innocent. The
moment they entered the room, he had expected her to start
stripping in a matter-of-fact way, only she hadn't done that.
She had approached him rather shyly, put her hands upon his
shoulders and stood on tiptoe to kiss him softly on the lips. It
was a hesitant, gentle kiss, almost chaste. They had exchanged
several kisses like that, very brief and tentative, and then she

had sighed as he pressed her against him and started undoing
the buttons on the back of her dress.

In bed, he had marveled at the soft, lithe suppleness of her,
the flawless, creamy skin, the gentle curves, the silky texture
of her hair. . . . They spent almost half an hour languorously
exploring one another's bodies, kissing and caressing and
whispering endearments to each other, and when they moved
beyond the foreplay and started making love, that too had been
nothing like what he'd expected. There were no melodramat-
ics, rather there had been a genuine, loving intimacy that took
him completely unprepared. He could not believe she was that
good an actress. He had climaxed quickly, carried away by the
intensity of his feelings, yet she had not gotten out of bed to use
the washbasin, dressed and gone away. Instead, she had
lingered, and they had held each other and talked, and then
they made love once more, and the second time, as she reached
orgasm, she had cried out softly and wept real tears. She left
shortly before dawn, after hugging him and holding him close
for a long time, and it was only after she had gone that he had
realized she had never even mentioned money.

He wondered what the hell he was getting into. Was he
falling in love with a hooker? Jesus, that would be really
stupid. Stupid and destructive. And yet, he couldn't stop
thinking about her. What they had shared was real. He had no
doubt of that. He did not know how he felt about it. Logically,
he told himself, he should forget it. Don't get involved. He had
a job to do and he could not afford distractions. Nor could he
afford to fall in love with someone who, when he was born,
had already been dead for over eight hundred years.

He could not reconcile the image of the tender and loving
young woman he had made love to with the image of a girl who
worked in a saloon and hustled drinks and would have sex with
any cowboy who could afford the price. A hooker with a heart
of gold? Come on, he told himself, get real. Don't be an
asshole. Yet, he kept thinking of her lying on top of him, with
her hand gently placed against his cheek, her beautiful blue
eyes gazing deeply into his, as if in wonderment. . . .

Don't *do* this, he thought to himself. It was just a brief
sexual encounter, nothing more. She had been excited by the
prospect of making it with a handsome, dangerous, young
gunfighter and there was nothing more to it than that. Hell, it
was probably only a come-on. Next time, she'd charge him. If

there was a next time. He knew it would be stupid. There would be no next time, he told himself. However, his resolution lacked conviction. He sat down on the bed and touched the pillow where her head had lain. Jesus, he thought, she had actually cried.

Why had she cried?

Hop Town was west of the Tombstone business district, just past Third Street, yet it might as well have been on the other side of the world. It was Tombstone's Chinatown, home to some five hundred Chinese immigrants, "coolies," as they were often called, who came to work on railroad construction gangs and in mining operations and in laundries and whatever other menial labor they could find. For most of the Chinese residents, it was a temporary situation, a way to find some work and make some money and return to the homeland, so they made little attempt to become acculturated to American society. As a result, Hop Town was like a little slice of China dropped into the frontier. Most of the residents of Tombstone never ventured there, preferring their own saloons to the Chinese opium dens and gambling houses. There was one exception.

Jennifer Reilly entered the opium parlour and held her breath as she walked through the smoke-filled room with its tiers of wooden couches, like cramped little bunk beds, most of them occupied by Chinese men reclining in states of drug-induced stupor. Jennifer had often thought that if there really was a Hell, it must be a lot like this. Heaven, she imagined, with a childlike simplicity, would be like some Elysian field, with waving heather and wildflowers and dreamy little thatch-roofed cottages from which harp music emanated while laughing little children, those innocents who had tragically died young, ran barefoot through the grass with little lambs and goats. It was a wistful vision, made melancholy by her certainty that she would never go there when she died.

She wasn't sure if she would go to Hell. She was a sinner, of that she had no doubt. She never went to church. Aside from the fact that it would have scandalized the respectable women of Tombstone if she had done so, she knew that she did not belong there. Church, like Heaven and Hell, was a place where people went. Real people. Not creatures like herself.

Often, when she looked in the mirror, she thought to herself that she *looked* real. She looked pretty—she knew that because so many men had told her so, and she knew they could not tell that she was not what she appeared to be. When she examined her own image in the mirror, she thought that she could not tell, either. But she knew. She would often think to herself, longingly, "How am I different?" And yet she knew she was. Because she had not been born. She had been made.

The nature of her creation was something that she didn't really understand. God created Man and Woman. The Master had created her. He was the closest thing to God that she would ever know.

He had made her in his laboratory, where she had been born not of a woman, but of an artificial womb, and he had molded her mind and placed her with others like herself, a man and a woman who had acted as her parents, though they were not her parents and could not be parents, ever, for they were just like her. She could never have a child. She could never be like other people. Real people. Those who had acted as her parents, until she was old enough to be of use to the Master, had taught her all about who and what she really was. She was not a human being, but a creature called a "hominoid," someone who only looked human but was really something less. She owed her existence, and her unquestioning allegiance, to the Master. And she had never questioned it, till now.

That she could even think of questioning the Master's wishes frightened her. Yet, it seemed impossible for her to think of Scott as being an enemy. The Master said he was. He had told her that he was one of those who came from the future, to seek him out and kill him. She knew that Scott could kill. She found it hard to believe that he could kill the Master, because the Master was so powerful and his enemies had always failed in the past. Yet the Master was concerned about them, concerned that they could interfere with his plans. If he had told her to kill Scott, she would have done it, without question. Only now, after what had occurred between them, she was not so sure.

She had been with many men since she had come to Tombstone. She had been told what to do and she had done it, though prior to coming to Tombstone, she had never been with a man and was not sure what to expect. The Master had told her, in brief, clinical terms, and explained that all she had to do was whatever the men wanted and act as if she enjoyed it immensely. She had not found it enjoyable. The first time, it had been painful and, despite her efforts, the man had not been pleased. She had cried afterward and felt terrible. But, as time went on, she found that it became less unpleasant, though it was never really pleasant. Most of the men were coarse and rough. Some of them had hurt her. A few, like Doc, were not so bad. She did not really mind doing it with Doc, though when he'd been drinking, he could be very rough, and Katie had told her that if she ever found out she was with Doc again, she'd cut her face up. Katie would do it, too. But Scott . . . with Scott, it had been different.

She'd felt differently about him from the very first. She knew that he was dangerous and that he was the Master's enemy, but she still found herself drawn to him. He was nicer than the other men. Cleaner. More of a gentleman. And he *had* been gentle. Tender. It had never been like that with anyone before. The orgasm she had experienced with him had been her first and she did not really understand what it was, but when it had happened, it had overwhelmed her. It had both thrilled and frightened her. So that's what it's like, she thought to herself later. That's what love feels like. Until then, she had not known. She had not thought herself capable of feeling it. Love, after all, was something only humans felt.

She had wept when it had happened, both because of the powerful feelings it had released in her and with joy, because she had discovered that she *could* feel those feelings, and at the same time, with utter misery, because she had deceived him. She had cheated him. She was not a real person and he believed she was. She had cheated others in that manner before, but it had never really mattered to her because she knew that she had never really mattered to them. Only Scott was different. She was in love with Scott. And she had no right to be in love. Not with any man, and especially not with Scott, who was the Master's enemy.

As she walked through the opium parlor toward the back room, no one except the attendants paid any attention to her. For most of them, she could have walked past them stark naked and it would have made no difference, but the attendants backed away from her, bowing deferentially, keeping their eyes averted. Not because of who she was, but because of who the Master was.

The people of Hop Town did not quite know what to make of the Master. He frightened them. He spoke their difficult language as well as any of them and he knew and understood their customs in a way no other white man did. He could do things that reduced them to a trembling awe. They believed that he was a powerful magician and it puzzled them, because they had not thought that there were wizards among the white men, yet he unquestionably was one. He had demonstrated to them what would happen if they did not do exactly as he said. As a result, he had become the lord of Hop Town. They would do his bidding, no matter what he asked. The penalty for disobedience was too terrible to contemplate.

Jennifer knew that what the Master did was not magic. It was science, which seemed like a sort of magic, since she didn't fully understand it. There was no need for her to understand. If there was a need for her to know or understand anything, the Master would give her that knowledge. He would also, if she performed her duties for him well, give her a child one day, and a man to live with, someone like herself, to act as father to that child. It would not be the same as having a child of her own, but it was the closest she would ever come to it and she had always dreamed of having that chance, that honor. Only now, she dreamed of something else. She had not thought she could feel love, but she had discovered that she could. Perhaps, if that was possible, there might be a way for her to have a child, as well.

She stepped through the door to the back room, where crates of supplies were kept, and continued on to a small closet at the very back. She unbolted the wooden door and opened it. Inside, assembled on the floor, were the softly glowing border circuits of a chronoplate. She took a deep breath, bit her lower lip, and stepped into the circle.

The weakness and dizziness struck her as soon as she stepped out into the room, a room that was thousands of miles away from Tombstone, and hundreds of years away, as well. She felt ill. Someone took her arm and steadied her.

"Come on," he said, "the Master's waiting."

She was conducted through a door and into an elegant living room in the penthouse of a luxury apartment building. Through the sliding glass doors at the back, leading out to the terrace, she could see the sun setting on 23rd-century London.

She knew it was the 23rd century, but she would not have guessed it from the furnishings. Nikolai Drakov was, at heart, a 19th-century man and he always liked surrounding himself with the trappings of that time. The wall-to-wall carpeting had been taken up when he moved into the apartment, the floors redone in handsome parquet and covered with expensive Persian rugs. The furnishings were all Victorian, from the sofa to the sideboard with its gasogene, and the reading chairs with their lace antimacassars. The apartment was lavishly decorated with sculptures and oil paintings and weapons of various sorts, from medieval broadswords to Zulu spears and shields to Kukri knives and pearl-inlaid jezail muskets. Not displayed, but available close by, were more sophisticated weapons.

Drakov stood by the bay window, staring out at the skyline of the city. He was dressed in wool slacks and a brocade smoking jacket. Jennifer could never quite get over how big he was, how powerful his arms looked. He heard her come in and spoke without turning around.

"This used to be a beautiful city," he said. "A city with character. Now look what they've done to it. I often recall the words of King Charles, spoken when he was still Prince of Wales. Referring to the Second World War, he said that you had to give one thing to the Luftwaffe. When they bombed London, they didn't replace the buildings with anything more offensive than rubble. The British themselves did that." He turned around. "Well, what have you managed to learn?"

"His name is Scott Neilson," she said.

Drakov smiled. "Ah. He is the one, then."

"There can be no mistake?" asked Jennifer. "Perhaps his having the same name is only a coincidence."

"In temporal physics, Jennifer, there is no such thing as a coincidence. Every event proceeds from cause and effect. If Neilson is here, then the others cannot be far behind. You have managed to establish a relationship with him?"

"Yes," she said, softly.

Drakov smiled. "Good. I had every confidence in you. Neilson is a professional, so you will have to be careful, but he is still very young, which means that he is emotionally vulnerable. I want you to play on those vulnerabilities. You've slept with him?"

She looked down at the floor. "Yes," she said, in a very low voice.

"Good. Very good. From now on, you will sleep with no one else. You will continue to work in the saloon, but you will no longer dispense sexual favors for money. If anyone questions you about that, and they undoubtedly will, you will tell them that it's because you have met someone very special. The implication will be that you're in love, and that the man you are in love with is Neilson. That you have given up prostitution for him will be certain to have an effect upon him. It will make him trust you."

Jennifer would have no trouble following those instructions. She had always hated allowing men to use her and, after what happened with Scott, the thought of going back to those rough and smelly cowboys was unbearable.

"Be careful not to crowd him," Drakov continued. "I want you to do nothing that could arouse his suspicion, but I do want you to report to me concerning everything he does and whom he sees. Especially anyone newly arrived in town. I'll have him watched, so I don't want you following him. But when you're with him, pay close attention to everything he says. If he asks you about Stone and Bailey, as he most assuredly will, play on his suspicions. You have already made a good beginning. Emphasize that both men have not been in Tombstone long and little is known about them, only be subtle. In particular, direct his attention at Ben Stone. You've been with Stone. Tell Neilson that there was something about him that seemed foreign somehow, something more than a little frightening, though you couldn't put your finger on it. Tell him he was cruel."

"He was," said Jennifer. She shuddered. "The things he made me do. . . ."

"Tell him that," Drakov said. "The way you just told me. With that little shiver of disgust. It's perfect. Neilson will ask what sort of things. Any man would. Only you will refuse to go into any details. You will beg him not to press you on the subject. It's painful and humiliating. Neilson's imagination will supply the rest."

"Master . . . forgive me, but is there no chance that you could be mistaken about him?"

Drakov stared at her and frowned. "Mistaken?"

"It's . . . it's just that he seems so nice . . . so kind . . . so gentle. . . . It seems so hard to think of him as an enemy."

"Ah, I see," said Drakov. "Do not allow his manner to deceive you, Jennifer. Naturally, he will not seem as coarse and rough as the men that you have grown accustomed to. He comes from another time. He is much more hygienic, more educated, more refined. That is only to be expected. His attitudes toward women are much different from those of the men you'll find in Tombstone. But take care not to let that influence you. Do not underestimate him. You have already seen that he is an accomplished killer. Think about that and not his gentle manner. If he were to discover what you really are, he would kill you without the slightest hesitation. Remember that."

Jennifer felt a chill run through her. "I . . . I will remember."

Drakov nodded. "Good. You have done well. Now go."

Jennifer turned and left the room. She was escorted back to the chronoplate and she stepped into its field. The border circuits flashed and she disappeared, to another place and time.

4 _____

George Spangenberg's gun shop wasn't much to look at, merely a small store with wood-plank floors and walls, a few wooden chairs, a cracker barrel and three glass-topped display cabinets, but to Scott, it was like entering a wonderland. The racks behind the counters displayed Winchester rifles, carbines and shotguns, and even a few Sharps buffalo rifles chambered in .50 caliber.

The holster rigs gave off the pleasant smell of brand-new leather. Some were made in the Territorial style, covering the entire gun except for the grips, so that the weapon sat very low in the holster. It was not a rig designed for a fast draw, but it provided greater security for the weapon. Others were cut slightly lower, such as the Main and Winchester holsters designed for percussion revolvers and the slim, open-bottomed holsters for metallic cartridge pistols. There were doubled-looped, Texan-style holsters, with wide leather skirts, some in plain, smooth leather, others border-stamped with decorations or carved with floral designs. The belts were looped for cartridges, some made in smooth leather, others in roughout, some plain and others carved, some sewn as money belts, so that coins could be slipped into them through an opening behind the buckle. There were leather carbine scabbards for carrying a rifle on a saddle, military-style flap holsters and leather pouches, handsome silver buckles and even Civil War

67

belts with the letters "C.S.A." on the buckles. Union buckles with the letters "U.S." on them were conspicuously absent.

But the guns in the display cases were what really caught Scott's attention. There was a profusion of Colt Single Action Armys, chambered in .45 and .44–40 calibers, most with the longer, seven-and-a-half-inch barrels, blued with color case-hardened finish and oil-stained walnut grips. There were a few Colts that would become known to future-era collectors as "U.S. Martials," those made under government contract and stamped on their wood grips with the date of manufacture and the government inspector's cartouche, as well as with the letters "U.S." on the left side of the frame. There were Colt and Remington derringers and pocket pistols, percussion pistols that had been converted to fire metallic cartridges, Smith & Wesson top-break revolvers, sidehammers, Colt Navys and Remington revolvers and even a couple of cased Walker Colts.

These monsters, with nine-inch barrels and a weight of four pounds and nine ounces, chambered in .44 caliber, were the largest production handguns Colt had ever made, named in honor of Captain Samuel Hamilton Walker, the Texas Ranger who had helped design them. When fired, they sounded like a howitzer going off. There were only about a thousand of them made. They were the rarest of all Colt pistols and Scott burned to have them for his collection.

"Help you, sir?"

The man who'd spoken was a small, trim, slightly bookish-looking individual who looked to be in his late forties. He had a receding hairline and wore little, round, wire-rimmed glasses and a leather apron over a white shirt and dark wool trousers.

"You'd be Mr. Spangenberg?" said Scott.

"No, sir, Mr. Spangenberg is out. I'm his assistant, Zeke Bailey. Is there something I can show you?"

"Oh, you're the gunsmith, then."

"Yes, sir."

"I was admiring these Walkers," Scott said. "Always wanted to get me a couple."

"I'm afraid those aren't for sale, sir. They are only for display purposes."

"I could make you a good offer."

"No, I'm sorry, sir, they're not for sale, as I said. They're my personal property. They belonged to my father. I couldn't possibly sell them. However, if you're interested in percussion pistols, I could show you some very fine Colt Navys that we have, just like Wild Bill Hickok's."

"No, I don't think so," Scott said. He would have liked to have them, but he reminded himself that he wasn't here shopping for his collection. "I think I need something a bit more practical."

"Well, then, you can't go wrong with one of these," said Bailey, opening up a display case, reaching in and taking out a Colt Single Action Army .45 with a seven-and-a-half-inch barrel, blued with a color case-hardened frame and walnut grips.

"I think I'd like a shorter barrel," Scott said.

"Ah," said Bailey, replacing the revolver in the case. "Something like this, perhaps?"

He took out a Colt with a four-and-three-quarter-inch barrel, blued and color case-hardened, with dark walnut grips. It was also a .45.

Scott took it from him and examined it. He pulled back the hammer to half cock and slowly rotated the cylinder, holding the gun close to his ear and listening to the lockwork.

"I see you know your guns," said Bailey. "You're the Montana Kid, aren't you? I've heard about you. Heard you shot three men in the Alhambra the very first day you came to town."

"It was two men, in the Oriental," Scott said, "and it was self-defense."

"Oh, I have no doubt that it was," Bailey said, hastily. "I merely wished to say that it's a privilege to have a shootist such as yourself in our store. In fact, I think we could even arrange a discount. I'll let you have that piece right there for twenty-five dollars and I'll throw in two boxes of cartridges."

"Sounds like a good deal to me," said Scott.

"Hear you use the crossdraw," Bailey said. "I have an unusual rig here that just might strike your fancy."

He turned around and took down a peculiar looking holster rig from a coat tree that was festooned with them.

"Fella came in about six months ago and ordered it made up special. Heard about that holster vest John Wesley Hardin used to wear and wanted a two-gun shoulder rig made up. Man was a greenhorn. You could tell straight off, but his money was just as good as anybody else's. When he picked it up, he put it on and stuck two brand-new Colts in it. Had them made up special too, ordered straight from the factory in Hartford. Had more money than sense, if you ask me. Right fancy lookin' things. Think I got 'em here somewhere."

He continued talking as he rummaged through one of the wood cabinets behind the counter. Scott picked the rig up and examined it, then took off his coat to try it on.

"Anyway," Bailey continued, still looking through the cabinet, "he puts on that there rig, sticks his fancy Colts in it, and goes straight down to the Oriental. God only knows what the damn fool had in mind. And who does he run into but Doc Holliday. Didn't know who Doc was, though. Like I said, a real greenhorn. Anyways, Doc sees the guns beneath his open coat and asks him if he knows that there's an ordinance against going armed in Tombstone. And the greenhorn opens up his coat to show off those fancy guns of his and says to Doc, so help me, 'Mister, I'd feel plumb naked without my shootin' irons.' Well, Doc just stares at him with his mouth open for a second and then commences laughin'. Pretty soon, the whole damn place is laughin' too and everybody's repeatin' what the greenhorn said. 'Mister, I'd feel plumb naked without my shootin' irons.' The greenhorn gets real hot under the collar and says to Doc, 'Mister, I don't take too kindly to bein' sported with.' Well, this only makes Doc start laughin' even harder. He just about split his sides. Ah, here they are. . . ."

Bailey straightened up, holding a wood guncase in his hands. He set it down on the counter.

"So the greenhorn says to Doc, real mad now, 'Mister, you stop that laughin' right now or I'll drill you so full of holes you'll look like a fountain every time you take a drink.' Well, as you might imagine, that only made things worse. Doc was laughin' so hard, he had tears comin' from his eyes. He's leanin' up against the bar and slappin' it with his hand and the whole place is in an uproar. So the greenhorn, God help him, goes to jerk his pistols. Only as he tries to cock and draw them both at the same time, the butts knock into each other and the guns go off, both of 'em. One bullet goes into the floor, the other one goes right into the greenhorn's foot. He screams and falls down, grabbin' his foot, and Doc falls down too, 'cause he's laughin' so hard he starts himself to coughin'. They had to get a couple of the boys to carry the greenhorn to Doc Warren's to get his foot fixed up and as soon as he was able to get up and about, he took the next stage out of town. Don't think he stopped till he got clear back to New York City. Sold me back the rig and fancy guns before he left. I paid maybe one-tenth what they were worth. Don't know what you'd think of them. They're right fine guns, but you might find them a bit gaudy. . . ."

He opened up the case and Scott almost gasped.

The silk-lined case held a matched pair of Colt Single Action Army .45s with four-and-three-quarter-inch barrels. They were silver-plated and profusely engraved, with scrollwork even on the barrels and the hammers. The grips were finely engraved pearl. They were the most beautiful guns Scott had ever seen. Not so much weapons as works of art.

"Good Lord," he said.

"Yeah, like I said, they're a bit gaudy," Bailey said, "but I could make you a good deal on 'em. Figure seventy-five dollars, for the whole kit and kaboodle. Guns and holster rig. I'll even throw in a couple boxes of cartridges."

Seventy-five dollars! Scott held his breath. The holster rig would have some curious collector value, but the guns would be almost priceless. He could retire from the service a rich man from what he could get from a collector for just one of them.

"Well, I don't know," he said, picking up one of the guns and examining it critically. "They certainly are a little on the showy side, aren't they?"

"Well, anybody else might get a little ribbing with a rig like that," said Bailey, "but I figure a serious shootist like yourself could carry them off without much trouble. And they'd be something that could add to your reputation, you know, like Bill Hickok and his brace of Navys. Tell you what, I'll let you have the whole thing for sixty dollars and it's a steal at that."

"All right," said Scott, barely able to hide his excitement. "Sold."

"Hear tell you're a good hand with a knife, as well," said Bailey. "Don't know as you'd be interested, but if you'd step over to this display case over here, I've got a few that I made up. Be anxious to see what you might think of 'em."

Scott walked over to the other case and once again, he caught his breath. The case held a number of Green River–style knives, popular among buckskinners, as well as several large bowies with staghorn grips, all extremely well-crafted specimens, but the blade that caught his eye was one forged of

Damascus steel. It was a seven-inch stiletto with a rib running down the length of the entire blade, giving it strength. It had a narrow wood handle, flaring slightly at the middle and tapering at the ends and toward the guard. It was completely useless for skinning or any other task but one. Killing. Except for being forged of Damascus rather than stainless steel, it was an exact copy of the famed Fairburn-Sykes commando knife used in World War II.

He was suddenly aware that Zeke Bailey was watching him carefully from behind his wire-rimmed spectacles.

"What do you think?" he asked.

"That one in the middle," Scott said. "I've never seen a knife like that before."

Bailey took it out of the display case and handed it over to him. "Don't know that I have either," he said, in a neutral tone. He shrugged. "The idea just sorta came to me one day. George, he took one look at it and said he couldn't see what use a knife like that would be. Said it would make a lousy skinner and thought it might break likely as not, but I made it pretty strong."

"I don't guess you'd use a knife like this for skinning," said Scott, feeling the perfect balance of the blade.

"Though it might make a nice boot knife for a gambler," Bailey said, "or somebody who might want a knife like that for serious business."

"It looks serious, all right," said Scott.

"It's balanced so as you can throw it," Bailey said. He pointed to a wood target mounted on the wall across the room. "Go ahead. Give it a try."

Scott grabbed the knife by the blade, holding it not by its point, but so that his hand was along the side of it, fingers on the central rib. He threw it in a smooth, practiced motion. The knife struck the target dead center.

"Guess you are a good hand with a knife at that," said Bailey.

Scott went over to the target and pulled the knife out. "How much do you want for this?" he asked.

"Well, it's a one-of-a-kind," said Bailey. "Twenty dollars."

"That's a lot of money for a knife," said Scott.

"It's a lot of knife. And I've got a leather sheath goes with it."

"All right," said Scott. "I'll take it. What do you call a knife like this?"

"I figured I'd call it a Bailey fighting knife." He shrugged. "Rezin Bowie made a knife up for his brother Jim and now everybody knows it as a Bowie knife. Maybe someday everyone will know that kind of knife as a Bailey. You never know."

"You never know," said Scott. "There might be a fair chance of that."

Bailey showed no reaction to his use of the word "fair," as in Fairburn. Scott paid for his purchases.

"Gunsmithing, knifemaking—you're a talented man, Mr. Bailey."

"Just tryin' to make a livin'," Bailey said. "And call me Zeke."

"Where you from, Zeke?"

"Oh, here and there. I've traveled some. Grew up back East, on a horse farm in Pennsylvania. Ever been there?"

"Can't say as I have," Scott replied. "Never been back East. You been in Tombstone long?"

"Not too long," Bailey replied. "But I kind of like it here. Lots of opportunities for a man in a boomtown like this. What brings you to Tombstone?"

"I came to look up some friends of mine," said Scott, "but all three of them were killed out at their claim."

"Heard about it," Bailey said, nodding. "Damn shame."

"Yeah."

"You lookin' to find who did it?"

"You have any ideas?"

"Could've been anyone, I guess. Maybe somebody only passin' through."

"Maybe," Scott said, "but somehow, I don't think so. I have a feeling that whoever killed them is still around." He casually inspected some of the guns in the display cases. "I figured I'd stick around a bit and see what I can turn up. Might be somebody knows something. Sure do have a nice selection here, Zeke. Say, isn't that one of those new Colt Bisley target models?"

"A Bisley?" Bailey said, with a frown. "No, that can't be. They didn't make those until . . ."

His voice trailed off.

"Until 1894," said Scott, softly. "That's thirteen years from now."

Bailey swallowed hard.

At that moment, the door to the shop opened and the proprietor, George Spangenberg, entered. "See we got us a customer, Zeke," he said. "Say, aren't you the Montana Kid?"

"That's right," said Scott, not taking his eyes off Zeke Bailey, who was suddenly perspiring. "I just told Zeke here I was admiring your selection. He sold me some nice guns." He held up the knife. "Bought one of his knives, too."

"Is that right?" said Spangenberg, with mild surprise. "Heck, and I told him we'd never sell that thing. No damn good for skinning, I told him. Not much you can do with a knife like that 'cept stick it in somebody."

"Be a pretty good knife for that, though," Scott said. He smiled at Zeke. "You might even say it's ahead of its time." He touched the brim of his hat. "Be seein' you, gents."

"Stop in anytime, Kid," said Spangenberg.

Scott paused by the door. "I'll do that. Nice talkin' to you, Zeke. We'll have to do it again real soon."

"Seemed like a nice fella," Spangenberg said, after Scott had left. "Heard he shot four men over at the . . . say, Zeke, you feelin' all right? You look white as a sheet."

"Okay, people, we've got a problem. According to history, there was never anyone known as the Montana Kid in this temporal scenario. So who the fuck is he?"

Tim O'Fallon looked around at the men seated at the table in the ranch house. He was young, slim, and good looking, with dark hair and a neat moustache. His eyes were large and expressive. His features were not entirely his own. They had been altered with cosmetic surgery to match the features of the man whose place he'd taken, a man who now lay buried in an unmarked grave in the Chiricahau Mountains a few miles outside of Galeyville.

"Could be just another young gun out trying to make a rep for himself," said one of the other men. "Somebody only passing through, someone who never achieved any real notoriety."

"I don't buy it," said O'Fallon. "Word is he's greased lightning with a gun. They say he's even faster than Wyatt Earp. It's hard to believe someone like that could have been a complete historical nonentity. What's more, both the *Nugget* and the *Epitaph* reported that shooting in the Oriental, when he killed Carter and Demming. And according to our research, neither paper ever made any mention of anyone known as the Montana Kid. So we're looking at a temporal anomaly. The question is, exactly what kind of an anomaly does he represent? It's possible that he could be the result of a disruption of some sort that occurred earlier in the timestream. Or he could be T.I.A. Or even S.O.G."

"He's been asking around about those three miners who were killed," one of the others said. "Word is they were friends of his."

"Friends? Or fellow agents?"

"You think those three might have been Observers?"

"It's possible. Or they could have been advance scouts for the S.O.G. Which makes their deaths much more significant. If they were Observers, then was the S.O.G. responsible? If so, then how did they manage to penetrate their cover when we couldn't? And if they were S.O.G., then who the hell killed them?"

"Maybe it was Temporal Intelligence," one of the other Network men said.

"Again, it's possible. But that means they would have had to discover their presence here somehow. If that's the case, then what tipped them off that we missed? And if the T.I.A. sanctioned those three men, then why is the Kid here asking questions?"

"Maybe the Kid is S.O.G."

"You think maybe Bailey killed them?" another man asked.

"I find that hard to believe," O'Fallon said. "Bailey's afraid of his own shadow. I can't believe he would have done anything like that without consulting me. He simply hasn't got it in him. We've got too many unanswered questions. I don't like that."

"You think we should put off the stage job?"

O'Fallon thought a moment. "No. No, I don't think so. There's a good shipment of bullion going out and I don't intend to miss it. Besides, it might help force the issue. All we've got to go on for the moment is the Kid. How he responds to the robbery might tell us something."

"I still think we should waste him, just to be on the safe side.

Demming's dying for a crack at him. He almost got him the other day at the hotel. If it wasn't for Doc Holliday—"

"From what I hear," said one of the others, "even if Holliday hadn't been there, the Kid might still have taken out both Demming and McLaury."

"So send Curly Bill along next time. He's been asking if the Kid's really as fast as people say. And Slim Carter was a friend of his. He's been wanting a chance to go into town and check the Kid out for himself."

"No, let's wait until after the stage job," said O'Fallon. "For now, the word to all the cowboys is to keep away from the Montana Kid. I don't want to do anything about the Kid until we know more about him. Meanwhile, get word to Bailey that—"

There was a loud knocking at the door.

"Paul, go see who it is," O'Fallon said.

A moment later, Paul came back in. "It's Bailey," he said. "He just drove up in his rig. He insists on seeing you. Curly Bill's outside with him."

"Damn it," said O'Fallon. "I told him never to come here. All right, bring him in."

Paul went back out and returned with a very worried-looking Zeke Bailey.

"What the hell's the matter with you, Bailey?" said O'Fallon. "I told you I didn't want you coming here."

"I'm blown," said Bailey.

O'Fallon frowned. "*What?*"

"It's the Kid," said Bailey. "He knows. Christ, I need a drink."

"Paul, get Zeke a whiskey," said O'Fallon. "Okay, now slow down and let's have it."

"He came in today and bought some guns," said Bailey. "I sold him a shoulder rig. And then I showed him the knives, like you said. He wanted to know about the Fairburn-Sykes right away, but I wasn't sure about him. He just seemed curious. I didn't see any recognition there and I was watching him carefully."

Paul handed him a drink and he gulped it down.

"Thanks, I needed that."

"Go on," said O'Fallon.

"I told him to go ahead and try it out. He threw the thing and hit the target dead center. He decided to take the knife, even though it was the most expensive one in the case. But I just couldn't be sure about him. He asked some questions, like how long I'd been in Tombstone, where I came from, that sort of thing. And then he tricked me up."

"What do you mean?"

"He was just sort of talking, and he was looking at some of the guns in the display cases. He stopped at this one case and seemed to be looking at one of the guns. Asked if it was one of the new Colt Bisley target models. It took me off guard and I just blurted out that it couldn't be, because Colt didn't make the Bisleys until . . . and then I caught myself and he was standing there, staring at me, and he said, '. . . until 1894. That's thirteen years from now.' And just then Spangenberg came back in and the Kid left. But he said we'd have to talk again real soon. I told Spangenberg I was feeling sick and came right over to tell you."

"You idiot," said O'Fallon. "He probably followed you right here."

"No, I was real careful, I made sure. . . ."

"You made sure," O'Fallon said, with disgust. "You never would have spotted him. He's probably sitting out there somewhere right now."

"I *had* to come," protested Bailey. "Look, you told me that if something like this ever happened, you'd get me out. I've done everything you said, O'Fallon. I've exposed this guy for you."

"Exposed him?" said O'Fallon, wryly. "What you've done was to expose *us,* you fool. You probably led him straight to us. Paul, I want security doubled right away."

"Got it," Paul said, as he turned to leave the room.

"No, wait . . ." O'Fallon said. "All he knows is that Bailey came straight here. He still doesn't know who he came to see. If he's out there watching and he sees increased security, that will only give away the operation. Let's keep him guessing. At this point, all he knows about for sure is Bailey."

"You said you'd help me, O'Fallon," Bailey said. "You promised!"

"You've put me in an awkward situation, Zeke."

"All right, at least give me back my warp disc!" Bailey pleaded. "I can't take the chance of staying around. He knows about me now! I've got to get out of here!"

"Yes," said O'Fallon. "I can't afford allowing you to be interrogated. You simply know too much."

Bailey paled. "Oh, Jesus Christ . . . you . . . you're not going to *kill* me?"

"You haven't given me a great deal of choice, Zeke," O'Fallon replied.

Bailey swallowed hard. "O'Fallon, please . . . you don't have to do this. You don't know for sure that I was followed. But if I was, and he doesn't see me leaving here, he'll know. He'll know for sure!"

"Yes, I'm afraid you have a point," O'Fallon said, rubbing his chin thoughtfully. "So what do you suggest I do, Zeke?"

"Give me back my warp disc," Bailey said. "I've got Underground contacts in other time periods who can help me. I'll never say anything about you or your operation, I swear to God. If I did, they'd cut me off, you know that. They wouldn't want to risk exposure."

"Yes, that's true enough," O'Fallon said.

"I'll leave here and start driving back toward town," said Bailey. "There's still plenty of daylight, I'll see the Kid coming if he's out there. If he gets anywhere near me, I'll just clock out. He'll never know where I went. Otherwise, I'll wait till I get back to my place and clock out from there."

O'Fallon thought about it for a moment. "I don't know," he said. "It's risky."

"I won't let him take me, I swear to God I won't."

For a long moment, O'Fallon didn't speak.

"O'Fallon . . ." Bailey said, his voice barely above a whisper. "*Please* . . ."

"I'll tell you what I'll do, Zeke," said O'Fallon. "I'll send Paul with you. I'll give him the warp disc I took from you. Perhaps we can turn this situation to our advantage."

"I'll do anything you say," said Bailey.

"Go back to your place, Zeke," O'Fallon said. "Paul will ride along. I don't think the Kid will try anything if you're not alone. He won't be certain of the situation. If he's out there somewhere, and I'm betting that he is, he'll follow you to your place, hoping to catch you alone. Paul will escort you that far, then he'll continue on to town. In the meantime, we'll clock some of the boys ahead to your place and see if we can't arrange a nice reception for the Montana Kid, whoever the hell he is. If we're lucky, we might even take him alive."

"What about me?" asked Bailey.

"After you've done your part, you'll be free to go," O'Fallon said. "Frankly, I couldn't care less what happens to you."

Bailey looked enormously relieved. "I'll do whatever you say, O'Fallon."

O'Fallon nodded. "All right," he said. "Paul, you go with Zeke. Steve, Randy, Allan, you'll pick up your ordnance and clock over to Bailey's place. At least now we know for sure the Kid is from the future. Let's see if we can find out *which* future."

As the men started to leave, O'Fallon said, "Steve . . ."

The man named Steve hesitated, waiting till the others had left.

"When Bailey gets back to his place," said O'Fallon softly, "kill him."

Scott watched from the ridge as Bailey's rig drove out through the gateposts of the ranch. He saw that Bailey was not alone. There was another man with him in the rig, his saddled horse tied to the back and following along. They took the road heading back toward town.

This wasn't what he'd hoped. He had hoped to catch Bailey coming out alone. The fact that he was not alone alerted him. Bailey had gone straight from Tombstone to the Clanton ranch. Interesting, thought Scott. Very, very interesting. It looked as if someone among the rustlers was not who he appeared to be. Maybe there were several of them. Only *who*? The Clantons themselves? The McLaurys? Ringo? Brocius? One or more of their hired hands? It could be any of them. He had no way of knowing. Not unless he could get Bailey alone to question him.

He had read Bailey exactly right. He had gone straight to whomever he was working with. Only who were they? The Special Operations Group? The Underground? The Network? The smart thing to do, he thought, would be to wait until Priest, Cross and Delaney showed up. Only he wasn't sure when they would be clocking in.

Perhaps they were already in Tombstone. But meanwhile, he was alone out here and he hated to take a chance on Bailey running, perhaps clocking out to some other time period. He had blown his cover purposely, setting himself out as bait, but if he could question Bailey, he could improve his chances of survival by learning where the attack might come from. The man with Bailey could be one of them. Or he might simply be one of the cowboys. There was no way of knowing. And when you don't have enough information, Scott told himself, the best thing to do is to do nothing.

He was sorely tempted to follow them, but he realized that could be exactly what they were expecting him to do. They could be trying to draw him into a trap. Whoever they were, he was at a disadvantage. They might try to catch him on the road or lead him into an ambush. It was possible they were unaware that he had followed Zeke, if that was really his name, but he was not about to take that chance. Better to gamble on the opposition being smart, not stupid. He had already discovered two valuable pieces of information—that Zeke Bailey was not what he appeared to be, and that whoever he was working with was involved somehow with the Clanton ranch.

The Network, he thought. It had to be. The whole setup had all the earmarks of a Network operation. He knew the Clantons were involved in rustling. They were part of a large outlaw faction that included the McLaury brothers, Johnny Ringo, and Curly Bill Brocius. Most of them were ranchers, people who had been here before the silver boom, and with the proximity of the Mexican border, rustling had grown commonplace. Men from both sides of the border frequently conducted rustling raids for horses and cattle. The rustled stock could then be cheaply sold to other ranchers in the area, to augment their herds and to be consumed in Tombstone. Consequently, rustlers frequently found a warm welcome at most of the ranches in the area and they often went out of their way to ingratiate themselves with local ranchers, who were, after all, their market. Many people in Tombstone and its environs did not really consider the rustlers outlaws. But that was slowly changing.

As Tombstone grew, it was inevitable that certain of its citizens would come to view the rustlers as a disruptive element. The community was polarized. There were those to whom the rustlers were their friends, hard-working cowboys just trying to make a living. And there were others to whom they represented a potential threat. Especially as it was just one short step from stealing stock to robbing stages, with their cargo of silver bullion.

It was a perfect setup for the Network. Not one of their

large-scale operations, obviously, but nevertheless one that afforded the opportunity for easy profit with a minimum of risk. How hard would it have been for them to infiltrate the rustlers and nudge them toward robbing stages? Or perhaps keep them out of it entirely and simply use their rustling operations as a cover for robberies of silver bullion? Either way, it would be relatively simple. A small operation, with no overhead to speak of, that would produce untraceable assets that could readily be liquidated. The Special Operations Group would not be interested in anything like that.

If there was a confluence point somewhere in this temporal sector, then it would be all the more reason for the S.O.G. to maintain a very low profile. They would set up a base of operations, carefully concealed, from which they could patrol the confluence point and stage hit-and-run operations in other temporal sectors. It would make sense that they would want to keep their involvement with the locals at a minimum. On the other hand, if it was the Network, then it would make sense for them to station someone like Zeke Bailey in town, keeping an eye on all new arrivals. That would explain the seemingly careless act of having a Fairburn-Sykes commando knife on display in the store. Most people in this time period would react to it the way George Spangenberg had. A knife that simply wasn't very useful for anything except maybe "sticking" people. Anyone with any sense would choose a skinner or a bowie. To people in this time sector, a knife like that would simply not appeal. But if anyone showed a marked curiosity about it, it could signal a warning.

What bothered him was Bailey. A Network man, it seemed to him, would have been too professional to have made that slip about the Bisleys. Bailey was a bundle of nerves. He simply did not fit the profile of a Network agent. But then, maybe he wasn't. At least, not part of the inner group. The Network was not above recruiting outsiders, often using criminals from the 27th century in their varied operations. They had contacts in the Temporal Underground, as well. Bailey could be a deserter from the future who was working for them. And, as such, he would be easily expendable.

The question was, what would they do now that they knew he'd broken Bailey's cover and revealed his own? Would they move against him or would they rush to shut down their operation in this sector and clear out? Much as he wanted to nail them, Scott had to recognize that the preservation of temporal continuity came first. If he alarmed the Network into shutting down and moving out, he would, in effect, have accomplished the primary goal of his mission. It would eliminate a potentially disruptive influence in this temporal sector. Taking the Network people into custody would be highly desirable, of course, but his first priority had to be safeguarding temporal continuity.

What would Forrester want him to do? The Old Man would not want him to take any unnecessary risks. He'd want him to wait until the others had arrived and convey what he had learned to Colonel Priest, who would take command of the mission. Much as he wanted to make a try for Bailey, Scott knew that the smart thing to do, for now, would be to wait.

"Play it safe, Neilson," he said to himself, out loud. "Keep a rein on it and play it safe."

He released the horse he'd rented and slapped it hard on the rump, sending it running down toward the road. It would make its way back to the corral in town. He'd clock back, to avoid any risk of being ambushed on the road, and simply say the horse had shied at a snake or something and had thrown him just outside of town. Then he'd wait and see who came for him. Would it be Wyatt Earp, unpersuaded by Doc Holliday and intent on seeing him on the next stage out of town? Would it be Demming, intent on avenging his brother's death? Or would it be the Network?

He grimaced, wryly. This was playing it safe?

5 ⎯⎯⎯⎯⎯⎯⎯⎯⎯⎯⎯⎯⎯⎯⎯⎯

Lucas and Andre got off the stage and waited for the driver to unload their bags. It hadn't been a very long ride from Benson, perhaps twenty-five or thirty miles, but it hadn't been very comfortable, either. Every jolt had been communicated to the passengers and the dust had seeped in everywhere. Both Lucas and Andre were well accustomed to discomfort, and there had been times in their careers when they had traveled in far less comfort. Lucas had never found anything to beat the sheer misery and exhaustion of forced marches with the Roman Legions and Andre had ridden for days on horseback, wearing full medieval armor. Nevertheless, they were grateful when the stage finally arrived in Tombstone.

Though they could easily have clocked into Benson, they had taken the Southern Pacific all the way from Lordsburg, the better to establish their cover. Lucas was posing as a writer from New York City, working on a series of articles for newspapers and magazines on the "Wild West." Andre was his wife, secretary, and personal assistant. Finn Delaney would arrive separately, on horseback, with the cover of a drifter, a cowboy looking for work in the boomtown or on one of the ranches in the area. Between them, they hoped to be able to cover all contingencies.

Their first step was to check into the Grand Hotel, where Lucas made sure the desk clerk knew why he was in town. A

promise to put the desk clerk's name in the article he was
writing immediately turned the man into a font of information
about "the town that had a man for breakfast every morning."
The next step was to stop in at the hotel bar, where Lucas
interviewed the bartender and some of the patrons, who regaled
him with stories about the Earps, Bat Masterson, Doc Holliday, and the young gunslinger who had recently arrived in
town, the Montana Kid.

"You missed Bat Masterson," the barman told him. "He had
to leave town and go to Dodge to help out his brother, Jim,
with some trouble he was havin' back there. But you'll still
find plenty to write about right here in Tombstone, mister.
There's trouble brewin', you mark my word."

"What sort of trouble?" Lucas asked him.

"There's bad blood between the Earps and some of the cowboys," said the barman. "Like the Clantons and the McLaurys.
And a lot of folks in town are startin' to choose up sides. Even
the newspapers are gettin' in on it."

"What's it all about?" asked Lucas, while Andre sat beside
him, taking notes. He bought another drink and invited the
barman to have one for himself.

"Well, near as I can tell, the bad blood between the Earps
and the McLaurys got started back around July of last year,"
said the barman, a loquacious sort who clearly liked to gossip.
He needed little prompting. "See, some soldiers came to town
one day to see the Earps. Seems some mules got stolen from
out at Camp Rucker and they wanted some help from the local
law to track the rustlers down. Well, sir, the trail took 'em
out to the McLaury ranch. They found some mules, all right,
but they couldn't prove that they were Army mules. Frank
McLaury said that they were his and the Earps thought that the
brands were changed. Anyways, they couldn't prove the mules
were stolen and the Army didn't get 'em back, but Frank
McLaury didn't like bein' called a thief and he went around
tellin' anyone who'd listen how the Earps were spreadin' lies
about him."

"*Did* Frank McLaury steal the mules?" asked Lucas.

"I'm not sayin' he did and I'm not sayin' he didn't," said the
barman, "but it wouldn't have been the first time stock was
rustled around here. There's been a lot of that sort of thing
goin' on. And lately, there's been some stage robberies, as
well. We got a lot of silver bullion goin' out and not all of it

gets to where it's goin'. See, lot of small ranchers around here have done a bit of rustlin' from time to time. There's nothin' unusual about it. Folks take a ride across the border and come back with some stock. Mexicans do the same damn thing. Been goin' on for years. Only now there's talk that some of the ranchers around here have taken to robbin' stages as well as rustlin' stock and some of that talk is comin' from the Earps and others. And that ain't the half of it."

"What's the rest?" asked Lucas, paying for another couple of drinks.

"Well, the McLaurys are real tight with the Clantons," said the barman. "And they're all friends of Sheriff Johnny Behan. Now Johnny, he's not a bad sort, you understand, but he doesn't go out of his way to look for trouble, if you get my drift. Now a while back, this girl showed up in town, name of Josie Marcus. She was an actress came to town with a show called *Pinafore on Wheels*. Seems she knew Johnny from before. Anyway, the two of them set up house together and Johnny was introducin' her to everybody as his fiancée. Only it seems that Josie didn't care too much for the sort of company that Johnny kept. Boys like the Clantons, the McLaurys, Curly Bill and Johnny Ringo. They'd have these all-night poker games out at Johnny's place and I guess Josie didn't like it. Anyway, it wasn't long before they had a fallin' out and Josie took up with Wyatt Earp."

"So you're saying there's a love triangle involved?" asked Andre.

"Well, now, I'm not tellin' you any secrets," said the barman. "The whole town knows all about it. Part of it's a question of property, too. In more ways than one. See, Johnny and Josie built their house on money Josie's daddy sent her, only Johnny owns the lot it stands on. One time, when Wyatt was away, Johnny came to try and dispossess her. Only Wyatt had asked Morgan to look in on her from time to time and Morg was there. They had some words and Morg knocked Johnny clear off the front porch. Johnny didn't bother Josie anymore after that, but you can see why he's never been too fond of the Earps. And it's like their trouble with property was just like the trouble many folks had here in town."

"How's that?" asked Lucas, plunking down for two more drinks.

"Well," said the barman, pouring, "Arizona's still a territory, you understand, and we ain't never had much in the way of law around here. Back when the boom got started, there was a good deal of lot jumpin' goin' on and it got so it wasn't very clear who owned what, you understand. Well, the mayor at that time, Alder Randall, went and transferred all the titles to the company of Clark and Gray. Seems the law let him do that, for the purpose of getting all the paperwork cleared up or somethin'. Only what Clark and Gray did was turn around and demand payment for all the lots in town and those who wouldn't pay were threatened with eviction. Some of the boys they used to do the dirty work were the same cowboys who were doin' a lot of the rustlin' in these parts. It turned into one big mess, let me tell you, and there's still lawsuits pending over the whole thing. It pretty near split the town in half. There was Clark and Gray and their friends in the County Ring, who own the *Nugget* and hold some of the offices in town, and there was John Clum, who's now the mayor and runs the *Epitaph* and a bunch of local businessmen around here who sided up with him.

"Now the Earps own some property in Tombstone," he continued, "and they got involved in the whole thing, as well. When they first came here, they were goin' to open up a stage line, only we already had two lines so the Earps got into other business. They own some mining claims around here and got interest in one of the saloons, plus a few more things. Virgil got himself a badge and Wyatt wrangled himself an appointment as deputy U.S. Marshal. Between them, they got the power to make Morgan deputy if need be and Wyatt's always got Doc Holliday and one or two others to back him up. Now on the other side, you got the County Ring, and Johnny Behan is their man, along with his deputies, Billy Breakenridge and Frank Stilwell. And Stilwell, for certain, with his buddy, Pete Spencer, has done some rustlin' with Ike Clanton. So we got ourselves one big kettle of stew on the boil, let me tell you."

"Sounds like something's bound to come to a head sooner or later," Lucas agreed. "Looks like I picked an interesting time to arrive in Tombstone."

"That you did, partner. And now that the Montana Kid's in town, there's no tellin' what's liable to happen."

"Tell me about the Montana Kid," said Lucas. "Who is he?"

"I don't rightly know," the barman replied, this time standing Lucas to a drink. He was clearly enjoying himself with his captive audience. "He came into town a while back lookin' for some friends of his. Three men named Ben Summers, Josh Billings and Joe McEnery had a small claim up in the hills. Only they'd been murdered 'bout two weeks before. Nobody ever learned who did it. Anyways, the Kid was in the Oriental, askin' questions, when this fracas breaks out between Bat Masterson and a couple of Ike Clanton's boys, Slim Carter and Jack Demming. Slim and Jack both jerked their pistols and it looked bad for Masterson, but the Kid shot 'em both quick as you please, dead center in the heart, each one. I didn't see it myself, sorry to say, but folks that did say the Kid's draw was the fastest thing they'd ever seen."

"Really?"

"That's what they say, and I can believe it, too. Why, just the other day, Ross Demming—that's Jack's brother—came in here lookin' for the Kid with Frank McLaury. The Kid was sittin' right at that table over there, with Jenny Reilly, she's a saloon girl over at the Oriental. Jenny's about the prettiest girl anyone's ever seen in town and she was real popular, I can tell you, but since the Kid arrived in town, Jenny won't have anything to do with anybody else, if you catch my drift—beg pardon, Ma'am," he added, with a glance at Andre. "So there's a lot of cowboys aren't too pleased to have the Kid around. Anyways, there the Kid was, sittin' right there and havin' himself a meal, talkin' to Jenny, when in comes Ross Demming, full of fight, with Frank McLaury to back him up. Both men wearin' guns, too, and the Kid had given his to Virgil Earp, 'cause of the ordinance, you know."

"So the Kid was unarmed?" asked Lucas.

"It sure looked that way," the barman said. By now, they had an audience. "Jenny tried to talk Frank into makin' Ross back off, but Frank wasn't havin' any of it. The Kid just sat there, quiet as you please, tellin' the boys he didn't want any trouble. When Frank found out he didn't have a gun, he offered to let the Kid use one of his. And right then Doc Holliday came in and got the drop on 'em. Made 'em both leave and as soon as they got outside, Virgil and Morgan took their guns and led 'em off to jail."

"So the Kid got lucky," Lucas said.

"Well, that's what Doc told him," the barman replied. "Asked him what he'd have done if it hadn't been for him showin' up when he did. And what happened next, I saw with my own eyes. The Kid makes a move like this . . ." the barman demonstrated, crossing his wrists, ". . . and pulls out two little knives and throws 'em, so fast you couldn't hardly see him move. And they went right into the wall there, where Frank and Ross were standin'. If you go on over there, you can see where they went in. Let me tell you, I've seen some fast men in my time, but never anything like that, not in all my born days! You want to get yourself a story, mister, the Kid's the man you want to see. Hardly old enough to take a drink, yet there's not a grown man in this town won't step aside to make way for him."

"Sounds like a fascinating individual," said Lucas. "Where can I find him?"

"Well, sir, he's got a room right here in this hotel. You stick around, you're bound to see him and I'll be pleased to point him out to you. Or you can head on over to the Oriental. Kid's been spendin' time down there, since he got sweet on Jenny. And there ain't been much trouble down there since the Kid has been around, no, sir! Even Wyatt Earp had to admit that."

"How do the Earps feel about the Kid?" asked Lucas.

"Virgil, he don't care one way or the other, long as the Kid stays out of trouble. Wyatt, he didn't care for him one bit and told him to leave town, but Doc Holliday seems to like the Kid and I guess he had a word with Wyatt. Anyways, since Wyatt has an interest in the Oriental, and the Kid bein' there keeps trouble down, seems Wyatt doesn't mind too much. But I don't think he trusts the Kid, entirely."

Lucas thanked the barman for all the information and left him a generous tip, then he decided to head over to the Oriental saloon.

"You might as well check out some of the local stores," he said to Andre. "Meet some of the local women, see what you can learn. Respectable women of this time didn't hang out in saloons."

Andre grimaced. "Right," she said. "I'll meet you back here later."

As they stood on the walk in front of the hotel, Finn Delaney came riding by. He nodded and touched the brim of his Stetson. Lucas nodded back.

"He's right on time," he said. "Which leaves only Darkness." He sighed. "Damn it. I hate not knowing what he's up to."

"From the way he talked, it's pretty serious," said Andre.

"Yeah. Here we are trying to pull off a temporal adjustment mission and meanwhile, we're part of something in his past that he's trying to change. Only he can't tell us what it is, any more than we can tell the people here. The only difference is that they don't know what they're caught up in and we do. Or at least we know that we're caught up in *something*. God knows what."

"There's not much point in worrying about it now, since there's nothing we can do about it anyway," she said. "At least not until Darkness tells us what it is."

"That's just what worries me," said Lucas. "What if he's wrong? What if whatever it is he expects us to do back here isn't the *right* thing to do? How the hell do we know?"

"We don't. We're simply going to have to trust him."

"Yeah. He wants our trust, only he won't give us his."

"Maybe he can't afford to," she said. "It's like he said, if we know more than we should, it could affect the outcome."

"Only what *is* the outcome?" Lucas asked, with exasperation. He paused as several people passed by, then turned to Andre. "What *happened* in the future, where he came from? Was it a timestream split? A chain reaction? An invasion from the parallel timeline? *What?*"

"There's no way we can know," she said. "We don't know what time period he came from. Even if we were crazy enough to take the risk and clock ahead, we wouldn't know which sector to check out. Or if we'd be able to make it back."

"He made it back."

"He's faster than light. We're not. Don't even think about it, Lucas. It would be crazy. It's against all the rules."

"How do we know *he's* playing by the rules?"

"We don't," she said. "But where he came from, the rules might have ceased to matter. We've got to trust him, Lucas. We have no other choice. Remember what he said. When the time comes for whatever it is we have to do, there'll be no time for doubt or hesitation."

"I know. I've been thinking about that. It tells me that whatever it is that's going to happen, or that has already happened from his temporal point of view, is going to happen so fast that a split second could make all the difference. And that scares the hell out of me."

"It scares me, too," she said. "But I have to believe that

Darkness knows what he's doing. After all, if it hadn't been for him, I would have lost you."

Lucas looked at her and took her hands in his. "I'm very much aware of that myself," he said. He smiled. "I wouldn't have come back from the dead for just anyone, you know."

"Just don't die on me again," she said, "or so help me, I'll kill you. Remember, you promised to marry me."

He grinned. "That promise was extorted under false pretenses."

"I might hold you to it just the same."

"We'll talk about it later. In about eight hundred years. Meanwhile, let's split up and see what we can learn. I'll meet you back here later."

Jenny was sitting beside a dapper man who was dealing in a card game when Scott came into the Oriental Saloon. The moment she saw him, she whispered something to the man, got up and rushed over to him.

"Hi, stranger," she said, with a dazzling smile. "I missed you."

"Who was that man you were sitting with?" asked Scott, as he stepped up to the bar. Frank Leslie set a glass of whiskey before him with a wink.

"You jealous?" Jenny asked, coyly.

Scott was surprised to discover that he was. That wasn't a good sign. It wasn't a good sign at all. He couldn't afford to get involved. Or was he already involved?

"Maybe," he said. "What if I am?"

"I think I like that," Jenny said, pressing up against him and rubbing his chest.

"Who is he?"

"That's Ben Stone. He's the gambler I told you about. Came to town just a little while before you did."

"About the same time my friends were killed?" asked Scott, softly.

She looked at him wide-eyed. "You think he might have had something to do with it?"

"I don't know," said Scott. "What do you think?"

She bit her lower lip. "I don't think I'd be surprised," she said. "Not that I know he did," she added quickly, seeing Scott's sharp glance. "Only there's something about him . . . something strange. And dangerous. He gives me chills."

"You ever been with him?" asked Scott, uneasily.

She looked up at him. "Scott, I've been with lots of men. You know that. But that's all in the past now. Oh, I still sit with cowboys and get them to buy drinks because that's my job here. Sometimes I might let them put their arms around me, but no more than that, honest. No more trips to the back room. All that's over now. It's been over ever since I met you. Things are different now. Does it really matter what happened in the past?"

"Sometimes it matters more than you might know, Jenny," said Scott, somewhat distantly. Then he smiled at her. "But that doesn't change the way I feel about you."

"Then that's all that really matters," she said.

Ben Stone put down his cards and got up from the table. He picked up his hat and cane and came over to them. Scott watched as he approached. He was a tall man, very fit looking, with short, neatly trimmed dark hair and gray eyes. He was clean-shaven except for a dark, close-trimmed, pencil-thin moustache. He was wearing an elegant dark suit and waistcoat, a gold watch chain, and a neatly tied cravat held down by a pearl stickpin. He would have looked like a fashion model, Scott thought, if it wasn't for those light gray eyes. They were alert, shrewd and calculating eyes. Eyes that didn't miss a thing.

"You must be the Montana Kid," said Stone. He offered his hand. Scott took it. "Benjamin J. Stone, at your service."

Scott nodded. "Mr. Stone."

"I've been looking forward to meeting you," said Stone.

"Is that right?"

"I wanted to see the man who managed to capture Jenny's affection. The moment she saw you, she excused herself and rushed right over to you. If I wasn't such an easygoing man, I might have taken exception. Jenny brought me luck. The moment she got up from the table, I started losing. A man can't afford to do much of that in my profession."

"No, I don't guess he can," said Scott. "Jenny's told me about you, but I don't believe I've seen you in here before."

"I've been playing down at the Alhambra for the past week or so," said Stone. "Thought I'd come back to the Oriental for a while. You never want to push a streak of luck too far in just one place."

"So you've been lucky, then?"

"I like to think that skill has a bit to do with it, but luck plays a part, as well. May I buy you and the lady a drink with my winnings?"

"It would be a pleasure, Mr. Stone, thank you."

"Call me Ben, Kid. All my friends do. And from what I've heard about you, I'd rather count you among my friends than among my enemies."

"You have many enemies, Ben?"

"Oh, a few, here and there. Some men like losing less than others. But I've always taken great care to stay on the right side of the law. Sometimes the only thing between you and a bullet is the local lawman, isn't that right, Marshal?"

Scott turned to see that Wyatt Earp had come up behind them.

"Isn't what right, Mr. Stone?"

"I was just telling the Kid here that a man always has to have respect for the local law, because sometimes it's all that stands between him and a bullet. Isn't that right?"

"I reckon I can go along with that," said Wyatt. He glanced at Scott's open coat. "See you got that fancy gun rig George Spangenberg had over in his shop."

"That's right, Marshal. But I made sure to get that special permit from your brother before I put 'em on. And I picked up that one that he was keeping for me, too."

"I know, I heard about that. Seein' as how you're workin' to keep order in here, I don't guess I mind that too much, so long as things don't get out of hand. And I suppose that havin' you wearin' your guns is a lot safer than havin' you without 'em. Otherwise you're liable to prove a temptation to certain folks around here."

"I appreciate your understanding, Marshal," Scott said. "Like I told you before, I'll do my best to stay out of trouble."

"Speakin' of trouble," Wyatt said, "you bought those guns from Zeke, didn't you?"

"That's right," said Scott, suddenly on guard.

"Mind if I see one?"

"Not at all." Scott took one of the Colts out and handed it to Wyatt.

"Sure is gaudy-lookin'," Wyatt said. "I figure folks will be talkin' about your guns as much as they talk about how fast you are with 'em. You seen Zeke since he sold 'em to you?"

"No, I can't say as I have. Why?"

"Just wonderin'," said Wyatt. "Seems after you left, he told George he was feelin' poorly and went home. After he closed up, George rode out to look in on him and see how he was feelin'." Wyatt shook his ahead. "Turns out Zeke wasn't feelin' too good. Fact is, he wasn't feeling anything at all. He was dead."

"Dead!" said Jenny.

"What happened?" asked Stone. "Was it fever?"

"Nope. It was a bullet. A bullet from a .45, just like this one." He handed the Colt back to Scott. "Zeke was shot right through the heart. And ole Ned, down at the corral, said you rented a horse from him this afternoon and rode out of town. Be about the same time Zeke went home to his place."

"Wyatt!" Jenny exclaimed.

"Are you suggesting that I killed him, Marshal?" Scott asked.

"I'm not suggesting anything, Kid. But I don't suppose you'd care to tell me where you went today?"

"I took a ride out to that old claim my friends had," Scott replied. "I thought maybe I'd file on it and find someone to work it for me. See if they were really going broke or if they'd made a strike and hadn't told anyone about it."

"And what did you decide?"

"I'm still thinkin' about it."

"Anyone see you go out there?"

"Wyatt, how can you suspect Scott of killing Zeke?" asked Jenny, shocked. "Why, Zeke never had an enemy in the world! Scott barely even knew him!"

"Like I said, Jenny, I'm not suggestin' anything just yet. I'm only making an investigation, that's all. What about it, Kid?"

"No, nobody saw me," Scott said.

"That horse you rented came back to the corral alone," said Wyatt. "What happened?"

"It spooked at a rattler and threw me, just outside of town," Scott replied. "I had to walk in. If you want to examine my other gun, Marshal, you'll see that it hasn't been fired, either. I haven't even had a chance to try 'em out yet. As for the one I came to town with, your brother still had that until *after* I got back." He offered the other gun to Earp, but Wyatt made no move to take it.

"So he did," said Wyatt. "I already checked on that. I don't think you had anything to do with Zeke's murder, Kid, but there's some that might. I don't really think you're a bad sort, but I still think you're trouble. Sooner or later, you're goin' to have to make some choices. Whether to walk on the right side of the law or the wrong one. For somebody like you, I don't think there's goin' to be any in-between. I'd think on that if I were you. Jenny, Mr. Stone . . ."

"Aren't you going to ask me where I was this afternoon, Marshal?" Stone asked.

"Why, you were right here, Mr. Stone," said Earp, "chasin' a big winning streak. I already asked."

He touched the brim of his hat, turned and left the saloon.

"Interesting things sure do happen around you, Kid," said Stone. "I wonder what Zeke Bailey did to get himself killed. Like Jenny here just said, he wasn't the sort of man that you'd think of as having any enemies."

"Then maybe someone ought to be lookin' at his friends," said Scott.

"I hardly knew the man myself," said Stone.

"Didn't say you did," said Scott. "Besides, you were here playin' cards all afternoon, in front of witnesses, isn't that right?"

They matched gazes for a moment. Stone smiled, but his eyes didn't.

"That's right. Too bad you weren't around to sit in, Kid. Looks like you could have used some witnesses yourself. I'll be seeing you around, Jenny."

He tipped his hat and left. Scott stared after him.

"There's something very odd about that man," said Jenny.

"Yes," said Scott, thoughtfully. "There is."

6 ———————————

Lucas sat across the table from Wyatt Earp in the Oriental Saloon, taking notes. On the other side of the room, Neilson was playing poker with several men. No sign of recognition had passed between them when Lucas came in. Good, thought Lucas, the kid's playing it smart. He decided to follow Neilson's lead for the time being. He was already on the scene and would be more on top of the situation. Maybe he was planning to make contact at the proper time. If not, and he was waiting for him to make the first move, Lucas knew he would have ample opportunity to do so in his cover as a journalist, when he sought to interview the Montana Kid. For now, he was more intent on firmly establishing his cover and getting his own reading on the situation in Tombstone. And in his cover as a journalist, he could hardly pass up the chance to interview the famous Wyatt Earp, who already possessed quite a reputation as a lawman from his days in Dodge.

He found Wyatt Earp to be amiable enough, a forthright, plainspoken man who talked easily and openly about his days as a lawman in Dodge City with Bat Masterson. He did notice, however, that while Wyatt Earp was not given to the sort of braggadocio that was often attributed to him later, he did have a tendency to give a version of events that placed him in the most favorable light. Lucas went through the obligatory questions that a writer could be expected to ask and listened to

Wyatt's stories about Dodge, then finally brought the conversation around to Tombstone.

"Would you say that Tombstone, in its own way, is as wild a town as Dodge was, Mr. Earp?"

Wyatt seemed to consider his response. "Well, in some ways, yes. And in some other ways, no. We don't really get the cattle drives the way that Dodge does, so there isn't as much trouble with the Texans comin' through. See, these cowboys spend a long time on the trail with nothin' much to do. Driving cattle's plenty of work, make no mistake, but there isn't really anything the men can do for entertainment on the trail, so when they get to town, they tend to run a bit hog-wild. That's understandable, so long as they don't get too out of hand. They gamble away most everything they've earned and what they don't gamble away they either drink up or spend on women. Trouble is, they get all liquored up and decide to hurrah the town, gallopin' through and givin' rebel yells and firin' off their six-guns. Somebody could get hurt and property could get damaged. So when that kind of thing gets started, you have to put a stop to it right quick.

"Now you take most men," he continued, "they get a little too much whiskey, they step out of line and usually all it takes is buffaloing one or two of 'em to put a stop to things. Man wakes up in jail in the morning with his head sore from too much drink and from a good blow with a six-gun barrel, he understands how things are. He pays his fine and says he's sorry he got drunk and caused a little trouble and he goes his way with no hard feelin's. None on my part, either. But some of them tend to be meanspirited and those are usually the real troublemakers. You need to come down real hard on them. You have to keep the peace. It's what you're paid for. Of course, every now and then, you get some cowboy who really ties one on and starts stalkin' through the streets, braggin' about how he's goin' to face down the local lawman. Clay Allison did something like that once. Well, so long as the gent isn't causing any real trouble, then you just keep out of his way and before too long, he'll get tired of it and go sleep it off somewhere.

"Now in Tombstone, the situation's a bit different. It's a boomtown and you get a lot of people comin' through. You get your businessmen and speculators, you get your greenhorns, you get your cowboys, you get your preachers and your gamblers and your bunco artists. . . . Wherever you find men makin' money, you find other men ready to separate 'em from it. We got us a sizable bunch of rustlers up in Galeyville and a few of 'em have ranches just outside of town. Many of 'em were here when Tombstone was no more than a few tents and empty lots, but now they get attracted by the money in this town and a few of 'em don't mind takin' a few shortcuts to get their hands on some of it."

"You're referring to the stagecoach robberies that you've been having lately?" Lucas said.

"That, for one," said Wyatt. "Once a man takes it in his head to steal some stock, he hasn't got far to go to holdin' up a stage. And he can make a lot more money that way. Then there's claim jumpin'. We've had our share of that, as well. Every now and then we have a shootin'. That's why we have an ordinance against carryin' guns in town, though that doesn't stop some people."

"I heard about some shootings you had here a little while ago," said Lucas, prompting him.

"That's right. Had two right here in this saloon," said Wyatt. "Matter of fact, that young fella playin' cards right over there was the one that did it."

"You're talking about the Montana Kid?" asked Lucas, turning around. Which one is he?"

"The one with the light blond hair, wearin' it long, like a plainsman."

"So that's him, is it?" Lucas said. "He looks very young."

"He's young, all right," said Wyatt, "but Billy the Kid was even younger when he killed his first man. You don't need hair on your chin to pull a trigger, mister."

"No, I guess you don't, at that," said Lucas. "But I was referring to the murders of those three miners out at their claim a little while back."

Wyatt Earp frowned. "Which three miners is that?"

"Let's see, I think I wrote their names down somewhere," Lucas said, glancing through his notebook as if he needed to refresh his memory. "Ah, here we are. Their names were Ben Summers, Josh Billings and Joe McEnery."

Wyatt Earp was still frowning. "You sure you got that right, mister? This is the first I've heard of it."

Lucas looked up at him sharply. "It would have been about a couple of weeks back," he said. "Three men found shot dead out at their claim. Very mysterious circumstances. Apparently, their murderers were never found."

"Seems to me like their bodies were never found, either," Wyatt said. "I think you must have got your information wrong, mister, or someone was feedin' you a story. I'm not aware of any men by those names bein' murdered."

Lucas stared at him, completely taken aback. "Ben Summers, Josh Billings and Joe McEnery? Those names mean nothing to you?"

Wyatt shook his head. "Never heard of 'em. Where'd you get this story?"

Lucas shook his head. "Why, I . . . I'm not exactly sure. I think I must have heard it in the bar over at the hotel. But I suppose I might have got it wrong somehow. You're sure those names mean nothing to you? Three men found dead in very mysterious circumstances?"

Wyatt smiled. "Sounds to me like somebody was pullin' your leg. You're liable to get some of that around here. City slicker like yourself, out to write about the wild frontier, folks are liable to string you along a bit. You'll have to watch out for that sort of thing."

Lucas was thoroughly confused. Why would Earp deny any knowledge of the killings? It made no sense, unless he wasn't anxious to have some reporter from back East writing about a case he couldn't solve. But then, surely he'd hear about it from others in town. Maybe it was just Earp's way of not wanting to talk about it.

"Well . . . I guess maybe I might've got taken in a bit," said Lucas. "I did tell people I was looking for interesting stories about life on the frontier. Somebody might have just made that one up to get a few drinks out of me."

"You offer drinks for stories, mister, you'll get more than your share," said Earp, with a smile, "and most of 'em right fanciful, to boot. But I don't guess that really makes much difference, does it? You writers like to spice things up a bit. I don't suppose it does much harm."

"No, I . . . I don't suppose it does," Lucas replied, still mystified by Earp's curious denial. "But I was wondering—"

"The stage's been robbed!" someone shouted.

Wyatt was on his feet in an instant, rushing over to the man.

"What happened?" he demanded.

"They shot Bud Philpot! Bob got the stage back, but Bud's

dead and one of the passengers was shot. They didn't get the silver shipment."

"I'm goin' to need a posse!" Wyatt called out, quickly taking charge. "Lem, you run down and get Virg and Morg. Where's Bob at?"

"He's outside with the stage," said the man who came running in with the news. "He got banged up some, but he's okay."

"You need some help, Marshal?" Neilson asked.

"I can use a good gun, Kid. Come along."

"Marshal Earp!" said Lucas. "I'd like to ride along, if I may."

"A posse's no place for a greenhorn, mister. No offense."

"I can ride," said Lucas. "I know how to shoot, too. I used to be a soldier. I'd like to help."

"All right, if you feel you're up to it, we'll get you a rifle. Come along."

Still no sign of recognition from Neilson, thought Lucas. All right, he'd wait and see. They went out into the street and hurried a short distance down the block, to where the stage had pulled up. Sheriff Behan was already there, along with several other men. A crowd was gathering rapidly. Wyatt pushed his way through to the man at the center of attention, the shotgun guard, Bob Paul. He was covered with dust and his clothing was disheveled.

"What happened, Bob?" asked Wyatt.

"I was just askin' him that," said Sheriff Behan, irritably. Lucas noticed a look of dislike between the two men.

"They got us a short way out of Contention," Paul said. "Bud was havin' stomach cramps, so I told him I could drive for a bit till they eased up. We'd pulled over and traded places, but we hadn't gotten more than a few miles north on the road to Benson when they hit us. We'd just gone across a dry wash and started up a hill when a masked man stepped out into the road and shouted, 'Hold!' Next thing we knew, there was a bunch of 'em around us. Three, four, maybe more, I couldn't tell, it all happened so fast. Bud went for the scattergun and they shot him. The horses bolted and then they were all shootin'. I lost the reins and had to climb down to retrieve 'em. Almost fell off into the road."

"They get the silver?" Behan asked.

"No, they didn't get it. They didn't have a chance. The

horses ran off soon as they shot Bud. One of the passengers took a bullet, too. Name of Peter Roerig, was sittin' in the dickey seat up back. He looked bad. They took him to the doc's, but I don't think he's goin' to make it."

Virgil and Morgan had arrived. "We're gettin' up a posse," Wyatt told them. "Outlaws just robbed the stage and killed Bud Philpot. If we get a move on, we might catch 'em."

"Wait a minute, Wyatt," Behan said. "I'm the sheriff, I'm takin' this posse."

"Fine, then, take it. But we're comin' along."

Behan looked as if he was going to make an argument of it, then changed his mind.

"I'm goin' too, Wyatt," Paul said.

"You sure you're up to it?"

"They got Bud," Paul said, with a hard edge to his voice. "I'm goin'."

Within moments, the posse was organized and mounted, galloping out of town on the road to Contention, about eight miles northwest of Tombstone. Lucas found himself riding next to Neilson, but aside from a curious look, nothing else passed between them. Lucas wondered if Neilson was being watched by someone in the posse and was aware of it. He was playing it very cool. Until he had a chance to speak with him alone, he'd have to follow his lead. Neilson could have discovered more about what was going on here since the time he'd last made his report.

It was late by the time they reached the place where the robbery had occurred and the darkness slowed them down, making the trail hard to follow. They were still tracking the outlaws when daylight came.

"Looks like the trail's leading to Len Redfield's place," said Virgil.

"Somehow I'm not surprised," said Wyatt, dryly. "Len's real friendly with Ike Clanton."

The trail, as Virgil had predicted, led straight to the ranch, where they discovered several horses in the corral that had been ridden very hard.

"Looks like they might have traded horses here," said Wyatt, as Lucas rode up beside him.

Suddenly a shot cracked out.

"Hold it right there, mister!"

It was Neilson who had yelled and fired. Lucas frowned.

That was getting a little too involved. The man who had taken off running from the corral, heading toward the house, stopped in his tracks and raised his hands in the air.

"Don't shoot!" he shouted.

"It's Luther King," said Behan, riding over to him. Wyatt and Bob Paul followed.

"Virg, you and the others go and check the house," he said. "And watch yourselves."

"I didn't do nothin'!" King protested. "What the hell did you shoot at me for?"

"Why'd you run, Luther?" Wyatt asked, looking down at the man from his horse.

"How was I supposed to know who you were?" protested King. "I thought you might be outlaws!"

"Did you, now?"

"Well, how was he to know?" asked Behan.

Wyatt gave him a hard look. "Why don't you go and check the house, Johnny? See if your friend Len can tell us anything."

Behan hesitated, again seeming as if he was about to argue, then once more thought better of it. He wheeled his horse and trotted toward the house.

"Been out ridin' tonight, Luther?" Wyatt asked.

"I've been here all night," King replied, nervously. "I didn't have anything to do with it."

"You didn't have anything to do with what, Luther?" Wyatt asked, calmly.

"With . . . with whatever it is you boys are out for."

"Somebody tried to rob the Kinnear stage tonight, Luther," Wyatt said. "Bud Philpot was shot and killed. I don't suppose you'd know anything about that?"

"How the hell would I know? Like I told you, I was here all night."

"Were you? What were you doin' out by the corral?"

"I . . . I came to milk the cows."

"You always strap your guns on when you go milkin', Luther?"

King hesitated. "Man can't be too careful these days. Might have been Indians around."

Morgan Earp snorted with disgust. "Indians, my foot! You were one of them Luther, weren't you?"

"I told you, I was here all night! I didn't have nothin' to do with it! Ask Len!"

"How do we know that Len wasn't involved?" asked Wyatt. "You've got some horses over there in that corral look like they were ridden pretty hard. You got anything to say about that?"

"Yeah, well . . . there was some riders came by not long ago. Wanted to trade some horses."

"Who were they?"

"I . . . I don't know. I didn't know who they were. I never saw 'em before."

"You're lyin', Luther."

"I ain't lyin'! I told you, I don't know anything about any robbery!"

"It's more than robbery, Luther," Wyatt said. "It's murder. Bud Philpot's dead."

"Passenger got wounded, too," said Virgil. "Looks like he might not make it. That'll be two murders."

"Three, Virg," Wyatt said. "Don't forget Katie."

Virgil frowned. "Katie?"

"Isn't that right, Bob?" Wyatt said, turning to Bob. "Didn't you tell me Katie Elder took a bullet? Killed her on the spot, you said. Doc just about went crazy when he heard about it."

Bob Paul picked up on it. "Yeah, that's right. I never saw Doc like that before. It was somethin' terrible."

"Doc Holliday's woman was on that stage?" asked King, his eyes wide.

"She was headin' out to Benson, to take the train and visit some relatives for a spell," said Wyatt. "When Doc found out she'd been shot, he swore up and down he'd get every last one of those outlaws if it took him the rest of his life."

"Oh, my God," said King.

"If Doc gets in his head you were involved, Luther, I don't know that there's anything in this world that will stop him," Wyatt said. "You know how he is."

"Listen, Marshal, you gotta promise me you'll tell Doc I had nothin' to do with it, I swear!" said King, in a panic.

"Well, now, I don't know that for a fact, Luther."

"Marshal, please! You gotta believe me! Look, you gotta tell Holliday it wasn't me! I didn't do any of the shootin', God's my judge! I only held the horses! You gotta tell Doc, I only held the horses! I never even fired my gun! I wasn't even there! I was just down the road a piece! I didn't know there was goin' to be any killin'! I swear, I didn't! Please, Marshal, you gotta *tell* him!"

"Well now, I might, Luther, if you were to tell us who the rest of 'em were."

"It was Head, Leonard and Crane!" said King. "I don't know which one of 'em shot Philpot! I heard the shootin', but I didn't see it! Like I said, I only held the horses!"

"Head, Leonard and Crane, eh?" said Wyatt. "Where are they now?"

"They rode out a while back. I ain't sure where they went and that's the truth, I swear it! The whole thing went wrong! But you gotta tell Holliday I didn't do any shootin', Marshal. You gotta tell him!"

Wyatt glanced at Bob Paul and grinned. "I always knew that bad temper of Doc's would come in handy one day."

Sheriff Johnny Behan and his deputy, Billy Breakenridge, took charge of the prisoner and rode back to town with him while the rest of the posse continued on the outlaws' trail. Lucas took the opportunity to ride back with the prisoner, expecting Neilson to volunteer to do the same, only the Montana Kid continued on with the posse. Not so much as a meaningful look had passed between them. Andre was waiting at the hotel when he returned.

"Did you learn anything?" she asked. "Did you have a chance to talk to Scott?"

"No, to both questions," Lucas said, easing himself onto the bed. It had been a while since he had been on horseback and he was saddlesore. "Neilson acted as if he didn't even know me. The only explanation I can think of is that someone in the posse was watching him and he was aware of it. He's still out there with them. I guess he thought that if he came back with me, it might tip off whoever's watching him."

"Any clue who it might be?"

Lucas shook his head. "It could've been any of them." He frowned. "I don't know. There's something bothering me."

"You, too?"

"You pick up on something?"

"You first."

"Actually, it's a couple of things, but I'm not sure if it means anything. For one thing, there's Masterson's leaving town to go back to Dodge City. According to our historical records, he shouldn't have done that until *after* the stage robbery. He should have been on that posse. But then, our records have been wrong before. Maybe that's all it is. The other thing is that Wyatt Earp claimed to know absolutely nothing about the deaths of those Observers. Said he didn't even know any men named Summers, Billings and McEnery. He told me that someone must have been pulling my leg and making up a story for my benefit. It's possible he just didn't want to talk about it and denied the whole thing because he didn't want to discuss a crime he couldn't solve. I can't think of any other explanation, but why would he want to lie about it? We could easily corroborate that story with anyone in town."

"You want to bet?" she said.

He glanced at her with a frown. "What do you mean?"

"I spent the evening last night visiting some of the stores and meeting some of the local women," Andre said. "I even managed to meet Wyatt's girl, Josie Marcus, and have dinner with her. And nobody would admit to knowing anything about those three Observers. Who they were, how they died, nothing. They all wanted to know where I came up with such a story. It was news to all of them."

Lucas simply stared at her. "What the hell is going on here?"

"I don't know," said Andre, "but it's as if somebody told the whole town not to talk about it."

"Wait a minute," Lucas said. "That barman downstairs, what's his name, Mehan, he talked about it, remember?"

"Good luck getting him to admit it," Andre said. "I spoke to him briefly after dinner. He looked blank when I brought it up. Said I must have gotten mixed up with a story about something that happened somewhere else. Denied ever telling us anything about it and looked at me like I was crazy."

"Somebody got to him," said Lucas.

"Apparently."

Lucas looked worried. "That might explain why Neilson didn't make any contact," he said. "Our cover might be blown already."

"How? We haven't done anything to tip anybody off," she said. "We've only just arrived in town."

"Maybe we were recognized," said Lucas. "There are people in the Network who know who we are. If one of them spotted us when we came into town, our cover could have been blown right there and then."

"I suppose that's possible," Andre said. "Only if that's the case, what would be the point in hushing up the deaths of those Observers? That would only put us on our guard."

Lucas shook his head. "You're right. It makes no sense. And how the hell could they get to everyone so fast and make sure nobody talked about it?"

"They were late getting to Mehan," Andre said.

"That makes no sense, either," Lucas said, with a frown. "You'd think he would've been the first one they'd warn to keep his mouth shut. And the fact that they could do that, whoever they are, would presuppose that they control the entire town. That doesn't seem possible."

"Maybe it doesn't seem likely," Andre replied, "but it's not impossible."

"That would mean that this *whole town* is a Network operation," Lucas said. "I can't believe that. There's got to be some other explanation."

"I'm open to suggestions," Andre said.

Lucas sighed heavily. "Yeah. The trouble is, I haven't got any. Did you talk to Finn?"

She shook her head. "I saw him going into the Oriental Saloon shortly before I went to dinner. He was with a couple of cowboys, so I didn't try to make contact."

"And he didn't make contact last night?" Lucas asked, with concern.

Andre shook her head. "No. But then he could have gotten into an all-night poker game or picked up a lead on a job at one of the ranches that the rustlers work out of."

Lucas shook his head. "I don't like it. He should have made contact by now."

"There's got to be a reason why he didn't," Andre said. "Maybe he learned something that warned him off."

"Or maybe something happened to him," Lucas said. He struck the bed with his fist. "*Damn* it! We only just got here and already things are out of our control! What aren't we *seeing*? What don't we *know*?"

"Whatever it is, we're not going to find out now," said Andre. "You look beat. Why don't you try to get some sleep? I'll stand watch."

She reached into her carpet bag, pulled out a laser pistol and double-checked its chargepak.

"I wouldn't mind lying down for a while," Lucas said. "But I don't know if I'll get any sleep."

"Try," said Andre. "Meditate or something. All we can do now is wait, anyway. Something's bound to break. And I don't need you tired when it does."

"Okay, you've got a point," said Lucas, lying back on the bed. "I'll try to get some rest. But I'd feel a lot better if I knew what Delaney was doing."

Moments later, he was fast asleep. Andre sat down in a chair and put her feet up, holding the laser pistol in her lap. She kept close watch on the windows and the door. Something wasn't right. She had the nagging thought that if she could just back off a bit and look at it a certain way, she'd see it.

She sighed. "Come on, Finn," she whispered, softly, so as not to disturb Lucas. "Where *are* you?"

"Dealer takes two," said Finn Delaney, dealing himself two cards. "It's your bet, mister."

"Well, let's see if we can't make this interesting," said Stone, putting down his bet.

"Feelin' sure of yourself, are ya?" said Delaney.

The gambler smiled. "Confidence is half the game."

"Luck is the other half," said Finn. "I'll see you and I'll raise you ten."

"Too rich for me," said one of the players, folding.

"I'm out," said another.

"Luck, is it? I thought it was skill," said Stone, his eyes twinkling. He matched Finn's bet. "Call."

"Three of a kind," said Finn, putting down three eights.

"Sorry, Mister," said Stone, putting down his cards. "Three ladies." He reached for the pot.

"And two aces make a full house," said Delaney, putting down his last two cards.

"Son of a bitch," said Stone.

"Whoo-eee!" said one of the other men, clapping Delaney on the back. "That's the way to play 'em!"

"Drinks on me, gents," said Finn, gathering up the pot.

"Looks like it's your lucky night, cowboy," Stone said. He gathered up the cards. "Tell you what. I'll cut you for that pot you just won. Double or nothing."

"No, not me," said Finn, with a smile. "I might believe in the luck of the Irish, but not enough to push it."

Stone smiled. "Suit yourself. We'll have to play again

sometime. Give me a chance to get some of that money back. Unless you're just passing through."

"No, I think I'll stick around a bit," said Finn, as the others got up from the table. "You go on and get your drinks, boys, and tell the bartender I'll take care of it," he said.

"Thanks, mister."

"Where you from, cowboy?" the gambler asked.

"Oh, all over," Delaney replied. "guess I'm what you'd call a drifter. I never seem to stay in any one place too long. What about yourself?"

"Boston," said the gambler.

"Boston? Is that right?"

"Ever been there?"

"Yeah, back in another life," said Finn. He smiled. The gambler seemed to hesitate a fraction of a second before he smiled back. "Got some of the finest food around in Boston. The old Oyster House by Faneuil Hall."

"I know it well. What brings you to Tombstone?"

"The wind, my friend, the wind," Delaney said. "I just follow where it blows me."

"You seem to have a touch of the romantic in your soul," said Stone. "That would be the Irish in you. A land of poets and dreamers."

"Aye, that it is," said Delaney. He grinned. "It's lucky for me I ran into you tonight, Mr. Stone. My roll was gettin' mighty thin. I'm much obliged to you."

"Well, you can't win them all," said Stone. "And call me Ben."

"My friends call me Finn."

"It's a pleasure, Finn. Jenny! Bring us a bottle, will you, dear?"

"Well, now, I said drinks were on me," said Finn.

"Very well. I won't argue. Feel free to pay."

Finn chuckled and stared appreciatively as Jenny brought a bottle of whiskey over to their table.

"Thank you, darling," Stone said.

She smiled. "Anytime, Ben."

They both watched as she moved off.

"Pretty girl," said Finn.

"That she is," Stone agreed. "But if you've got any ideas along that line, I'd advise you to forget them. Time was, not too long ago, she'd have been happy to accommodate you, but not since the Montana Kid arrived in town. Now she's got eyes only for him. A big, husky fellow like yourself might not be deterred by that, but I'd think twice if I were you. The Kid's one hell of a fast gun."

"Is he, now?"

"Killed two men right here in this saloon. And they knew their business, too. He's young, but don't let that fool you. The Kid is deadly."

"I'll keep that in mind," Delaney said. "Sounds like this town can get a mite rough for a man."

"Well, it isn't Boston, that's for sure," Stone replied.

"You get many killings here?"

"More than our share."

Finn fought back the temptation to ask about the dead Observers. He didn't want to ask too many questions. He was aware of Stone's light gray eyes watching him carefully, not smiling when his mouth smiled. Neither one of us are too sure about each other, are we? he thought. He had a feeling about Stone and he was pretty sure that Stone had the same feeling about him. Not quite a certainty, but close enough for government work, as they said. They were both gambling men and Finn would have bet Stone was a pro. Stone would probably have made the same bet, too. There were all sorts of telltale little things that ordinary people would have missed, things that, to a pro, couldn't really be disguised. Body attitude and language. A sense of fine control. Alert and watchful eyes, eyes that picked up much more than most people's did. But mostly, it was a feeling like two predators sensing each other. It was possible that Stone was simply the same breed of man. Capable, crafty, dangerous. Delaney knew he could be wrong. But he didn't think he was.

"Seems like a man could do all right for himself in a town like this," said Finn.

"Well, I guess it would all depend on what he had in mind," Stone replied.

Finn shrugged. "I'm in no hurry. I think I'll just sort of stick around and get the feel of things before I make any decisions. Find out who's who around here, what sort of opportunities there are."

"There anything special that you had in mind?" asked Stone.

"I said, let *go* of me!"

Stone turned around. "Oh-oh. Looks like trouble."

A cowboy sitting at a table had Jenny by the arm and was refusing to let go. She struggled, but he was much stronger and held on firmly.

"Come on, now, honey, don't be like that! You weren't too good for me last week!"

"That was last week!" Jenny said. "Things are different now. I don't do that anymore. Now let me go!"

"The Kid's not going to like that," Stone said.

"He around?"

"No, he went out on that posse with the Earps. And Frank Leslie rode out with the sheriff when they went back out after they brought in their prisoner."

"I said, let me *go*!"

The man pulled her down on his lap, laughing. "Playin' hard to get, eh? Well, I know what *you* like!" Jenny struggled as the man started roughly fondling her breast. The other men at the table were laughing and egging their companion on.

"Excuse me," Finn said, pushing back his chair. He went over to their table. Jenny was making angry, whimpering sounds as the man forced his kisses on her. "I think I heard the lady ask to be let go," said Finn.

The man stopped kissing Jenny and stared up at Finn belligerantly, though he still held onto her tightly.

"What the hell business is it of yours?"

"I just don't like seeing women bullied, that's all," Finn said.

"Is that so? Well now, just what do you intend to do about it?"

"How about if I break your knees?" asked Finn, with a smile.

"Hey, now! I don't want any trouble in here!" the barman shouted.

"You stay out of this, Lem! It ain't none of your concern!" shouted the cowboy.

Lem didn't seem inclined to make it his concern. The cowboy let Jenny go and stood up. He was a beefy man, as big as Finn, though heavier and not as muscular.

"Mister, you just bought into a pack of trouble."

Delaney hit him in the face with a quick, sharp blow and the man dropped like a felled tree. His three friends were on their feet in an instant. One of them swung at Finn. Delaney caught his fist in his left hand, then brought his right hand up to cover it, gave a quick, sharp twist and the man howled as his wristbone snapped like a twig. The other man had picked up a chair and was bringing it down hard. Delaney swung the man with the broken wrist around and made him take the blow. The chair broke over the man's head and Delaney released him as he went down. The third man was reaching into the pocket of his coat. Delaney snatched up a half empty whiskey bottle from the table and smashed it into the man's face. Whiskey, broken glass, blood and a few teeth spattered on the table as the man went down.

The man who'd swung the chair came up with a bowie knife he had in his boot. Delaney just looked at him and grinned. The man with the knife found the grin highly disconcerting. The knife made sweeping arcs in front of him as he bent over in a crouch. Cards, glasses and coins rained to the floor as Delaney picked up the table and ran it at him.

"Jesus . . . !" yelled the man with the knife as the table struck him and he was propelled back against the wall, struck it hard and remained there, pinned by the table. The knife fell to the floor. Delaney dropped the table on the man's feet.

"Yowww!"

And then Delaney struck him once and knocked him out.

"Great day in the mornin'!" someone said.

A few people applauded and whooped. Delaney turned and gave them a small bow.

"I'd like to thank you, mister."

Finn turned to see Jenny standing behind him.

"My pleasure, Ma'am."

"Can I buy you a drink?"

"I'd be delighted."

He glanced at Stone, who was watching him thoughtfully. Stone gave a slight smile, inclined his head and raised his glass to him.

"My name is Jennifer," the girl said. "Jennifer Reilly. What's yours?"

"Delaney. But my friends just call me Finn."

"You sure do handle yourself well, Finn. Those boys can be pretty mean."

"Oh, I thought they seemed right sociable," said Finn.

Jenny smiled. Oh, dear, thought Finn, not immune to its effects. What's a heartbreaker like you doing in a place like this? One of the men behind him groaned from the floor, but made no move to get up.

"I'm afraid that coming to my rescue might have brought you trouble," Jenny said. "Those men are Johnny Ringo's boys. And they've got friends."

"I'd be happy to make their acquaintance," Finn said, raising his glass to her.

"I'm not sure you'd like that too much," she replied. "What you did was very gallant, but I don't want to mislead you. I'm spoken for."

"So I heard," said Finn. "I'd say the Montana Kid's a lucky man."

"He'll appreciate what you did for me tonight," said Jenny. "I'll be sure to tell him when he gets back to town. I think the two of you might like each other."

"Well, if you think highly of him, then I'm sure that I will, too," said Finn. He turned around and glanced toward Stone's table. The gambler was gone. He felt a light touch on his arm.

"You're pretty good with your fists there, cowboy," said a husky, female voice. "My! Strong, too!"

He turned to see an attractive young redhead smiling at him.

"Finn, I'd like you to meet my good friend, Becky," Jenny said. "Becky, this here's Mr. Finn Delaney."

"Pleased to meet you," Finn said.

"That was a nice thing that you did for Jenny," Becky said. "Those boys had it comin'."

"I thought so," Finn replied.

"Too bad that Jenny's already spoken for," said Becky. "But I'm sure she wouldn't mind if I was to thank you for her."

She stood up on tiptoe and kissed him. She took her time about it and she seemed sincere.

"You're welcome," Finn said somewhat breathlessly, when she broke off the kiss.

"Well now, I haven't thanked you, yet," said Becky, with a smile and a smoldering look. "That was just to introduce myself. Jenny, you'll send up a bottle, won't you, dear?" She took Finn by the arm. "Would you be so kind as to escort me to my room, sir?"

7 _____

"Now let me get this straight," hissed Andre, furiously. "I was up all night, worried about where you were, and you were off getting your ashes hauled with some *bimbo*?"

"It wasn't exactly the sort of situation I could have backed out of," Delaney protested, whispering so as not to wake Lucas, who was stretched out on the bed.

"Oh, really? What did she do, *force* you?"

"Come on, Andre, give me a break, for Christ's sake! It would have looked a little strange for a cowboy fresh off the trail to turn down a proposition from a woman like that! Besides, I thought I might learn a thing or two."

"Well, I hope she was a good teacher," Andre said.

"That *isn't* what I meant, dammit!"

"What's going on?" Lucas mumbled from the bed. He sat up and rubbed his eyes. "Finn! What happened?"

"He was out getting laid, that's what happened," Andre said.

"What?" said Lucas.

"It wasn't like that," Delaney protested. He quickly brought Lucas up to date on what had occurred the previous night. "I knew you'd gone out with the posse," he said, when he'd finished, "and I figured Andre would try to get some sleep. The Oriental Saloon is one of the big social centers in this town and I figured if anything unusual was going on, there was a chance that Becky knew about it. I'm sorry if I worried you, but I figured that if I didn't make contact, Andre would realize I was following up a lead."

"Oh, is that what you call it?" she asked, wryly.

"All right, never mind," said Lucas. "The important thing is, did you find out anything?"

Delaney nodded. "Yeah. She knows a lot about what's going on in this town. Mostly stuff that we already know, but a few things that we didn't. Like about Ben Stone. I think he's a ringer. And I'm pretty sure that he suspects me, too. He saw me pull a martial arts move on one of those guys during the fight and if he's a pro, it must have tipped him off."

"What did you learn from the girl?" asked Lucas.

"He's apparently loaded. He's always got a roll on him. He rents a room in Fly's Boarding House, but he doesn't seem to spend much time there. When he's not gambling in the Occidental, or the Alhambra or the Oriental, nobody seems to know where the hell he goes. He simply disappears. Apparently, there's been some talk in town that he might be in on some of the stage robberies, but he was always around somewhere in front of witnesses when they went down. That still doesn't mean he's not involved, though. And after those three Observers were killed, he seemed real interested in the investigation."

"She *told* you about that?" said Andre. "About the Observers being killed?"

"Yeah," said Delaney, faintly puzzled. "Why?"

"Because it seems no one else in town will talk about it," Lucas said. "It's as if it never happened. When I spoke to Wyatt Earp, he claimed he didn't know anything about it, had never even heard of anyone named Summers, Billings or McEnery."

"You're kidding," said Delaney, startled.

"It's as if somebody went around to everyone in town and told them not to talk about it," Andre said. "They all act as if it simply never happened. As if those men had never even been here."

"That doesn't make any sense," Delaney said, mystified. "The whole *town*?"

"Well, apparently not the whole town," Andre said, "since Becky spoke to you about it. But when we first got in, we spoke to the bartender here in the hotel, Andrew Mehan, and he talked about it. Later, when I asked him again, he denied he'd ever said anything and looked at me like I was drunk or something."

"That's weird," said Delaney. "What the hell is going on?"

"That's what I'd like to know," said Lucas.

"You get a chance to make contact with Neilson on the posse?" Finn asked.

Lucas shook his head. "He acted as if he didn't know me. I figure whoever's behind all this, one or more of them were on the posse and Scott knew that he was being watched."

"You figure it's the Network?" asked Delaney.

"I don't know," Lucas replied. "If it is, there's a good chance we might have been blown as soon as we got into town. We're known to some of those people. But it could also be the S.O.G. One way or another, we'll probably find out before too long, because someone's bound to make a move against us."

"What bothers me is why suddenly no one will talk about those murders," Andre said. "Could it be possible that the Network is actually in control of this whole town?"

"I wouldn't have thought so," said Delaney. "But I can't think of any other explanation." He compressed his lips into a tight grimace. "I'll bet that bastard, Darkness, knows. Only he's not going to tell us anything until he's good and ready. And then we won't have any time to think about it. Son of a bitch. Just once, I'd like to get my hands on him. . . ."

"I keep thinking that there's something we're not seeing," Lucas said. "Something we're not taking into account. So far, we're just floundering around back here, waiting for something to happen. I don't like it. I've got a real bad feeling about this whole thing."

"We're going to have to make contact with Neilson as soon as he gets back," Delaney said. "He's got to know something. Something must have happened between the time he clocked in with his report and the time we got here."

"Obviously," said Lucas. "Only what?"

"He's apparently become involved with Jenny Reilly, who works at the saloon," Delaney said. "From the way she spoke, it sounded pretty serious."

"You apparently got yourself involved, as well," said Andre.

"I went to bed with Becky," said Delaney. "I'm not 'involved' with her. This sounds different. The Montana Kid and Jenny Reilly seem to have become an item in this town. Did you have a chance to check out that other guy Neilson mentioned in his report? The gunsmith, Zeke Bailey?"

"He's dead," said Lucas. "He was murdered at his home just outside of town by person or persons unknown. Shot with a .45."

"That's interesting," Delaney said. "You think he might have been killed to keep us from talking to him?"

"I don't know what to think," said Lucas. "I'm not even sure where to start."

"I am," said Delaney. "Ben Stone."

There were things that went on in Hop Town that no one else in Tombstone knew about. The Chinese had a very closed community. There were a lot of them living in a relatively small space and the other residents of Tombstone tended to avoid the area. Not out of fear, but out of bigotry. They didn't like being around them. They liked having them do their laundry, they liked having them perform menial jobs and hard labor in the mines and on the railroad, mainly because they worked cheaply, and they liked having them as cooks, so long as they didn't cook that slop they ate themselves, but when it came to treating them as equals, that idea simply didn't occur to anyone. They were, after all, the "heathen Chinee," an inferior race altogether, with their own incomprehensible language, customs and beliefs. They were different and it was better if they just kept off to themselves.

The law in Tombstone did not overly concern itself with what went on down there in Hop Town. If they wanted to cook their funny-smelling food, and smoke their opium and gamble in their own establishments and chant and light their prayer sticks and have their own little internecine conflicts, so long as the trouble didn't spill outside of Hop Town, nobody really gave a damn. After all, they had to live somewhere, didn't they, and as long as they kept to themselves and didn't cause any trouble and stayed out of the way, let them live any damn way they pleased. So Tombstone had its own little Chinese ghetto and, for Nikolai Drakov, that had certain advantages.

With their superstitious beliefs in magic and mysticism, instilling fear in them had been pathetically easy. Intimidating the leaders of the community had posed no problem whatsoever. In effect, he now controlled an entire section of Tombstone and because of the close-knit, segregated nature of the Chinese community, no one in town even suspected it. It had, however, involved a certain element of risk.

For a time, it had been necessary for him to be visible in Tombstone as Nathan Drake. He had tried to keep that to a minimum, but it had been necessary in order to make his preparations. He had eliminated the threat of the Observers, but he had been concerned about the Network and the Special Operations Group. The unique nature of this time sector was such that none of those groups was as yet aware of the others, except that the Network had discovered Bailey's secret, that he was a deserter from the Temporal Corps, a member of the Underground. Bailey had become careless and he had paid the price for it. Now he was dead. The situation was starting to develop rapidly. The temporal instability was increasing and Drakov wondered how long it would take for the Network, the S.O.G. and the T.I.A. agents to realize what was going on. With luck, by the time they put it all together, it would be too late.

He turned as the women came into the room. It was an elegant study, furnished comfortably in the best Victorian style, a room above the opium parlour. All the residents of Hop Town knew about it, no one else did. They knew that this was where the powerful sorcerer lived and they treated him with utmost, groveling respect whenever they came in contact with him. Otherwise, they gave him a wide berth.

"They're here," said Becky. "I spent the night with one of them. His name is Finn Delaney. He asked a lot of questions."

Drakov smiled as he drew on his long pipe. "Excellent."

"And two more strangers have just arrived in town," said Becky. "They've been asking a lot of questions, too. A man and his wife. The man's name is Priest and he's a writer from back East. His wife's name is Andrea and she is his assistant. Priest went out with the posse looking for the stage robbers. His wife stayed in town, going into all the stores and asking questions."

"Lucas Priest and Andre Cross," said Drakov. "My old enemies. They're not even bothering to use false names. That means they're uncertain of the situation. They have devised a cover for themselves, but they've kept their real names, in an effort to draw out whoever might recognize those names. Which means that they suspect the Network. They undoubtedly have reinforcements waiting to clock in whenever they give the signal. Perfect. Only we're not quite ready for that yet. We need to keep them off-balance for just a little while longer. Mr. Stone should serve that purpose admirably. Have you been able to direct their suspicions toward him?"

"I've spoken to Scott about him," said Jenny. "I've told him that I had been with Stone and that he was very rough with me, that there is something very strange about him, something that frightens me. And that no one really knows anything about him, who he is or where he really came from."

"Finn Delaney asked about him, as well," said Becky. "He already seems to suspect him. I told him that Stone spends most of his time gambling in various saloons, but that when he isn't gambling, no one seems to know where he goes. Stone acts mysterious and secretive."

"Good," said Drakov." "Very good, indeed."

"What about Scott Neilson?" Jenny asked, hesitantly.

"You've established a relationship with him," Drakov replied. "I want you to maintain it. Keep him off-balance, emotionally. He will draw the attention of the Network while the others will be preoccupied with Stone. They will suspect that Stone is a Network man, himself. Meanwhile, Stone will bring in his fellow S.O.G. agents to move against the T.I.A." He chuckled. "That will accelerate the instability. Things are about to become quite interesting."

"Will it be necessary for Scott to die?" asked Jenny, softly. Becky glanced at her, puzzled.

Drakov gave her a long, appraising look. "Are you becoming emotionally involved, Jennifer?"

Jenny looked down at the floor. "I . . . I think I'm in love with him."

Drakov raised his eyebrows. "Really?"

"It's what I feel when I'm with him," Jenny replied, unable to look her master in the eyes. "He is so kind and gentle, when he touches me, he . . . He makes me feel something that I've never felt with any other man."

"Oh, I see," said Drakov. "That is merely lust. A purely physiological response. Men of this time period, of most time periods for that matter, are not very sensitive to women's emotional needs, which are much more bound up with the physical than male needs are. Neilson is apparently more perceptive. I suppose he has brought you to orgasm. It was probably your first. But that is only a physical sensation, Jennifer. A biological response."

"But . . . but it feels so overwhelming," Jenny said.

"Indeed, it does," said Drakov. "But it is most emphatically not love. I know something of how you must feel. I made the same mistake myself once, many years ago, much to my regret. You were created from human genetic material, Jennifer, and so you are subject to the same procreative urges humans are. Those feelings can be very powerful and there is no reason why you should not enjoy them at every opportunity. In fact, the more frequently you indulge them, the quicker the novelty will wear off and you will find those feelings diminishing in intensity. Because it is merely sex. Love is something else, entirely."

"How is it different?" Jenny asked.

"It arises from shared values and mutual respect," said Drakov. "And your values and Neilson's could never be the same, Jennifer. You are not human. If Neilson knew that, he could never respect you. He would, in fact, be furious at having been deceived. I have told you that if he suspected your true nature, he would kill you. The only reason he treats you as he does is because he does not know what you really are. And even believing you to be human, like himself, he wishes to manipulate you, to use you to help him on his mission. If he truly loved you, he would be honest with you."

"I had not thought of it that way," she replied, softly, still looking at the floor. "I was afraid you would be angry with me."

"Why should I be angry with you?" Drakov asked. "Have you failed me in any way? I created you. I gave you life. And it is I who care about you, enough to tell you the truth. I have no wish to see you hurt."

Jenny nodded and swallowed hard, torn by conflicting emotions. "Thank you. I do not wish to disappoint you."

"You won't. Enjoy yourself with Neilson. Indulge those feelings and you will soon find they are not nearly so profound as you suspect. He uses you. Use him in return to explore the depths of your sensations. But don't deceive yourself with thoughts of love. Love is for humans."

All Scott wanted to do was sleep. The posse got back to town without catching the outlaws. Head, Leonard and Crane had led them on a merry chase throughout the countryside and they were never able to catch up with them. They had ridden so hard one of the horses died. They were tired, they were thirsty, they were sore, and they had simply given up. On their return, the Earps had received even more bad news. Luther King, the prisoner they had taken back at the Redfield ranch, had managed to escape.

The whole thing was ludicrous. He had simply stepped out the back door of the jail while the deputy was engaged in selling his horse. Accusations were flying back and forth. The Earps were convinced that Behan and his deputies, being involved with the rustlers, had simply allowed him to escape. Which certainly seemed likely. Behan and his men were claiming that King had help, that Doc Holliday had been waiting behind the jail with two horses and had spirited King away.

Holliday, conveniently, had been out of town when the stage was robbed and the posse left. He was known to have been acquainted with one of the outlaws before, Bill Leonard, when the two men were in Las Vegas, New Mexico. On the strength of that association, Behan and others in his faction were claiming that Doc had been involved in the robbery and had helped King to escape. (Though no one explained how Holliday knew that King would have a chance to simply stroll out through the back door of the jail while the deputy's back was turned, or why he hadn't been locked up in the first place.) Behan was even spreading rumors that Wyatt Earp and his brothers had been involved in the robbery, tipped off by Morgan, who, in his capacity as a Wells Fargo guard, would know when silver shipments were going out. The town was becoming polarized, with the hostility between the factions rapidly growing worse.

Scott wished that Priest and the others would show up. He couldn't understand what was keeping them. He felt certain now that the Network was behind it all, but he couldn't take them on all by himself. That would be crazy. He felt exposed and vulnerable. He felt the situation was completely out of his control.

There was a soft knock at his door. He quickly grabbed a gun from the holster rig he'd hung up on the bedpost.

"Who is it?"

"It's Jenny, Scott. Can I come in?"

He opened the door. She was alone. She saw the gun and her eyes grew wide.

"What's that for?" she asked.

"I had to be sure you were alone," said Scott.

"Who did you think might have been with me?"

"Well, I did make some enemies in this town," he replied. "Man can't be too careful." He closed the door behind her and eased the hammer down on the Colt.

"Did you really think I'd be part of anything like that?"

"You might have had no choice, Jenny. Someone might have been holding a gun on you, or a knife."

"That wouldn't make any difference," she said. "They'd have to kill me before I'd go along with doing anything to hurt you." She suddenly started crying.

"Jenny! What's wrong?"

"Hold me, Scott."

He put his arms around her. She was trembling.

"What's wrong, Jenny?" he asked, with concern. "What is it? What's happened?"

"Everything's wrong," she sobbed. "I wish I were dead!"

"Jenny!" She was holding onto him as if for dear life. "What *is* it? Tell me! Is it something I've done?"

She shook her head. "No," she said, quietly. "It isn't anything you've done. It's me."

He took her over to the bed and sat down with her. He took her hands in his.

"Whatever it is, Jenny, you can tell me. I'll understand."

"I don't think you would," she said.

"Try me. At least give me a chance. If there's anything I can do to help, you know I will."

"I don't think anyone can help me," she replied, sniffling.

He kissed her. "If I possibly can, I will. I love you, Jenny."

"Oh, God," she said, her voice barely audible. "How can you say that?"

"Because it's true. I love you."

She pulled away from him. "Scott . . . there are things about me . . . things you don't know. And if you knew, you'd hate me."

"I could never hate you, Jenny. I know what kind of life you've led. It makes no difference to me."

"I wasn't talking about that," she said, not looking at him.

"There are things . . ." she bit her lower lip. "Oh, Scott, if you really knew the truth about me, you'd want to kill me."

He stared at her, astonished. "How can you say that? That's crazy! What could you possibly have done—"

"It isn't anything I've done," she said. "Well, yes, it is, but it's also what I am. If you knew . . ." She got down on her knees before him and took his hands, holding them tightly, looking up at him with fear and confusion. "If I tell you the truth, I know I'll lose you. You'll hate me and you'll want to kill me, but even if you do, I don't care anymore. I just don't want anything to happen to you. You have to leave, Scott. You have to leave Tombstone as quickly as you can and go back where you came from, before it's too late!"

"Jenny, what are you talking about?"

"Scott . . . before I tell you . . . kiss me. Please, kiss me one last time."

"Jenny . . ."

"Just do it, Scott. Please."

He kissed her. She clung to him with desperation and he could taste the saltiness of her tears.

"Oh, God, I love you, Scott," she said. "I don't care if it's not possible, I *know* I love you. I've never felt this way about anyone before."

"I love you too, Jen," he replied, bewildered.

She shook her head and placed her forefinger up against his lips. "Maybe you think you do," she said. "But you can't. You mustn't."

"*Why?*"

She stared at him with fear in her eyes. "Because . . ." she swallowed hard and took a deep breath. "Because I'm not human, Scott."

"*What?*"

"I'm not a real woman. I only look like one. And, God help me, somehow I feel like one, too, but I'm not a human being. I wasn't born. I was created. The Master made me in a laboratory."

Scott simply stared at her, speechless with astonishment.

"I know he's your enemy," she continued. "I know who you really are. I know you're from the future. I know why you're here. And no matter what you do to me, you *must* go back. Please, you must go back before it's too late!"

Suddenly, comprehension dawned. "My God," said Scott.

He felt as if he'd been punched in the stomach. "You're one of Drakov's hominoids."

She nodded, staring at him, her face streaked with tears, her eyes wide with fear.

"He said love is only for humans," she whispered, "and that what I feel toward you isn't really love, and that you couldn't possible love me if you knew what I really was. An imitation of a human being. He said you'd kill me, but I don't care! I don't want to live like this! It hurts! It hurts too much. If I can't be human, then I just don't want to *be*!"

"Jesus Christ," said Scott. He reached out for her and she cringed. "That bastard. That lousy bastard. What's he done to you?"

He put his arms around her and she became very still, as if afraid to move, afraid to breathe.

"You poor girl," he said, stroking her long blonde hair. His own eyes were misty. "Jesus, it must have been awful for you."

"I . . . I don't understand. . . ." she said in a small, frightened voice.

Scott held her away from him, so he could look into her eyes. "He had you believing you weren't human?"

She stared at him with incomprehension.

"Oh, Jenny, you don't even realize what you are," he said. "How much do you really know about Nikolai Drakov?"

She shook her head, dazed, still unable to believe he wasn't furious with her, that he wasn't striking out at her.

"He's insane, Jenny. He's brilliant, a genius, but he's a madman and a criminal. God knows, maybe he even believes that the hominoids aren't human. It would certainly fit with his insane megalomania. The thought that he's created an entirely new species, that he's some sort of God . . ."

"What are you saying?" she whispered.

"Jenny, the first hominoids that Nikolai Drakov created were androids. They weren't really human, but crude imitations. They weren't really capable of independent thought, or of human feelings and emotions. But later, Drakov resorted to genetic engineering to create clones in a laboratory. . . ." He trailed off as he watched her. "God, you don't understand the first thing about what I'm saying, do you?"

She shook her head.

He stared up at the ceiling. "How on earth can I explain it to you? You don't know the first thing about science. . . ."

"I understand a little about science," she said, in a small voice, still confused by his lack of a violent reaction, which was what she had expected.

"Well, genetic engineering is a science," Scott told her. "What Drakov did was to . . . to give birth to humans in a laboratory without the benefit of parents. What I mean is, there *were* parents, human parents from whom Drakov obtained the raw material, but the hominoids—he still called them that, even though they were different from the first ones—were born without the necessity of a man and a woman having sex. The eggs were fertilized in a laboratory and the fetuses came to term in artificial wombs. . . ."

He saw that he was losing her again and he felt exasperated. There had to be some way that he could make her understand.

"What I'm trying to say, Jenny, is this: Even though you were never born in the normal way, even though you never had a father or a mother, you are *still* a human being. Drakov lied to you. He wasn't really your creator, he . . . he was more like a midwife. It's much too complicated for me to explain to you, but you have to believe one thing. You are as human as I am."

She shook her head, slowly. "Is it possible?" she whispered.

He grabbed her by the arm. "That's human flesh, Jenny." He put his hand on her breast. "That's a human heart beating in there." He kissed her. "Those are *human* lips," he said, softly. "I couldn't love you if you were not human. And I *do* love you."

She gave a small cry and clutched at him, burying her head against his chest as her small body was wracked with sobs. He held her tightly, stroking her hair and kissing the top of her head. Meanwhile, his mind was racing. Drakov, here! Then it *wasn't* the Network or the S.O.G. Or perhaps the Network was here, as well. Or maybe the S.O.G. He was no longer sure of anything except two things. One was that with Drakov here in this time sector, the threat was even greater than he had imagined. And the other was that he was deeply in love with this poor, tortured girl.

He couldn't begin to imagine what her existence must have been like. Cloned in a laboratory, she had been raised to believe she wasn't human, but some sort of clever simulacrum.

It was simply monstrous. Unlike other hominoids that Neilson had encountered, she had not been artificially mutated into some sort of frightening creature, her mind had not been destroyed, her personality—severely damaged though it was— had been left more or less intact. Only she had grown up believing that she was some sort of an inferior creature and that Nikolai Drakov was her "master," her god, to whom she owed unquestioning obedience. Except that he had triggered feelings in her that had been powerful enough to upset a lifetime of conditioning.

Apparently, she had been told that if he found out "what she really was," he'd kill her. And yet, she had disobeyed her master. Convinced that he would kill her if she told him the truth, she had told him anyway. Because she loved him. At that moment, Neilson would have died for her.

She needed help. It would probably take years of therapy to overcome all the damage that had been done to her. But before he could even think of that, he first had to make sure that he could get her away from Drakov. And that Drakov would be stopped. Only he wasn't sure if he could do it alone.

If he kept her from going back to him, wherever he was, Drakov would realize what must have happened and it would force his hand. But he could not bear the thought of having her go back to him. Obviously, Drakov had placed her in Tombstone, in the saloon, so that she would be in a position to report to him. Which meant he had to know about him. Scott was torn. He didn't know what to do.

Where the hell were Priest, Cross and Delaney?

Lucas Priest came over to the table in the hotel dining room where Neilson was eating his dinner and sat down.

"Mind if I join you, Kid?" he said.

"Looks like you just did, mister."

"I'd like to introduce myself. The name's Priest. Lucas Priest. I'm a writer and, from what I hear, you're somebody worth writing about." He lowered his voice and said, "We have to talk."

"Go ahead and talk, Mr. Priest. I'm listenin'."

"I'm writing some articles about the West for a magazine back in New York and I believe you're someone my readers would be very interested to know about." He lowered his voice again. "Why the hell haven't you made contact? Are you being watched?"

Neilson put down his fork and frowned. "Beg pardon?"

"I hear you're mighty fast with a six-shooter," Lucas said. "I'd like to ask you some questions, if you don't mind." Then lowered his voice once more. "Are you under surveillance?"

"No, sir, I ain't no surveyor. Don't know anything about it."

Lucas stared at him. "What the hell's the matter with you, Neilson?" he whispered.

Neilson frowned. "I say somethin' wrong?"

"Lower your voice, for Christ's sake!"

Neilson's eyes narrowed, but he complied with the request. "Why?" he asked, softly.

Lucas frowned. "Scott, are you all right?"

Neilson regarded him with puzzlement. "I'm just fine, mister. But I seem to be a mite confused. We met before?"

Lucas didn't say anything. He was completely taken aback. He looked at Neilson and saw no recognition in his face. None whatsoever.

"You don't *know* me?" he asked, gazing at him intently.

"If we met before, Mr. Priest, I'm real sorry, but I don't seem to recall. Where was it that we met each other?"

"You don't remember London?"

"London? London, *England*?" Neilson shook his head. "I ain't never been there, mister. I grew up in Montana Territory. Spent most of my life there. Ain't never been to England. Ain't never even been east of the Mississippi. I'd say you've got me confused with someone else, only you seem to know my name. You got somethin' mixed up, that's for sure, only I don't know what it is. I've never seen you before in my life. Leastwise, I don't believe so."

Lucas was speechless.

"You okay, mister?" Neilson asked. "You been drinkin'?"

"The name Forrester mean anything to you?" asked Lucas, uncertainly.

Neilson shook his head. "Can't say as it does."

"What about Cross? Delaney? Steiger?"

"Don't know any of those people," Neilson said, with a frown. "What's this all about?"

"How long have you been in Tombstone?"

"Only a few days. Why?"

"Were you injured in any way? A knock on the head or something?"

Neilson shook his head. He seemed thoroughly confused. "Mister, I don't know what you're talkin' about."

Lucas sat back in his chair, stunned. "Never mind," he said. "I . . . I must be mixed-up somehow. I guess I . . . I guess I thought you were someone else."

"Someone else named Neilson?"

"I guess that must be it. I knew someone else with the same name and I thought you were him."

"Oh, I see. I take it there was a resemblance?"

"Yes. A truly remarkable resemblance. You could be his twin brother."

"No foolin'? You mean there's somebody in London, England who looks like me and has got the same name?"

"Yes. Hell of a coincidence, isn't it?"

"Well, I'll be damned. I guess that explains it. Tell you the truth, Mister, for a minute there, I thought you might be drunk or off your head or somethin'."

"I was thinking the same thing about you," said Lucas.

Neilson grinned. "Well, ain't that somethin'? Somebody who looks like me and has the same name, too! And you say you met him in England?"

"Yes, that's right. He was a soldier."

"I'll be. No wonder you seemed all mixed-up. You thought I was him."

"I was certain of it."

"If that don't beat all. I'd sure like to meet this fella. But I don't know as I'll ever get to England. Sure is a long way off. This other Neilson, he a shootist, too?"

"Yes. He is. A remarkably good one."

"Is that right? Boy, ain't that somethin'?"

"Yes, it's an amazing coincidence," said Lucas. "Astonishing, in fact."

"I guess it is, at that. I never heard of such a thing."

"You ever hear of three men named Summers, McEnery and Billings?" Lucas asked.

Neilson chuckled. "Hell, this other fella must really look a lot like me," he said. "You still don't believe it, do you? I'm tellin' you, mister, I ain't him. I never heard of those people. They're friends of his, I take it."

"Fellow soldiers," Lucas said.

Neilson shook his head. "Well, I ain't never been a soldier. You got my word on that. And I don't know any of those folks you mentioned."

"Well, I'm sorry I bothered you," said Lucas. "I was sure that you were him."

"No trouble," Neilson said. "It sure has been interestin'. You still want to ask me those questions?"

"Perhaps another time," said Lucas, getting up from the table. "This whole thing took me so much by surprise, I can't remember a single thing that I was going to say."

Neilson smiled. "Well, I'll be around, you want to talk some more. And maybe you can tell me some more about this other fella. I sure am mighty curious."

"Yeah, maybe we can have a drink later," Lucas said.

"Anytime."

They shook hands and Lucas went back up to his room. Delaney had left, but Andre was still there, stretched out on the bed and getting some rest.

"You get a chance to talk to Scott?" she asked, sitting up as he came in. Then she saw the expression on his face. "What is it? What's wrong?"

Lucas shook his head, looking dazed. "We're in a lot of trouble," he said.

8 _____

"Twenty-five thousand in silver bullion," said O'Fallon. "And it slipped right through our fingers. What the hell went wrong?"

"Those three idiots, Head, Leonard and Crane, went wrong," replied Paul Zaber. "I gave them the plan myself. I told them, soon as the stage pulls up, shoot both the driver and shotgun guard, but they blew it. Leonard shot all right, but the other two hesitated and the horses bolted, so they only got Philpot. Then instead of chasing the stage down when the horses bolted, they had King holding their horses a short distance away, so the stage had a good head start on them by the time they got mounted. They still could've caught it, but they gave it up as a bad job and took off. Had to run from the damn posse with nothing to show for it."

"Exactly the way it happened in the original scenario," said O'Fallon, thoughtfully. "We seem to be swimming against the current of temporal inertia. I wouldn't have thought something like this would have made much difference to the scheme of things, but perhaps I was wrong. This time sector may have more temporal significance than I'd imagined."

"If that's true, then we're taking a big risk," said Zaber. "You think we should pull out?"

"I'd hate to do that without having this operation show more of a profit," O'Fallon replied. "Remember that none of us can depend on our agency pensions anymore, thanks to Moses Forrester. And I always intended to retire a very wealthy man, with a ludicrously expensive lifestyle. That means I'm going to have to convince the board to put me in charge of more profitable operations. They're not going to do that if they're not sufficiently impressed with the way I conducted this one."

"We've done all right," said Zaber.

"'All right' is not enough," O'Fallon replied. "They're not going to be impressed with just 'all right.' I went to a lot of trouble to set this operation up. I don't intend to pack it in until we've pulled everything we can out of it."

"It could be risky staying around," Zaber said. "There's still the question of the Montana Kid, whoever the hell he is. If he's a temporal agent, you can be sure he won't be alone. If he's an advance scout for the S.O.G., we're liable to wind up in the middle of a temporal disruption."

"That could be very bad for business, all around," O'Fallon said.

"Hey, as far as I'm concerned, the S.O.G. isn't my headache. Let Forrester's people handle them. There's no money to be made going up against commandos."

"Perhaps not, but there is money to be lost," said O'Fallon. "A significant disruption in this sector could affect our operations further down the timestream. The S.O.G. isn't just a threat to Temporal Intelligence, Paul. It's a threat to the entire timeline. And that means us, too. If the S.O.G. mounts an operation here, and the T.I.A. isn't around to stop them, it's going to be up to us. Don't forget, we *were* Temporal Intelligence ourselves at one time."

"Yeah, but there are only five of us," said Zaber. "We can use Clanton's rustlers to help us pull off operations, but sending them up against trained commandos would be ludicrous. The thing to do is get word to Forrester's people and let them handle it. And make sure we're long gone by the time they get around to it."

"That could be rather difficult to do, considering we won't know when they would be clocking in," O'Fallon replied. "Besides, we don't know that it *is* an S.O.G. infiltration. The Kid could be T.I.A. In which case, something must have tipped them off. It could have been Bailey. He wanted to get out from under. He might have contacted them and tried a double cross in return for immunity. Warning us about the Kid the way he did could have been part of the setup, or just Bailey burning his candle at both ends, trying to keep his ass covered. Either way, we don't have enough information."

Zaber shook his head. "And either way, we could be buying into one shitload of trouble."

"I'm not sure we have much choice, Paul. But keep one other thing in mind. If the Kid is an advance agent for the T.I.A., and if Bailey sold us out and they know we're conducting a Network operation back here, they'll send in one of their old First Division teams. If we could take them out, we'd not only enhance our standing in the organization, we'd collect a bounty that would go a long way towards making our retirement very comfortable."

Zaber took a deep breath and let it out slowly. "You've got a point. I can't decide for the others, though."

"Allan will go along with it," said O'Fallon. "He's young and he's hungry. And he's anxious to move up. Randy's more cautious, but I think he'll see that there's no avoiding the risk no matter what we do. Steve won't like it, but he'll understand the necessity. Especially if you and I are together on this."

"All right. So what's our first move?"

"The Kid didn't take the bait when you left here with Bailey. And I'm positive he followed Bailey here. So that means he's playing it smart. He knows there's something going on here, but we haven't been hit, so either his backup hasn't clocked in yet—assuming he's T.I.A.—or Bailey didn't tell him everything. Assuming Bailey tipped them off." He grimaced. "That's too many assumptions, but the one I think we can safely make is that he knows we're here, but he doesn't know exactly who we are. Let's put a little pressure on him. See if we can force his hand or get any backup he might have to reveal themselves."

"One of them already might have," Zaber said.

"Oh?"

"I was going to tell you about it when I came in, after we discussed the stage job. A few of Clanton's boys were in town and got mixed up in a fight with a cowboy who just arrived in town. You know Jenny, down at the Oriental? Sam wanted to tear off a piece, only she turned him down. It seems she's taken up with the Kid and given up turning tricks. Anyway, Sam got a little rough with her and this cowboy came over to play hero. He dropped Sam with one punch, broke Joey's wrist, used a whiskey bottle to make a mess out of Luke's face and hit Walt with a table."

"With a *table*?"

"Picked it up and used it to slam Walt against the wall, then knocked him out. Walt said he snatched up that table as if it didn't weigh a thing. Big guy, Walt said. Fast with his hands. Hits like a pile driver. Dark red hair, beard and a real shit-eatin' grin."

"Finn Delaney," O'Fallon said.

"You know him?"

"Oh yeah, I know him. It was a few years ago, back in the old days before Forrester took over. I ran into him on a mission, when I was working with the Mongoose. He and Carnehan did *not* like each other. And Delaney had a real hard-on for spooks. First Division time commando all the way, only a real maverick. Crazy son of a bitch. He was a noncom in those days. Kept getting busted for punching out officers who gave him a hard time. Yeah, I know Finn Delaney, all right."

"So then the Kid *is* T.I.A."

"Yeah. And that probably means Priest is heading up their team. And Cross will be in on it, as well. Foxy lady, and nasty as a snake. Looks like Forrester sent in the first string."

"That's not what I'd call good news," said Zaber.

"Are you kidding?" O'Fallon replied. "You know what the bounty is on those three? Shit. We just struck it rich."

"I wouldn't start counting that bounty before we collect it," said Zaber. "And if they're as good as you say they are, that's not going to be easy."

"Nothing worth doing is ever easy, Paul," O'Fallon replied. "But we've got the home-court advantage. I'll check with the others, but I'm pretty sure that I'm the only one they know. And they'll never recognize me with this face. All we have to do is identify the targets and send the rustlers out to take care of them. We may not even have to get involved ourselves. Because they're concerned about temporal continuity, they'll think twice before taking out any of the locals in this time sector. Our boys won't have any such compunctions." He smiled. "God damn. This operation is turning out to be a lot more interesting than I thought."

"You want me to call in the others?"

"Yes. We'll tell Allan and Steve to cancel their plan for the next shipment. Then we'll get some of the boys together and take a ride into town. It doesn't sound as if Delaney's had any cosmetic surgery. They usually don't, unless they're going to assume specific identities. I want to make sure. I want to find out where they're staying and what their covers are. I don't want any mistakes on this one. Once we've got them spotted and the situation cased, then I'll tell the boys I'm putting a bounty on them."

"I've got a better idea," said Zaber. "Have Ike Clanton do it. That way, if anything goes wrong and anybody talks, they'll go after Clanton first. And while they're doing that, we can make our move."

O'Fallon smiled broadly. "That's very good, Paul. That's what I call good thinking."

"Yeah, well, if we're going to take on the First Division's number one team, we're going to need a lot of that," said Zaber. "I'll go get the boys."

"What do you mean, he didn't know you?" Andre asked, staring at Lucas with astonishment.

"Just what I said," Lucas replied, taking off his coat and dropping down into a chair. He exhaled heavily. "He didn't have the faintest idea who I was. Said he'd never seen me before in his life. Thought I had him mixed-up with someone else. I came up with some story about his having a double that I met in England and he seemed to swallow that, but it gave me one hell of a turn, I can tell you."

"I don't understand," Andre said, an expression of complete confusion on her face. "Why would he do that? You think he was under surveillance?"

Lucas snorted. "He acted like he didn't even know what the word meant. I asked him that and he thought I was asking him if he was a surveyor."

"You're kidding."

"I wish I was."

"What the hell does he think he's doing?"

Lucas shook his head, helplessly. "I don't think he's playing games, Andre. You should have been there. You should have seen him. It was spooky. He really didn't know me. Your name, Finn's name, Steiger's name, the Old Man, they didn't mean a thing to him. There was no glimmer of recognition. None whatsoever."

She stared at him with disbelief. "My God. You think he's got amnesia?"

Lucas shrugged. "I don't know. I'm at a loss to account for it. I asked him if something had happened to him recently, if he'd gotten hurt or something, and he just looked at me as if I were crazy. It's as if the role has completely taken him over. He's not Sergeant Scott Neilson, temporal agent. He's Scott Neilson, the Montana Kid."

"You think the opposition got to him and brainwashed him?"

"I suppose it's possible, but *why*? Why go to all that trouble? Why not just interrogate him and then take him out? It doesn't make any sense."

"Does Finn know about this yet?"

Lucas shook his head. "I haven't had a chance to talk to him. But we're going to have to warn him. I don't know what the hell's happened to Neilson. Maybe he's had a breakdown or something, but we can't count on him anymore. He's become a liability."

"Maybe this is it," said Andre. "Maybe this is what Dr. Darkness meant. Maybe something has happened to Scott and he forgot who he really was and somehow disrupted temporal continuity."

Lucas sat very still, staring at her for a long moment.

"It's possible, isn't it?" she asked.

Lucas nodded slowly. "Yes. It's possible. The question is, what are we supposed to do about it?"

"No," said Andre. "That's not the question. The question is, what is it that we're *going* to do—or not do—that we're going to have to do differently to save the future?"

"Jesus," Lucas said. "How the hell are we supposed to know?"

"Darkness said he's going to tell us."

"Yeah. At the last moment. Only *why*? Why wait till the last minute?"

"Maybe to make sure that we don't have a chance to think about it," she said. "Lucas . . . it's possible that we may have to kill him."

Lucas closed his eyes. "Oh, hell."

"Maybe . . . maybe I'm wrong. Maybe there's another way . . ."

"No," said Lucas, shaking his head. "No, I don't think so.

I think you're right. Under ordinary circumstances . . . if you can possibly call this situation ordinary . . . that's what we'd do. We'd look for some other way. We'd take him and clock him out and get him to a hospital . . . and somehow, that's what would interfere with temporal continuity. That's got to be it. Neilson has to be the key. That's why Darkness didn't tell us any more than he did. It's the only possible explanation that makes any sense. Whatever it is we have to do regarding Neilson, we're going to have to do it at a specific time. And there's no way we could know what that time is unless Darkness tells us. Only if he told us in advance we'd have to kill him, we'd do everything in our power to find some other way around it. He's trying to make sure that we won't have a chance to do that. Damn. Damn, damn, *damn!* "

"We've got to find Finn," she said. "If he runs into Scott before we warn him about this, he's liable to take it on his own to do something."

"You're right. He took a room over at the Aztec Rooming House. You head on over there, and if he's not in, check the Capitol Saloon over on Fremont, then the Can Can Restaurant over on Allen. I'll start at Hafford's across the street and work my way down through the Occidental, the Alhambra and the Oriental. If he's not in his room, he's got to be in one of those places, following up on Ben Stone. We'll meet back here."

"Got it."

"God, whatever it is, I hope it doesn't happen tonight, before we get a chance to find Delaney." He got up and put on his coat.

"Then let's not waste any time," she said, heading for the door.

Ben Stone was in the last saloon Finn checked, the Oriental. Going by his own statements, Stone was breaking his pattern. He said he liked playing in different saloons after he lost, "to keep his luck fresh." Only here he was, in the Oriental once again. Why? Because this was where they met the last time?

"You're waiting for me, aren't you, you son of a bitch?" Finn mumbled under his breath as he spotted Stone sitting at a table in the back. He glanced around at the room. There were some cowboys sitting in a group at a couple of tables, a few card games going on. None of the Tombstone lawmen were in evidence. Holliday sitting in on a card game with Stone and a couple of the townspeople. And Scott Neilson at the bar, talking to Jenny. The moment Jenny spotted him, she waved him over.

"Finn, I'd like you to meet Scott, the Montana Kid. Scott, this is the kind gentleman who helped me the other day."

"We already know each other, Jenny," Neilson said, keeping his voice low and checking to see that they weren't overheard. "Finn's one of the people I was telling you about."

Delaney glanced at him, startled. He couldn't possibly have . . . no, he must have devised some sort of cover story for the girl. Which could pose a problem, since he hadn't admitted knowing Scott before, when he'd met her. But there was nothing else to do but play along with it.

"How're you doing, Kid? It's been a while."

"Where have you *been*?" Neilson said, in a low voice. "Did you just clock in? Are Lucas and Andre with you?"

Delaney stared at him with disbelief, then glanced at Jenny with alarm.

"What the hell are you doing?" he whispered.

"It's okay," Scott replied. "She knows all about it."

Delaney couldn't believe what he was hearing. "You *told* her? *Are you crazy?*"

"Finn, we have to talk," said Scott, quietly. He glanced at Jenny. "She's not who you think she is. She's one of Drakov's hominoids."

Delaney caught his breath. "Holy shit! What the hell—"

"You're the fella that busted up some of my boys the other night, ain't 'cha?" said a voice behind him, before he could finish.

Scott's hands flashed to his coat and the two pearl-handled Colts leaped from their holsters. There were several audible clicks as he cocked them.

"Say, take it easy there, Kid," the man said, slowly opening his coat. "I'm not heeled." There were two other men standing beside him. "My friends ain't, neither."

"What do you want, Clanton?" Scott asked.

"We don't want any trouble," said Ike Clanton, as Delaney turned to face him. He was a large man, with light, curly hair, a moustache and a thin goatee. One look and Delaney didn't like him. "And I wanted to be sure you understood that, seein' as how you seem friendly with this here gentleman and your girl, Jenny, was involved."

"Say your piece, Ike." Scott lowered the hammers and put away his guns.

"You met my friends, here?" Clanton said, indicating the two men with him. "This here's Johnny Ringo. And this gent is Curly Bill Brocius."

"Any friends of yours, Ike, ain't no friends of mine," said Neilson.

"Say, now, I was just bein' polite," said Clanton. "I don't believe I know this gentleman."

"The name's Delaney," Finn said, watching the men carefully. "Finn Delaney."

"Irishman, eh?"

"What can I do for you, Mr. Clanton?"

"Well, I just wanted to come over and apologize on behalf of my boys," said Ike. "They had a mite too much whiskey yesterday and got out of line a bit."

"More than a bit, I'd say," Delaney replied. "And any apologies should be addressed to this young lady."

"I reckon so," said Clanton. "Jenny, I'm right sorry about what happened. There wasn't no call for it. I sure hope you won't go bearin' us a grudge."

"I accept your apology, Ike," she said.

"I ain't gonna be so easy," Scott said.

"Well, now, I figured that," said Clanton, "which is why I'm keepin' those boys out of town for a while. Fact is, they're feelin' poorly anyway, after what Mr. Delaney here did to 'em."

"They got off lucky," said Scott. "If I'd been here, I would've killed them."

"Well, now, that's what I wanted to talk to you about," said Ike. "I don't want any bad blood between you and my boys if I can help it. They're right sorry about what they done. I talked to 'em and made sure they wouldn't be bearin' your friend here any grudges. I don't want any trouble. Now they promised to behave themselves and they didn't really understand about you and Jenny. They do now. Seein' as no harm was really done, except a little to my boys, I'm hopin' we can just patch things up and forget about the whole thing. That is, if you're agreeable."

Scott stared hard at Clanton. "If you really mean that, Ike, then I'm agreeable. But you keep your rustlin' lowlifes away from Jenny or I'll have something to say about it, understand? And I'll be sayin' it to *you*."

"Hey," said Ike, raising his hands up to his chest, "I got no problem with that. Looks like we understand each other. I'm happy we could work it out. Will you have a drink on it? I'll buy. That goes for you too, mister," he added, looking at Delaney. "Frank, whiskey for my friends here."

Delaney was paying less attention to Ike Clanton than to the two men with him, Brocius and Ringo. Both hard-looking men, with eyes that met his gaze dead on. Gunfighters. Men who looked as if they knew their business.

Brocius shifted his gaze to Neilson. "You're pretty quick with those fancy guns of yours," he said.

"I hear tell you're pretty quick, yourself," Scott replied.

"I wonder which one of us is quicker," Curly Bill said, with a smile.

"You want to find out?" asked Neilson.

"Scott!" said Jenny.

"Hey, now, wait . . ." started Clanton.

Delaney took Scott by the arm. "Don't push it," he said, firmly.

"Anytime, Kid," Brocius said.

"Now hold on just a minute," said Delaney.

"Relax, Finn," said Scott. "We can find out right here and now, without anybody getting hurt. You game, Curly Bill?"

Brocius narrowed his eyes. "What you got in mind?"

"I see you're wearing a two-gun rig, too," said Scott. "You take one gun and give it to Ike. I'll take one of mine and give it to Finn. Then we each take the gun we got left and give them both to Frank, here, to unload. We put the empty guns back in our holsters and Frank will say the word. Then we draw and dry fire."

By now, the other people in the saloon were aware of what was going on and they had started to gather around.

"What do you say, Brocius?"

Curly Bill was aware of the attention on them. "I'm game."

He took out one of his guns and handed it to Clanton while Scott took out one of his and handed it to Finn. Then they each took their remaining gun and passed it across the bar to Frank Leslie, who opened the loading gates, held them up one at a time, barrels up, rotated the cylinders and let the bullets drop out.

"Five each," he said, after making sure both guns were empty. He put the bullets down on the bar and handed the guns back to them. They replaced them in their holsters.

"Anytime you're ready, Frank," said Scott.

Curly Bill nodded. They stood about three feet away from each other.

"I'll count to three," said Leslie. "On three, go for your guns. You ready?"

Everyone in the saloon gathered around. There was utter silence.

"I'm ready," Scott said.

"Ready," said Curly Bill.

"Okay, here goes," said Leslie. "One . . ."

Curly Bill flexed his fingers.

"Two . . ."

Scott stood perfectly relaxed.

"*Three!*"

Curly Bill's right hand darted toward his holster, but his gun hadn't even cleared it when he suddenly found himself looking down the barrel of Scott's Colt .45. He froze.

Scott squeezed the trigger and the hammer fell with a loud snap.

"*Damn!*" said someone in the crowd.

Someone else whistled and the whole crowd started talking excitedly. Brocius simply stood there, staring at Scott, his eyes like anthracite. Clanton cleared his throat.

"How about that drink, boys?"

Curly Bill snatched his bullets off the bar, took his other gun from Clanton and stalked away without a word, going out through the double doors into the street.

"Some other time, Ike," Scott said. "I feel like a walk. Jenny . . ."

She took his arm.

"I'll walk with you," Finn said.

They went outside. There was no sign of Curly Bill.

"Was that smart?" asked Jenny. "He knows you're faster now. He'll look to shoot you in the back."

"He probably would have done that anyway," said Scott.

"Scott, what the hell is going on here?" Delaney asked, as they walked down the street. "Drakov's *here*?" He glanced at Jenny. "And where does she fit into this?"

"I'm in love with her, Finn. And she's in love with me."

"Oh, Jesus Christ!"

"She's the one who warned me about Drakov. He knows about me. He knows about you, too. That girl, Becky, is one of his."

"Shit. Where is he?"

"I'm not sure. Neither is Jenny. Part of the time, he's basing himself in Hop Town, in a room above an opium den. He's also got a chronoplate stashed there, which leads to London in some future time period, Jenny's not sure which. She isn't told any more than she needs to know. He *is* protected there. As far as any other bases of operations he might have back here, she doesn't know. We're in it up to our necks, Finn. It's not only Drakov back here. It's the Network *and* the S.O.G."

"Good God! Stone?"

"He's S.O.G. But he's the only one that Jenny knows about. The Network and the S.O.G. apparently don't know about each other. And there's a hell of a good reason for that. Are Lucas and Andre here with you?"

"Yeah. They're over in the Grand Hotel. But wait a minute. You *saw* Lucas!"

"I did?"

Delaney frowned. "He went out on that posse with you. He said he saw you. And he said you acted as if you didn't know him. He figured you were under surveillance from someone in the posse and knew about it. What kind of game are you playing here, Scott?"

Scott had stopped dead in his drinks. "He saw *me*?"

Delaney looked at him with a frown. "What is this? Are you telling me you don't remember?"

Scott gave a low whistle. "Finn, Lucas wasn't with that posse. At least, not the posse *I* was on."

"What the hell are you talking about? Of course, he was there! I saw him ride out! He *saw* you, for God's sake!"

"No. He didn't. He didn't see *me*. I'm beginning to understand what's going on here. And it's even worse than I thought. Finn, everything that we suspected about this temporal scenario is true. Not just one of the possibilities we considered, *all* of them together. The S.O.G. is here. At least one of them that I know about, but there's probably more. There's got to be. The Network is here. They're running an operation out of the Clanton ranch."

"You mean *Ike Clanton* is a Network agent?"

"Not Clanton. And not Curly Bill, either. The other one, Johnny Ringo. Only he's not really Johnny Ringo. His real name is Tim O'Fallon."

"*O'Fallon!*"

"You know him?"

"Hell, yes. He was one of Jack Carnehan's field agents. You remember the Mongoose?"

"No, Carnehan was before my time. But I've heard about him."

"So that means he recognized me," said Delaney. "I thought he was looking at me funny. He's got himself a new face."

"Yeah. Johnny Ringo's," Scott said. "They must have killed the real Ringo."

"But I still don't understand about you and Lucas. How could you be on the same posse together and not see each other?"

"Because we weren't on the same posse," Scott said. "We were on *different* posses. In different timelines. Only I didn't realize until now that there's another Scott Neilson in that other timeline. That puts an entirely new twist on things. Finn, this whole damn town is one big confluence point."

Delaney stared at him, stunned. "The whole *town*?"

"I was able to piece it together from what Jenny told me," Scott replied. "And she doesn't quite understand it all. As near as I can figure, the location of this town is also the location for a massive area of temporal instability. It's a confluence, but more than that, it's that one-in-a-million shot, a confluence where both timelines intersect at the same, exact corresponding space and time. You're the one who went to R.C.S., so you probably understand the zen physics a lot better than I do, but as a result, the temporal instability here is incredible. It's like . . . like the town sort of *flickers*, like a strobe light, not so anyone here would actually notice, of course, but at different times, first you're in one Tombstone, then you're in the other."

"Holy shit," whispered Delaney.

"The thing I've been batting my brains out about is what the effect of temporal inertia is here. It doesn't seem as if the people from *this* Tombstone can cross over into the *other* one, and I don't even know if the Network and the S.O.G. are in the same timeline together, but apparently, we *can* cross over. Or at least *you* can. You have, obviously, if you've talked to

Lucas, because he and Andre are in the other timeline. Or at least they were. Maybe they're here now. Hell, I don't know. It's a fucking mindblower. But it looks as if I may not be able to cross over, because there's another Scott Neilson in the other timeline and temporal inertia is keeping us apart. Either that, or I've become too deeply involved in this scenario and I'm part of whatever's going to happen here."

"So that's what Darkness was talking about," said Finn. "That's what he didn't tell us. And that's why he wasn't able to tach back here, or at least he won't be able to until a certain point in time."

"I don't understand," said Scott.

"Darkness isn't sure what effect crossing over would have on his subatomic structure," Delaney explained. "It's unstable and gradually disintegrating. He seems to have periods of . . . remission, for lack of a better way of putting it, but he thinks that one of these days, he's going to pass the point of no return and he'll simply discorporate, depart at multiples of light speed in all directions of the universe. Being in the vicinity of temporal confluence could accelerate that."

"Wow," said Scott. "And he's been *living* with that?" He exhaled heavily. "No wonder he's so flaky around the edges."

"There's something else that you don't know, Scott," said Delaney. "Darkness is from the future. Not our time sector, but *our* future."

"I'll be damned," said Neilson, softly. He nodded. "That figures. It would explain a lot about him."

"There's more," said Finn, grimly. "We're not sure what time he came from, but whatever century it was, something devastating happened up ahead. Or *is going* to happen. Some kind of terrible temporal disaster. He wouldn't tell us what it is, but it's got to be a massive timestream split, possibly even a chain reaction. And that's what Darkness is trying to prevent. Actually, he isn't trying to prevent it, because from his temporal standpoint, it's *already* happened. He's trying to change it. He's trying to change history, Scott, and somehow we're a part of it. Whatever it is that is going to bring on that temporal disaster is going to happen right here, in this scenario. Maybe tomorrow, maybe next week, maybe five seconds from now, for all we know. And we haven't got any idea what it is. Darkness wouldn't tell us. It could involve the S.O.G., it could involve the Network, it could involve Drakov or all or even none of them. But Darkness told us that we're going to be in a position to change it. And whatever it is we're going to have to do, we're not going to know about it until we have to do it, until the very last minute. Now I know why. Darkness is taking a big gamble. He's putting his life on the line. He's got one chance, just one, to tach in and tell us what to do . . . because whatever it is, it's got tō be something heavy. Something he can't even give us a chance to think about. And he knows that the instant he arrives here, he might discorporate."

"But he doesn't know for sure?" said Scott.

"No, how could he? He's gambling that he won't. Or that if he does, he'll have enough time to tell us what to do before it happens."

"God damn it. It's even *worse* than I imagined," Scott said.

Delaney suddenly had another thought. He recalled back when Darkness had appeared to them in the First Division Lounge. He had indicated that the three of them would be in a position to do whatever it was that would have to be done. He hadn't said anything about Neilson.

He racked his brain for what he knew of the metaphysical complexities of temporal physics, popularly known as "zen physics," trying to think back to the problem modules he had studied back in Referee Corps School. He had never graduated. He came close, but he had washed out, ultimately because of his personality, not because of any inability on his part. He was convinced of that, despite the fact that he always told people he'd washed out because he couldn't cut the mustard academically. There was no shame in that. In all the world, only a handful of the most brilliant graduate students in the field of temporal physics were selected for R.C.S. and it was one hell of an achievement and an honor simply to be chosen. But Delaney had realized early on that he lacked two essential personality traits to be a Temporal Referee. Patience and detachment.

In the old days—they *were* the old days now, although it didn't seem like so very long ago—when nations waged their conflicts through the medium of the Time Wars, the Referees had functioned as the temporal arbiters, choosing and defining the conflict scenarios and arbitrating their results. Now, they functioned as a sort of temporal high command, the final guardians of temporal continuity, a Supreme Court of time travel. It wouldn't have been easy, for R.C.S. was brutally demanding, but Delaney could have become a Temporal Referee after graduating from the world's toughest post-postgraduate school and serving a lengthy tour of internship. He would have enjoyed the highest pay scale in the world, commensurate with the most prestigious job in the world, but he would have been an old man by the time he had finally achieved his goal. And about midway through R.C.S., he had realized that he had misjudged his aspirations.

He didn't have the patience to finish his schooling and go through all those years of internship. And he lacked the personal detachment to play with human lives as if they were nothing more than chess pieces. What he really wanted, he had realized, was to be directly involved, hands on, with history. So he had dropped out of R.C.S. and enlisted in the Temporal Corps.

He was already a veteran of many temporal campaigns when he had first met Lucas Priest on what was to become the very first temporal adjustment mission ever conducted in Minus Time, when Professor Mensinger's worst fears came true and it was discovered that history was *not* an immutable absolute, that it *could* be changed, with consequences that could prove disastrous. He and Lucas had been part of the team who were the very first Time Commandos, even before the First Division had been organized under Moses Forrester, who had acted as their training officer on that mission. It seemed so very long ago.

Priest had only been a sergeant major back then and had just clocked in from a hitch served in the Second Punic War. Delaney, himself, had been a Private First Class—again—and if anyone had told him back then he would one day become an officer, he would have laughed in his face. Half the team never made it back from that mission. Johnson and Hooker had both bought it and their names were the first to be listed on the Wall of Honor, the first of many. Too many.

It had been on that mission that they first met Andre, although their real relationship with her did not begin until centuries had passed. When Lucas had first met her, he had not even known she was a woman. She was a native of that time period, in 12th-century England, a woman passing as a young man. She had called herself Andre de la Croix and had carried her deception off so far as to become a mercenary knight in the service of Prince John. She and Lucas had first met in the lists at the tournament of Ashby de la Zouche, an encounter Lucas was never to forget. He had almost failed to survive it.

They had met again in 17th-century France, when they went up against the Timekeepers, and were stunned to learn that Andre had been brought there from the past by a deserter from the Temporal Corps named Reese Hunter. Hunter had been assassinated by the Timekeepers and Andre had helped them to avenge his death and successfully complete their mission, after which they had brought her back to Plus Time with them, to the 27th century. She became a soldier in the Temporal Corps, transferring to the First Division as soon as she completed her training.

They had served on many missions since then, but never one like this, never one where all the laws of Temporal Relativity seemed to be suspended . . . the *theories* of Temporal Relativity, Delaney corrected himself, for zen physics was anything but an exact science. Mensinger had never anticipated anything like the Temporal Crisis or confluence points. They had studied Mensinger's theories exhaustively in R.C.S., pushing themselves to the verge of nervous breakdowns trying to solve the theoretical problem modules posed by the instructors, temporal riddles more mystifying than zen koans. What would happen if . . .

But the one hypothetical situation that no one had anticipated was the one that faced them now. What would happen if two separate timelines in two parallel universes converged in a confluence point at the exact same space and time? How would the Theory of Temporal Inertia be affected? Where and how would the Fate Factor come into play? What definition would apply to the Principle of Temporal Uncertainty? Or, given such a situation, could it even *be* defined? And what about the potential for a timestream split? Would it occur here and now or . . .

No, not here and now, Delaney thought, but in the future Darkness came from. Here and now, where two timelines intersected, the immeasurable surge in temporal inertia would somehow affect the currents of both timestreams, inducing a profound rippling effect, like a timewave that would gradually swell into a tsunami as the centuries rolled by until, somewhere in the future, it broke and . . . *and what*? Ultimate entropy? An end to all of time? A disaster that would make all the prophecies of Nostradamus and the biblical Apocalypse seem like nothing more serious than a mild spring shower? He shuddered at the thought.

"Finn? You okay?" said Scott.

Delaney snapped out of it. "Yeah . . . yeah, I guess so."

"For a moment there, you looked . . . you looked as if the world was coming to an end."

Delaney took a deep breath and let it out slowly. "It is, Scott. Not only the world, but everything. And the whole shebang hinges on one whacked-out scientist saying the right word at the right time. Then, for probably about one second, it's going to be up to us."

Scott moistened his lips and swallowed hard. "Nothing like a little pressure," he said, with a weak smile.

9 _____

The Alhambra and the Oriental were the last saloons left for Lucas to check. If Delaney wasn't there, he only hoped that Andre would find him and get him back to the hotel. Unless Finn had picked up some sort of lead and left town to pursue it, he had to be around somewhere. Lucas couldn't imagine him leaving town without letting them know. But there was no sign of Delaney in the Alhambra. Lucas decided to check the Occidental Lunch Room, which was attached to the saloon. As he entered, he walked right into the middle of an altercation.

"There ain't a word of truth to it!" Ike Clanton was shouting at a man sitting at a table. "I ain't never made no deal with him! And if Wyatt Earp says I did, then he's a damn liar and I'll make him pay for it!"

"You're a son of a bitch, Clanton," said Doc Holliday, getting up from a nearby table, "and you talk too much!"

"Man goes spreadin' lies about me, I intend to speak up about it and you ain't got no say in it, Holliday!"

"You're the one's been spreadin' lies about the Earps, Clanton, and I tell you I won't stand for it," said Holliday, a dangerous edge to his voice. "And I hear it's you been tellin' people I was the one held up that stage and helped King get away."

"I don't know nothin' about that," Clanton protested. "And I don't know nothin' about no reward for Leonard, Head and

Crane, neither. It's your friend Wyatt Earp's been tellin' folks I made a deal with him in secret to double-cross those three for the reward and I ain't never done no such thing!"

"You're a liar, Clanton," Holliday replied. "You'd sell out your own mother for a dollar. I've had about enough of you and your damn mouth. Jerk your pistol!"

"I'm not heeled," said Clanton, nervously. "Hell, you know the law."

"Yeah, and it seems like you obey it only when it's convenient for you," Holliday replied.

The door behind Lucas opened and Virgil Earp came in. Apparently, someone had run to fetch him.

"Trouble, Doc?" said Virgil.

"Clanton here's been spreadin' lies about us all over town," said Holliday. "I've had about enough of it. You talk big, Clanton, let's see how big you are. You want a fight, you son of a bitch, you can damn well have one!"

"I told him I'm not heeled," Clanton said to Virgil. "I ain't breakin' any laws."

"You're a liar," Holliday said. "If you haven't got a gun, then go and get one! I'll wait right here!"

"I'm not going to have any shooting around here, Doc," said Virgil. "Come on, let's step outside and talk about this."

"I'm through talkin'! And I'm through listenin' to this lyin' rustler, too!"

"Doc, I'm askin' you as a friend," Virgil said. "Let's go. Let Clanton have his mouth. He's just a blowhard, everybody knows it."

Clanton glared at Virgil, but said nothing.

Doc pointed his finger at Clanton. "I'm not through with you, you bastard. This ain't finished!"

He walked out with Virgil.

"You heard him!" Clanton said, to the people in the room. "You heard him threaten me! That's what this town has come to! Outlaws like Doc Holliday can threaten law-abiding citizens just because he's got the Earps there to protect him! Now they're goin' around throwin' dirt on my good name! Well, if they want a fight, then Ike Clanton will oblige them!"

Lucas beat a hasty retreat before he got caught in the middle of something. He knew what this was all about and he knew what it was leading up to. Wells Fargo had offered a reward for the capture of the outlaws who had killed Bud Philpot and tried to rob the stage. Leonard, Head and Crane had managed to elude the posse and Wyatt Earp was still smarting from it. He wanted the glory of capturing the outlaws and he hoped to do it before the next election, when he planned to run for sheriff against Johnny Behan.

According to history, he'd secretly offered a deal to Ike Clanton, Frank McLaury and another rustler named Joe Hill, to trap the outlaws. And rather than manifest the outrage that he claimed to have over being asked to betray his friends, all Ike Clanton had wanted to know was if the reward was good dead or alive. Obviously, if the outlaws were killed, they'd never be around to tell the other rustlers who betrayed them. And the size of the reward was more than a suitable inducement.

Ike was going to set them up for an ambush and then collect the reward, only nothing ever came of it because Leonard and Head were killed in an attempted store robbery in Hatchita, New Mexico and Crane was killed shortly thereafter, rustling cattle with Old Man Clanton, Ike's father. However, word of the deal leaked out and soon spread all over town, primarily because of Clanton's vocal protestations to anyone who'd listen. It only added to the bad blood between the Clantons, the McLaurys and the Earps and it would lead to the most famous gunfight in western history—the shoot-out at the O.K. Corral.

The situation in Tombstone was tense enough without agents from the future contributing to temporal instability in the time sector. Lucas only hoped that whatever was supposed to happen would happen soon. Yet, at the same time, he wasn't ready for it. He hurried down the street to the Oriental Saloon.

Delaney wasn't there, either. Cursing to himself, Lucas hurried back to the hotel. He had the terrible feeling that he was running out of time. He hoped Andre had found Delaney. They had to tell him about Scott. Somehow, Lucas was certain, Scott Neilson was the key to the whole thing. Only what, exactly, were they supposed to do? And *when*? There was still no sign of Darkness. Why was he cutting it so close?

He ran into the hotel and hurried up the stairs to their room. Andre was already there. There was no sign of Finn Delaney.

"You didn't find him?" she asked, anxiously.

Lucas shook his head. "I looked everywhere. I can't imagine where he could have gone."

"He hasn't been in at the boarding house all day," she said. "And he hasn't been seen in any of the other places that I checked. Hell, they didn't even know who the hell he was. You'd think they'd remember a guy built like a gorilla with red hair and a beard."

"Something may have happened to him," Lucas said. "Maybe he pushed Stone too close. Christ. Where *haven't* we checked?"

Neither Lucas nor Andre were registered at the Grand Hotel. Delaney stared at the desk clerk with astonishment. "Are you *sure*?" he asked.

"We don't have anyone by the name of Priest registered here, mister," said the desk clerk. "You must have made a mistake."

"Finn," said Neilson, from behind him.

"Excuse me," Delaney said to the desk clerk and went over to join Scott and Jenny.

"They're not at this hotel," said Scott. "They're at the *other* Grand Hotel, in the other timeline. It's me. Somehow, you've been crossing over from one timeline to the other, but you can't do it now because of me. There's another Scott Neilson over there and if I crossed over, it would be a temporal anomaly."

Delaney frowned. "That doesn't make sense," he said. "Lucas had a double in the other universe and he was able to cross over. Why should I be prevented from crossing over because of you? And why should *you* be prevented from crossing over?"

"Come on, Finn, you must have figured it out by now," said Scott. "There's only one explanation that makes any sort of sense. It's not the Network, it's not the S.O.G., it isn't Drakov, it's me. *I'm* the focal point of the disruption. Whatever's going to happen here, I'm at the center of the instability and when it reaches the breaking point, I'm the one who's going to trigger it somehow. Jenny, excuse us for a moment."

He drew Delaney aside and spoke to him in a low voice, so she couldn't hear.

"She turned on Drakov because of me," he said, "and I don't want her to hear this, but you've got to promise me one thing. When all of this is over, you'll take her back with you. She needs help, Finn. Drakov had her thinking she wasn't even human."

"What are you talking about, Scott? You know we can't possibly—"

"She doesn't *belong* here, Finn. Look, let's be honest with each other. Ever since Jenny told me what was going on, I've been wracking my brain over it, trying to figure all the angles. Drakov, the Network, the S.O.G., they're all here contributing to the instability, but they're not the real threat, are they? It's me. Somehow, in the other universe, I *was* the Montana Kid. I lived in another time, in another place, and I didn't know anything about the T.I.A. or temporal disruptions. You know, it's a funny thing, but I've always felt that I was born too late. That I didn't belong in my own time, that I really belonged *here*. And in the other timeline, that's how it was! I don't even pretend to understand the metaphysics involved, but somehow, I was fated to be here. Only I'm not *supposed* to be here. Whatever's going to happen to bring about the disaster up ahead, maybe the Network's going to start it, or maybe the S.O.G. or Drakov or maybe even all of them, but I'm the one who's going to finish it. Don't ask me how I know. I can just *feel* it. And I also have a feeling that to stop whatever's going to happen, you may have to kill me."

"Scott, you don't know what you're saying. You've been under a lot of strain and—"

"Damn it, Finn, don't patronize me! You've thought about it, haven't you? Tell me the truth!"

Delaney took a deep breath and nodded. "Yeah. I've thought about it."

"Suppose that's what Darkness wants you to do," said Scott. "Suppose you're going to have to kill me. You *are* going to go through with it, aren't you?"

"Scott . . ."

"Damn it, Finn, if that's how it turns out, you'll *have* to do it! You *know* you'll have to! I just want you to know I understand. Whatever happens now, if I'm really at the focal point of all this, I'm simply going to have to assume that there's nothing I can do about it. If I'm the one, then whatever it is I'm going to do, we know from Darkness that I've already done it and chances are the only way to stop me is to kill me. But only at a certain time, apparently."

"Scott, this is all conjecture," said Delaney. "You don't really know that—"

"No, I don't really know, but *if* that's how it's going to be, I want you to know that I understand and I want you to do what you have to do. I've only got one last request. Take Jenny with you."

"Scott . . ."

"Please, Finn. Is it really asking all that much?"

Delaney nodded. "No. No, I don't suppose it is."

"Then you promise?"

"Okay, I promise."

"All right, we're getting out of here, so you can find Lucas and Andre. We'll be over the Oriental. Tell the others good luck for me."

"I will."

"And tell them . . . just tell them that I understand."

Delaney watched as they walked out the door. He sighed heavily. "Damn it."

"Finn! Where *were* you?"

He turned to see Lucas and Andre coming down the stairs.

"Where were *you?*" he asked, astonished.

"We've been all over town looking for you! Where —"

"Did you just come down from your room?"

Lucas stared at him. "Of course we just came down from our room! Where did you think we were?"

"In another universe," said Delaney. "I'll be damned. He was right."

"Who was right?"

"Incredible. Nothing changed. I didn't notice or feel a thing."

"Finn, what the hell are you talking about?"

Delaney exhaled heavily. "We'd better go back up to your room," he said. He shook his head. "You're not going to believe this."

Zaber came back into the saloon and sat down at the table with the others. "They're registered at the Grand Hotel, as Mr. & Mrs. Priest," he said. "And Delaney's got a room over the Aztec."

"Are they there right now?" O'Fallon asked.

"Priest and Cross are. I don't know where Delaney is. And I haven't seen the Kid. . . ."

"He just walked in," O'Fallon said, looking toward the door.

"What's the plan?"

"We wait. We act nice and polite—like Clanton said, we

don't want any trouble. We stay right here, in front of witnesses. And when he leaves, Curly Bill plugs him."

"What about the others?"

"I've got six of the boys waiting for Delaney at his rooming house. I made it clear to them that he's extremely dangerous and if they screw up, it could mean their lives. The moment they spot him, they'll open up. As for Priest and Cross, I've got four of our best riflemen stationed on the roof of Hafford's Saloon, across from their hotel. As soon as Delaney gets it, someone's going to run inside and tell them he's been shot. The minute they step outside, the snipers will open fire with their Winchesters. Meanwhile, we'll all be sitting right here, having a nice, friendly game of cards and establishing our alibis."

"How are you going to prove to the organization that we got them?" Zaber asked.

O'Fallon smiled. "We won't have to, Paul. Forrester is going to do that for us. We'll be able to collect on that contract as soon as their names appear on the First Division's Wall of Honor."

Zaber smiled and nodded. "Nice."

"Minimum risk, maximum profit," said O'Fallon. "That's the way to run things. Then as soon as it's over, we fold the operation and pull out, before any of their backup can arrive."

"What happens if anything goes wrong?"

"Relax and have a drink. Nothing will go wrong." He pushed a pack of cards toward him. "Shuffle the deck and deal."

Scott stood at the bar with Jenny, watching the Network men out of the corner of his eye. He was torn with indecision. He felt certain, somehow, that he was at the center of this whole temporal scenario. What should he do? Would he have to think twice about every single action he was going to take from now until . . . whenever? Or should he simply attempt to do nothing? Maybe he should just hole up in his room and not come out until the time for whatever was supposed to happen had passed. Only how was he to know when that would be?

What troubled him the most was Drakov. Drakov troubled the others, too. Not only because of who and what he was, but because somehow he had found out about everything that was going on in this scenario. What Scott knew, he knew only from what Jenny had told him, and from what he had deduced from that, but clearly Jenny did not know everything. Drakov had told her only as much as he felt she needed to know to do her job for him. Obviously, he himself knew a great deal more. Only *how*?

He knew about the Network and who they were. He knew about Ben Stone being S.O.G. and if there were others—and it would seem there had to be—he probably knew about them, too. He knew about Zeke Bailey. *How could he know all that?* How could he know about all the forces at work in this scenario without any of them knowing about him?

"Scott?"

He looked at Jenny.

"You look so worried."

He took her hand and gave it a gentle squeeze. "Everything's going to be all right, Jen."

"What did you and Finn talk about before?"

"Oh, we were discussing what our plans should be," he lied. "What we should do about Drakov and the others."

"I watched Finn's face while you two were talking," she said. "He didn't look as if he thought everything would be all right."

"We're all worried, Jen. It's a dangerous situation. I just want you to stay out of it, that's all. I don't want to see you hurt. And I don't want you going back to Drakov."

"If he sends for me, I'll have to," she said.

"No. It's too risky."

"It would be too risky if I didn't go," she said. "It would warn him that something was wrong. I have to go on pretending, Scott. For your sake as well as mine."

"What if he finds out you've betrayed him?"

"He won't find out," she said. "Nobody knows but you and your three friends. And he would never suspect that I could even think of turning against him. After all," she added, with a grimace, "he's the Master."

"He isn't *your* master, Jen. Not anymore."

"I could kill him myself," she said, vehemently. "Not only because of what he wants to do to you, but because of what he's done to me. All those years, all my life, I've believed that I was something less than human. I've believed that ever since I was a little girl, because that's what I was taught. I'd stand before the mirror and stare at my reflection, trying to see *how* I was different, how I was inferior. . . ."

"You weren't born the same way other people are born,"

said Scott, "but that's the only difference. That and the fact that Drakov had poisoned your mind. I know you're in the grip of powerful, confusing feelings right now, Jen, but you've got to try not to dwell on them. When this is over, I'll take you back with me and you'll get some help from doctors who can help you sort out those feelings. They'll help you to overcome all the damage Drakov has done to you. It will take some time, Jen, but you'll be all right. I promise."

"And you'll be with me? We can be together?"

Scott felt a tightening in his stomach. "Yes, we can be together."

"I feel afraid. Take me out of here, Scott. I want to be with you now. I need you to hold me. Just you and me, alone, together, the way it's going to be."

Across the room, O'Fallon watched over his cards as Scott and Jenny headed for the door.

"There goes the Kid," he said. "Another minute or two and we'll have one less temporal agent to worry about."

"So there you have it," said Delaney. "We seem to be stuck right smack in the middle of a giant confluence point and it looks like there's no telling which damn universe we're in. You seem to have been primarily in this one, which is theirs. . . . I think, or maybe we're back in ours again. Anyway, it looks like I've been crossing over from one to the other. Don't ask me how. I don't know if there are specific areas in town where you can cross over if you happen to be in the right place at the right time or if one timeline sort of winks out while the other one blinks in. Theoretically, since none of us happen to belong in either time sector, we're getting tossed around like corks on the ocean."

"Jesus. That would explain a lot of things," said Lucas. "Unfortunately, it raises more questions than it answers. How do we happen to know which universe we're in at any given time? And how do we know which timeline it is we're supposed to act in? Are the Network and the S.O.G. caught up in this, the same way as we are, or are we the only ones subject to this peculiar phenomenon for some reason? And, if we're in the wrong timeline when whatever is supposed to happen happens, how do we know we can get back?"

"There are two more questions we have to consider," Andre added. "One, how did Drakov manage to learn about everything that's going on and, two, how do we know that we can trust Jenny Reilly? She's still one of his hominoids, after all."

"She seems on the level," said Delaney. "At least, Scott believes her. And I believe Scott."

"Scott is also infatuated with her," Andre pointed out.

"I think it's much more than just infatuation," Finn replied. "He made me promise that we'd take Jenny back with us and get her therapy for the damage Drakov has done to her. He said it was his last request, in case he didn't make it out of this. He said he . . . he had a feeling that he wouldn't. And he wanted me to tell you that he understood."

Lucas exhaled heavily. "God, what a mess."

"Yeah," Delaney agreed. "But even if we're not going to trust Jenny—and I'm entirely convinced we should—why would Drakov want to warn us about everything that's going on back here? Why warn us of his presence? I can see no reason for it. Except that Jenny has actually betrayed him for Scott's sake."

"Well, either way, it makes no difference," Lucas replied. "We got us a whole new ballgame. The only advantage we have, assuming Jenny's on the level, is that Drakov doesn't know she's come over to our side. But there's no way of knowing how long we'll have that advantage, so we're going to have to move fast."

"Take Drakov first," said Andre.

"We'll have to. And we're going to have to do it right now."

"What about Scott?" asked Finn.

Lucas shook his head and sighed. "I don't know. I just don't know. All we can do at this point is play it by ear and hope for the best. But we'll have to hit Drakov fast and hit him hard. Take him alive, if possible. Did Jenny tell Scott how many people he's got with him?"

"Scott said she saw at least four at that baseops he's got in London, on the other side of the chronoplate in the opium den. He's got Becky, over at the saloon, and some guy named Indian Charlie. Neither Scott nor I have seen him. That's all we know about. There could be others. Plus he's got an undetermined number of the Chinese residents of Hop Town that he can call upon. It seems he's got them thinking he's some kind of sorcerer. They're all afraid of him, but whether or not they'll actually fight for him is anybody's guess."

"Considering the risk involved, we'd better call for back-up," Andre said.

"I've been thinking about that," Lucas replied, "and I'm not sure if we should. The more people from the future we introduce into this time sector, the greater the odds of increasing the instability that's already present here. If we bring in reinforcements, it may force Stone's hand and we would wind up fighting a pitched battle in the streets of Tombstone, with no one being certain which timeline they're fighting in. For all we know, that's exactly what Darkness doesn't want to happen. Damn it, if only he'd told us more!"

"Only what happens if we go after Drakov by ourselves and we don't make it?" asked Andre. "Who's going to stop the S.O.G. and the Network? Who'll be around to send up the balloon?"

"There's still Neilson," said Delaney.

"No good," said Lucas. "I don't want to count on him. For one thing, he's gotten too mixed-up in the scenario. For another, he's too vulnerable. We'll need somebody else. We'll have to bring in someone who can take charge immediately and call in the strike if anything goes wrong and we don't make it."

"Cooper?" Andre said.

Lucas nodded. "Yeah, Cooper. We need somebody who won't get nervous and jump the gun, but who can hit and run with maximum effectiveness if need be. Cooper would be perfect. Under any other circumstances, he'd be the one we'd pick and we're just going to have to go on our best instincts. We've got to treat this as if it were any other mission. We can't afford to question our decisions and wonder if we shouldn't be doing something different than what we ordinarily would have done, because of Darkness. He told us that whatever's going to happen, we'll be in a position to affect it, so I've got to assume we're going to live at least that long."

"Well, that's a cheery thought," Delaney said.

"We've got to consider all the possibilities," Lucas continued. "The key point may come when we make our move against Drakov. Or it may come before that, in the next five or ten minutes, for all we know. Or it may come afterwards, involving either the Network or the S.O.G. or maybe even both. It may come when Cooper brings his troops in. There's no way we can know, but we *do* know that we're going be there when it happens. When it does, Darkness is going to clock in and give us the word and we'll have to act immediately. So I want to know right now if anybody has any problems with that."

"I take it you don't," Delaney said.

"Yeah, I do," Lucas replied, with a nod, "but I've made up my mind that I'm going to do whatever he says without asking any questions. It's too great a risk not to. He's never let us down before. We're just going to have to trust him."

"Speaking hypothetically . . . I hope," Delaney said, "what if what we're going to have to do involves killing one of us?"

"Good Lord," said Andre. "You don't really think . . . no, that can't be. Darkness said that whatever happened didn't happen as a result of anything we did, directly. Just that we're going to be in a position to change it."

"Yeah, but what if changing it means that one of us is going to die?" Delaney asked. "What if something that one of us is supposed to do indirectly triggers whatever disaster is going to occur? And the only chance the others have to stop him . . . or her . . . is to shoot?"

There was a long silence.

"We have to consider that possibility," said Delaney, finally. "Suppose you had to kill me, Lucas. Or Andre. Could you do it?"

Lucas swallowed hard and stared at him for a long moment. Finally, he nodded. "Yeah. I could. I don't know how I'd ever live with it afterward, but if I had to . . . with everything that's at stake . . ." He shook his head. "I'd have no choice. What about you?"

Delaney nodded.

"What are you guys *saying*?" Andre whispered, her eyes wide.

"Andre?"

"This is crazy. It isn't going to happen. It can't—"

"Maybe that's why Darkness didn't tell us any more than he did," Delaney said.

"I can't believe that," she said. "I *won't* believe it!"

"But what if it comes to that?" asked Lucas. "Could you kill me? Or Finn?"

"How in God's name can you ask me that?"

"Because I have to."

She shook her head. "*How?* How *could* I?"

"Because billions of lives in the future could depend upon it, that's how," Lucas replied. "There's a chance, maybe a remote chance, but a chance that it could all come down to you. And if it does, Lieutenant, I'll expect you to do your duty."

She glanced from him to Delaney with a stricken look.

"*Lieutenant!*"

"Yes, sir," she said, softly, looking away from them.

"I didn't hear you!"

She jerked around, looking at him as if he'd struck her. "I said, *yes, sir!*"

Lucas nodded. "Right. Let's not waste any more time. Finn, I want you to clock back to Plus Time and get Colonel Cooper back here. He's to bring no more than two men with him. Use your room over at the boarding house as the transition point. Tell him he's to stay there and not budge from that room, no matter what, till we get back. If we're not back by morning, or if he's attacked, then he's in charge. Brief him on the situation and get back here as quickly as you can."

"I'm on my way."

Delaney got up and popped the cover on his warp disc, then clocked out.

"Andre . . ." Lucas said, gently.

She got up, turned away from him, walked over to the window and stood there looking out, not saying a word.

10 ⸻⸻⸻⸻⸻⸻⸻

"I count six," said Ben Stone, standing in the vacant lot next to Fly's Boarding House on Fremont Street. "How many do you make?"

"That's what I've got, sir," said Lieutenant Victor Capiletti, of the Special Operations Group. "Two across the street, two over on Third, around the corner, and the two that just ducked inside the alley. What do you think, Captain?"

"I'm not sure," said Stone, using the corner of Harwood's house, on the west side of the lot, as a cover from which to check the street. They were looking toward the Aztec Rooming House. "It looks like a loose security perimeter to me. They don't want to attract attention, but they've got the place pretty well covered. They could be getting ready to clock in a strike force, using Delaney's room upstairs as a transition point."

"Can't have that," said Capiletti.

"No, we can't, can we?" Stone replied. "Our timing couldn't have been more perfect. We set out to take one T.I.A. agent and we may just wind up getting their entire strike force. All we have to do is secure the transition point and take them out as they clock in. It'll be like shooting fish in a barrel."

"We'll have to take out their external security first, without alerting whoever's inside," said Capiletti.

"I want your team to handle it without making any noise,"

said Stone. "The last thing I want is interference from the locals."

"Leave it to me." Capiletti spoke into his radio. "Okay, people, we're gonna take 'em. No noise. Repeat, *no noise*. And I want the bodies disposed of. Robbins, Mattick, Howard, Stein, you take the two in the alley. Andrushack, Washburn, Kent and Sagretti, you take the two on Third. Donninger and Miller, you stand by. On my signal, repeat, on my signal, use stingers to drop the two out front. Lethal dose. Okay, everybody got it? Move out!"

It was just a short walk down Allen Street to the hotel, but they hadn't gone more than a few steps past the corner of Allen and Fifth, where the Oriental Saloon was located, when Scott heard the ominous clicking of a hammer being cocked.

"Don't move, Kid," said Curly Bill Brocius. "Keep your hands out at your sides and turn around, real slow."

Scott stood perfectly still. Beside him, Jenny stiffened with a gasp and looked over her shoulder.

"Curly Bill! What are you *doing*? Have you gone crazy?"

"You step away from him now, Jenny. This is between the Kid and me."

"Do as he says, Jen," Scott said.

"But—"

"Do as he says!"

She moved away from his side,

"Why didn't you just shoot me in the back, Brocius?" said Scott, tensing.

"I don't think I want to do that," Curly Bill replied. "You're gonna get it from the front, so everyone will know I can beat you to the draw when it counts."

"I see," said Scott, not turning around. "Only you've already got your pistol out. That's not exactly beating me, is it?"

"Bill, don't—"

"Stay out of it, Jenny!" Scott snapped.

"I will *not* stay out of it! Bill, this is murder! You'll hang for it!"

"Maybe I will and maybe I won't," Curly Bill replied. "I'll take my chances. I'll give you a fair chance, Kid. Pistols loaded this time. Let's do it for real."

"How do I know you won't just shoot me as soon as I turn around?" asked Scott.

In reply, Curly Bill lowered the hammer on his Colt and put it back in its holster. "I've holstered my pistol. Ask Jenny if you don't believe me."

Scott frowned. "Did he do it, Jenny?"

"Yes," she said, in a small voice.

Scott glanced at her. "You're too close. Move back."

"Scott, I—"

"I said, move back!"

She stepped back up on the boardwalk, watching them both fearfully.

"Go ahead, Kid. Turn around and make your play."

Behind them, some people saw what was going on and made haste to get out of range of any stray bullets. Scott moistened his lips. Something was wrong here. Curly Bill knew he could beat him. Surely he wasn't going to give him an even chance. Unless, of course, there was another gun pointed at him somewhere. . . .

Still standing with his back to Brocius, Scott said, "I'd like to give Jenny a kiss, Curly Bill. Just in case. That all right with you?"

"Sure. Why not? Be quick about it, though."

"Jenny . . ."

She came running to his arms. "Scott . . ."

"Listen, Jenny," he whispered in her ear, urgently, as he put his arms around her. "Look up at the roof of the saloon and tell me if you see anybody up there."

He felt her stiffen, then she pressed her cheek against his as he hugged her close, so she could see behind him. He heard her sharp intake of breath.

"Oh, God," she whispered. "Scott, I can see a man up there! He's got a Winchester!"

"Okay, Jenny, keep calm," Scott whispered back. As he held her close, with his hands behind her back, he popped open the hinged cover on his warp disc. Pretending to kiss her neck, he looked down behind her and quickly programmed the disc, hoping he could correctly estimate the height and distance. . . .

"That's enough!" said Brocius. "Let's get on with it!"

"Jen, as soon as I let you go, I want you to get out of here," said Scott. "Don't ask any questions, just run. Can I count on you?"

She nodded. He gave her a quick kiss and let her go. She ran back toward the saloon.

"Okay, Kid. Turn around and make your play."

Instead of turning around, Scott quickly hit the button on his warp disc and disappeared.

Brocius quickly drew his gun, then blinked and stared with disbelief. "What the . . ."

Scott reappeared on the roof of the Oriental Saloon, directly behind the rifleman. The man still hadn't recovered from his shock at suddenly seeing his target vanish into thin air.

"*Psst!* Over here," said Scott.

As the startled man spun around, Scott fired. The bullet took him in the chest and he went flying off the roof to land in the street below.

Scott moved to the edge and looked down. Brocius, having heard the gunfire, was staring up at him, his jaw hanging open. The moment he saw him, he lifted his gun and let off a wild shot, then took off running.

Scott ducked back from the edge as soon as Brocius fired at him. When he heard his running footsteps on the boardwalk below, he moved forward again and looked down at the body of the sniper, sprawled on the street below. It was Ross Demming.

Scott's lips were set in a tight grimace. It was possible that Demming and Brocius had been acting on their own, but he didn't believe it for a second. It had to be O'Fallon, in his guise of Johnny Ringo, setting him up for an ambush. The gloves were off. He moved back from the edge of the roof as people came running out into the street to see what happened. He set the transition coordinates on his warp disc for his room back at the hotel and clocked out. As soon as he materialized, he spun around quickly, his guns out, but the room was empty.

It would no longer be safe to stay here. Only where else could he go? It would no longer be safe anywhere. Brocius didn't seem in the least bit worried about having Jenny witness the shooting. Nor did he try to stop her when she ran. Which could only mean one thing. He was not concerned about the Earps. He checked the date on his disc. October 25, 1881. The eve of the O.K. Corral shoot-out.

He frowned. That couldn't possibly be right. That was still

days away. But the warp disc couldn't be wrong. He had never heard of one malfunctioning. And if it had malfunctioned . . . no, he didn't want to think about that. It was getting late. He hurried downstairs to the bar and got a copy of the *Tombstone Epitaph*. He stared at the front page with disbelief.

"Like a drink, Kid?" asked the barman.

"Yeah," said Scott, dully. "Whiskey. Make it a double."

The date on the front page was October 25, 1881. It seemed impossible. Somehow, without even being aware of it, he'd lost an entire week.

He downed the whiskey in two quick gulps, feeling the fire as it burned down his throat and in his stomach. *A whole week?* How was it possible? He paid for his drink, put the paper down on the bar and went back up to his room, in a daze. He locked the door and sat down on his bed, his mind racing.

He could think of only one possible explanation. The temporal instability was increasing rapidly and dramatically. Either he had somehow crossed over from one timeline into the other without realizing it, and lost a week in the process, or the timeline had started to ripple and the effect was concentrated in this sector. Somehow, a week had passed in a matter of hours. And he hadn't even noticed. It was as if he'd been picked up by a timewave and deposited farther down the shore.

He tried to think what implications this new development could have for the mission. Had he alone experienced this effect, or were Priest, Cross and Delaney caught up in it as well? And, if so, were they aware of it? Would he be able to warn them, or were they still in the other timeline? And what would happen if they'd been caught in the ripple effect and carried farther down the timestream than where he was now?

He had no answers. No idea what to do. Priest was in command of the mission. Only Priest was not around to give commands. There was no going by the book because the book had never covered situations such as this. There had never *been* a situation such as this before and, quite possibly, there never would be again. Was this where the whole thing fell apart? Was the temporal instability in this sector going to grow into a timewave that would travel down the timestream, eventually breaking somewhere in the future in a massive timestream split? Was it possible that he was the only one who could prevent it?

No. Not prevent it. *Change* it. Because whatever it was he was fated to do, according to history as it was seen from the time that Darkness came from, he had already done it. If, in fact, he *was* the one. Perhaps he wasn't. Perhaps it wouldn't have anything to do with him at all, in spite of the powerful gut instinct that he had, telling him that he was about to be involved in something of monumental significance.

We *can* change history, Scott thought. We learned that the hard way. Everything that's happened from the first time a man traveled back into the past has led to this point. And it was a point of no return, because they had learned that there was really only one chance to effect a temporal adjustment. If it failed the first time, and another effort was made to clock back to a point before the original adjustment mission was attempted and try again, it only contributed to the instability of that temporal scenario and increased the odds against them.

If a temporal anomaly or disruption was discovered and a team was clocked back to effect an adjustment, they were already working against the force of temporal inertia and their very presence meant there was a chance that instead of adjusting the disruption, they would only make it worse. If they failed, and another team was clocked back to try again, they would be clocking into a time sector that was already unstable to begin with and they would also encounter the original adjustment team, which in itself could bring about a temporal paradox. They had learned that the hard way, too.

Temporal anomalies that had been brought about by the actions of the Time Wars had resulted in historical disruptions that had to be adjusted, but the adjustment missions themselves, even though successful, had undoubtedly affected temporal inertia in ways that manifested themselves as more anomalies and disruptions further down the timestream. Nor was there any way of knowing how many temporal anomalies brought about by time travel had gone completely undiscovered. It was like trying to plug a hole in a pipe that had sprung a leak, only each time one leak was stopped, two more appeared. There seemed to be no end to it.

Only what if this *was* the end? What if, this time, history could not be changed? What if, this time, they had run out of time?

Scott took his pistols out of their holsters and laid them on the bed, beside him. One had been fired when he had killed Ross Demming a short while ago. Or was it a *week* ago?

He picked up the fired piece in his left hand, pulled the hammer back to half cock and opened the loading gate on the right side of the frame. Strange, he wondered, how for so many years no one had thought to question that. It was simply accepted. To load or unload the gun, a right-handed shooter had to transfer the weapon to his left hand, open the gate on the right side, and manually rotate the cylinder, using the ejector rod to push out one empty brass casing at a time, then load with the right hand. For a left-handed shooter, the procedure was much simpler and more natural. One simply continued to hold the gun in the shooting hand, pulled back the hammer halfway, opened up the gate and proceeded to reload. Colonel Sam Colt had been left-handed and he had designed the Peacemaker as a left-handed gun. Thereafter, the entire world had unquestioningly used the left-handed design for well over a hundred years, until the late 20th century, when a man named Bill Grover had finally hit upon the idea of manufacturing a right-handed Peacemaker with the loading gate on the *left* side of the frame. It seemed incredible that no one had ever thought of that before. It was a testimony to the genius of Sam Colt that his Single Action Army had been considered so perfect that for over a hundred years, no one had thought of modifying the design.

As he ejected the fired brass casing and slipped in a fresh cartridge, Scott wondered what it meant that he knew about things like that. In the 27th century, it was completely useless, trivial knowledge, and yet he had researched such obscure facts with relentless fascination, long before it ever occurred to him that he might one day enlist in the Temporal Corps. Why, in a time when lead projectile weapons had been obsolete for several hundred years, had he become so fascinated with them? Why had he devoted so many long hours to practicing with them, going to all the trouble of making his own bullets from scratch, only to perfect an arcane form of marksmanship and self-defense that would have no use whatsoever for him in modern life? Why had he been so intensely interested in the history of the Old West, moreso than in that of any other time, and in the lives of the men who became frontier legends? Was it fate?

All his life, Scott had felt he had been born in the wrong

time. Then when he had first clocked into this temporal scenario, he had felt suddenly and inexplicably at home, as if this was where he truly belonged. In the other timeline, he—or his twin—apparently *did* belong here. Maybe *that* was the anomaly. Maybe he should have been born in this time in the first place, only because of some temporal disruption brought about by time travelers before him, something had gone wrong and he had been born about eight hundred years too late. A man out of time, returned by Fate to the time in which he really belonged, completing some sort of temporal cycle, a missing piece of the puzzle finally dropped into place. Only now that he was here, was it his fate to live or die? The fate of billions of future lives could rest on the answer to that question.

He held the handsome, engraved and silver-plated Colt in his hand. It felt as if it had always belonged there. He had dreamed of owning such a revolver all his life. He thumbed back the hammer and sat for a long moment in silent thought. What would happen if he stuck the barrel in his mouth, angled upward, and squeezed the trigger? The big .45 caliber bullet would smash through the roof of his mouth and into his brain in a mere fraction of a second. There probably wouldn't be time to feel any pain.

Perhaps that was the solution. If he killed himself, then he wouldn't be able to do anything to upset the balance of the timestream and bring on that disaster in the future. If he was, in fact, at the center of the whole thing, then killing himself might be the perfect solution to it all. It would absolve Priest, Cross and Delaney of having to do it. And if it could save lives, then he was prepared to do it.

But, on the other hand, what if that was exactly the *wrong* move? What if the act of his suicide triggered off whatever was supposed to happen? But, if that were the case, then Priest, Cross and Delaney would be in a position to do something about it. To stop him, perhaps. Wasn't that what Darkness had told them? In that case, maybe he should go ahead and do it . . . and see if they arrived to stop him in the nick of time. Only if they didn't . . .

Scott was in an agony of indecision. He had never wanted to live so much as he did now. He had never felt as vibrantly *alive* as he did now. He had never been in love the way he was with Jenny. It was as if, after all those years of living out of time, he had finally found himself. Only what was he to do?

He started at the loud knocking on his door. He picked up his other gun and cocked it.

"Who is it?"

"Wyatt Earp. Open up, Kid."

Scott holstered his pistols and went to open the door. The tall figure of the marshal confronted him.

"You'll have to come with me, Kid," said Wyatt.

Scott stared at him. Then he looked down and saw the gun.

"I'm putting you under arrest for the murder of Ross Demming. Hand over your guns."

The two rustlers waiting in the alley never knew what hit them. One moment, they were standing near the entrance to the alley, staying out of sight and keeping a watch out for Delaney, the next, they were suddenly being grabbed from behind by black-suited commandos. They felt hands being clapped over their mouths and then an agonizing, incandescent pain as the razor-sharp, nine-inch combat blades did their grisly work. Their bodies slumped to the ground. Without wasting any time, the S.O.G. commandos quickly strapped warp discs to the corpses' wrists and clocked the bodies out. One of them spoke into his wrist communicator.

"Mattick to Team Leader."

"Go ahead, Mattick."

"Two down."

"Roger. Stand by."

On Third Street, just around the corner of the Aztec Rooming House, two gunmen were shocked out of their wits when two black-uniformed men in commando masks suddenly appeared before them out of nowhere. That one second of shock was plenty of time for the two men who clocked in behind them to move up and slit their throats.

"Sagretti to Team Leader. . . ."

"Go ahead, Sagretti."

"Four down, two to go."

"That's a roger. Stand by and stay out of sight. Okay, Miller, Donninger, you got a clear shot at the two out front?"

"That's a roger."

"Drop 'em."

The two commandos stationed on the roof across the street from the rooming house fired. One of the rustlers slapped his hand to his chest.

"Ow! Jeez, damn skeeters—" then he spasmed and dropped dead as the fast-acting poison did its work. His partner collapsed a fraction of a second later.

Capiletti spoke into his radio. "Okay, Sagretti, get those bodies out of there! Now! Move it!"

The black-clad commandos blended with the shadows as they quickly ran around the corner and up to the fallen rustlers. Seconds later, the bodies were gone.

"Well done, Lieutenant," said Stone. He pulled back his sleeve and spoke into his own radio. "Listen up. This is Stone. I'm going in. Give me five seconds once I go through the front door, then move in behind me. We're taking that house. Miller, Donninger, you keep to your posts. Cover the street."

"Roger, Captain."

"Okay, here we go," said Stone. He turned to Capiletti who, unlike the other commandos, was dressed in period clothes. He was wearing jeans, a cotton shirt, boots and a Stetson hat. Only beneath his coat, his holsters held a laser and a plasma pistol. "Let's go," said Stone.

Together, the two men started across the street, heading toward the rooming house.

O'Fallon stood among the crowd, looking down at the body of Ross Demming. There was a slight tic at the corner of his mouth. He balled his hands into fists. Idiots, he thought. Goddamn idiots! A simple job, one shooter on the street, another on the roof to cover him. How in hell could they possibly have bungled it? And where in hell was Brocius?

"All right, move aside," said Wyatt Earp, pushing his way through the crowd. He looked down at the body sprawled out on the street. "Demming," he said, with a grimace. "Had a feelin' he'd wind up like this, sooner or later."

He bent down and picked up the Winchester that was lying next to the corpse. He checked it. "It hasn't been fired." He glanced around at the crowd. "Anybody see what happened?"

"I saw the whole thing, Marshal," said O'Fallon. "It was the Montana Kid. He shot Ross down in cold blood. Never even gave him a chance."

"He's lying!" Jenny shouted.

Wyatt turned toward her. "What do you know about this, Jenny?"

"I was right here," she said. "I was leaving the saloon with

Scott when Curly Bill came up behind us and jerked his pistol!"

"Then what's Demming doing here?" asked Wyatt.

"He was up on the roof of the saloon, with his rifle," Jenny said. "Bill wanted Scott to turn around and make his play and Demming was going to shoot him down as soon as he turned around."

"So what happened to Curly Bill?" asked Wyatt.

"He ran after Scott shot Demming," Jenny said.

"And Demming was up on the roof, you say?" asked Wyatt. He turned and looked up at the roof. "How did the Kid happen to see him up there?"

"He didn't," Jenny said. "I did. I saw him and I warned Scott."

"*You* saw him," Wyatt said. "What made you think to look up there?"

"Scott told me to look."

"I see," said Wyatt, pursing his lips thoughtfully. "Why couldn't he look himself?"

"Because he had his back turned."

"And with his back turned, he knew there was someone on the roof behind him?"

Jenny saw how it was going and it wasn't going well. "He . . . he knew that Curly Bill knew he couldn't beat him and he figured out that someone else had to have a gun on him."

Wyatt grunted. "So he shot Ross Demming."

"It was self-defense!" said Jenny.

"Head shot," Wyatt said. He turned to look at the roof again. "Clear up there, eh? In the dark, too. What was Curly Bill doing all this time?"

"I told you," Jenny said, "he ran."

"Why didn't he just shoot the Kid while the Kid was shooting Demming? He had the drop on him, didn't he?"

"He . . . well, he couldn't because . . . " Jenny's voice trailed off.

"Marshal, she couldn't have seen anything," O'Fallon said. "She was inside, in the saloon. Ain't that right, boys?"

"Yeah, that's right, I saw her," Zaber replied.

"And Curly Bill left quite a while ago," O'Fallon said. "After the Kid called him out back there in saloon."

"The Kid called him out?" asked Wyatt.

"It's a lie!" Jenny said. "He just offered to show Bill who was faster."

"Ain't that the same thing?" asked O'Fallon.

"They drew on each other with empty pistols!" Jenny said. "Ask anybody! They all saw!"

"And once the Kid saw he could take Curly Bill, he decided to do it for real," said O'Fallon. "Curly Bill left and the Kid went out after him, but he ran into Ross Demming first and decided to take care of some old business."

"It isn't true!" shouted Jenny. "He's making it all up!"

"What was Demming doing with a Winchester?" asked Wyatt.

"He had it on his horse," O'Fallon said. "He was gettin' ready to ride out of town when the Kid came out. When the Kid saw him, he jerked his pistol. Ross went for the rifle in his scabbard, but just barely got it out when the Kid shot him. You know how fast the Kid is."

"What happened to his horse?"

"Ran off when the shots were fired," O'Fallon lied, smoothly. "I don't know where Jenny got this roof business, but you have to know, Marshal, she's in love with the Kid. Wouldn't have anything to do with anybody else ever since the Kid showed up. You can ask anyone. She's his woman. You can't blame her for tryin' to protect him. I'd like a woman of mine to do the same."

"Is that true, Jenny?" Wyatt asked.

She shook her head. "Surely, you don't *believe* him?"

"I know how you feel about the Kid, Jenny," Wyatt said. "Everyone in town knows. And if it happened like you said, I can't see how the Kid could have shot Demming down from that roof without having Curly Bill shoot him. Nobody's that fast."

"But . . . but that's the way it happened! I swear!"

Sheriff Behan pushed his way through the crowd. "Heard there was a shootin'," he said.

"You don't say," said Wyatt, wryly.

Behan shot him an angry look. "Ross Demming, eh? Looks like the Kid finally got him."

"How do you know it was the Kid?" asked Wyatt.

"Heck, everybody knows there was bad blood between those two," said Behan, "ever since the Kid gunned down his brother. I understand they had a near set-to in the Grand Hotel a while back. Fact, you were there, weren't you, Wyatt?"

"I was there," admitted Earp.

"Wyatt, you're not going to *believe* these men?" said Jenny.

"It appears I'll have to believe them enough to put the Kid under arrest, Jenny," Wyatt replied.

"But you know what kind of men they are?" she argued, with exasperation.

"That's right, Jenny," Wyatt said, looking at her sympathetically. "I know. And I also know what kind of man the Kid is. He's a gunfighter and there's enough information to make him a suspect. I'm going to have to take him into custody and let the court decide."

"But you don't understand," she protested. "You can't!"

"I have to, Jenny," Earp replied, misunderstanding the reason for her distress. "And for his sake, I hope the Kid comes along quietly. He'll get fair treatment, I promise. I'll continue to look into this. I have no intention of letting a man hang on the word of someone like Johnny Ringo."

He gave O'Fallon and his men a hard stare.

"Just tellin' the truth, Marshal," said O'Fallon, with a shrug. "I saw what I saw."

"That's what you say, Ringo," Wyatt Earp replied. "But I think I'll ask around just the same and find out if anybody else saw the same thing."

Jenny felt someone come up beside her and touch her elbow. She turned to see Indian Charlie standing by her side. He merely nodded at her once, then slipped away through the crowd. She felt a tightening in her stomach. Drakov wanted to see her.

As she moved away from the crowd, she felt herself torn by indecision. If she refused to respond to Drakov's summons, he would know that something had gone wrong. If she went to him now, Scott would be placed under arrest and thrown in jail and there would be no one to warn his friends of what had happened. Perhaps if she could find them quickly and let them know that Scott was in trouble, then go back and see Drakov. . . .

She ran down the street, toward the Grand Hotel. She ran inside and up the stairs, to Lucas Priest's room. She pounded on the door. There was no answer. In desperation, she pounded again and this time, the door opened, but it wasn't Lucas

Priest. It was another man, with a large, bushy moustache and red-rimmed eyes. His nightshirt bulged out over his paunch.

"What in tarnation . . . ?"

"Where's Mr. Priest?"

"There ain't no one by that name here, Missy. But say . . . will I do?"

She backed away, then turned and ran down the stairs and out into the street.

Ike Clanton stood at the bar in Hafford's Saloon, hunched over a whiskey. In defiance of the town ordinance, there was a six-gun stuck in his belt, beneath his coat, and a Winchester .44-40 rifle lying on the bar before him. The bartender kept glancing at the rifle nervously. Clanton was working up a real snootful and guns and whiskey didn't mix.

"Want me to hold on to that gun for you, Ike?" the bartender asked.

Clanton slapped a beefy hand on top of it. "It's stayin' right here," he replied, in a surly voice. "There's men in this town lookin' to murder me and if they come lookin' for a fight, they'll get one!"

He glanced around at the other patrons in the bar. "You all heard that!" he said, loudly.

"I don't want any trouble in here, Ike," the bartender said.

"Ain't me that's causin' trouble," Clanton replied. "I was mindin' my own business when that Doc Holliday invited me to jerk my pistol! I couldn't defend myself because I wasn't heeled, but that Virgil Earp was right there with him and you think he arrested Holliday for makin' a play against an unarmed man? No, sir! I tell you, they're all in it together, those Earps and Holliday! They've been spreadin' lies about me, tryin' to frame me, and now they're out to murder me, as well!"

He patted the rifle once again. "That's stayin' right there! Man's got a right to protect himself! Gimme another whiskey!"

"Maybe you'd better go home and go to bed, Ike," said the barman. "You've already had quite a lot to drink—"

"*I said, another whiskey!*" Clanton shouted, slamming his hand down on the bar. "I ain't goin' nowhere! I ain't goin' to bed. I'm goin' to stay right here in town and as soon as the Earps or Holliday show themselves out there on that street, the ball opens! They're gonna have to fight!"

The bartender nervously poured him another shot of whiskey. Clanton tossed it back. He was tired of being caught in the middle of this whole thing. First Ringo and the others coming in and taking over, telling him and his boys what to do, then the Earps and Holliday, with their high and mighty ways, doing everything they could to run him off, acting like they were the lords of the roost and trying to turn people against him. He was tired of it. Sick and tired. Things were working out just fine till those damn Earps showed up with Holliday.

He had complained bitterly to Johnny and the others, telling them what lies Wyatt Earp was spreading. A lot of the boys were even acting as if they believed it. And Wyatt *was* a liar. He'd promised that he would keep their deal secret and he'd lied about that. He probably never intended on paying that reward money, after all. Son of a bitch would probably have kept it for himself. Now he was left was nothing. There was no reward money, because Head and Leonard had to go and get themselves killed in Hachita, and Crane was dead, as well. So the whole thing fell apart, only Wyatt had broken his promise and told about the deal and now some of the boys weren't sure if Clanton wouldn't also double-cross them for some reward money if he were to get the chance.

"Those damn Earps are always gettin' in the way!" he'd said to Curly Bill, earlier that day. "And I've had about all I can take of Doc Holliday, as well!"

"Then maybe you ought to do something about it," Curly Bill had said.

"Yeah, maybe I oughtta."

"Maybe you should fight."

"What, just me? Against the four of 'em?"

"Take Frank, Tom and Billy with you," Curly Bill had said. "We'll back you up."

"Yeah?"

"Yeah. I've had a bellyful of the Earps myself. I'll get the boys together and we'll ride on into town tomorrow. You call the Earps out for a fight. When they come out, we'll all be waitin' for 'em."

"One more time," said Ike now, pointing at his shot glass.

"Don't you think you've had enough, Ike?" asked the barman.

Clanton fixed him with a baleful glare. "You gonna give me another drink or not?"

"And we're looking at possible hostilities from Drakov, the Network *and* the S.O.G.?"

"What we've got is what we've got," said Cooper, curtly. "We're going to have to make the best of it." Colonel Cooper, commander of the elite Ranger Pathfinder division based in Galveston, was tall and trimly muscular, with sharp, angular features and curly, light brown hair. His high-cheekboned face was covered with coarse stubble and his eyes had an unsettlingly direct and intense gaze. He spoke in sharp, clipped tones and had the air of a man who assessed situations quickly and took firm charge.

All three men were dressed in period costumes. Tilley wore jeans and boots, a denim shirt, a bandana, a gray Stetson and a long trail duster. His dark hair hung down to his shoulders and he had a full beard. He would have looked perfectly at home on horseback, driving a herd of cattle or perhaps robbing a bank. Georgeson had on a pearl gray bowler hat, a black frock coat, dark trousers, jodphur boots, a white shirt and a gray silk vest. He was clean-shaven, his blond hair slightly shaggy, and he looked like the sort of man who might be a professional gambler or a big city dandy. Cooper wore black trousers, high-heeled boots, a black frock coat and a white shirt with a black vest. His curly hair fell loosely to his shoulders from beneath his black Stetson, yet for all his western accoutrements, he looked more like the leader of a motorcycle gang than a cowboy. None of the three looked "regular Army." In any other time but the 27th century, when the service had special need of men with their distinct talents, they would probably have been mercenaries or contract assassins.

Beneath his duster, Tilley had a short plasma rifle slung from his shoulder, barrel pointed downward, so that he could quickly grab it, swing it up and bring it into play. He also wore a laser pistol in a cordura holster at his hip. Georgeson had two laser pistols in tanker-style shoulder holsters underneath his coat and Cooper was armed with a disruptor in a special snap holster on one hip and a curious weapon that was regarded by most of his contemporaries as being out of date, though the Ranger leader seldom went anywhere without it. It was an antique, late 20th century, Israeli Desert Eagle semiautomatic finished in matte black and originally chambered in .44 Magnum. It was a massive piece, almost as large as the disruptor that he carried, weighing almost four pounds, with a ten-inch barrel. It had been specially adapted to fire rocket-powered, explosive 10 mm. rounds, with enough power to flatten an elephant, and it was equipped with a specially made silencer and flash suppressor that extended its barrel another four inches. In addition to the sidearms, all three men carried fighting knives and wire garrotes, several throwing knives concealed about their persons and a number of small fragmentation grenades hidden in their pockets. They had also brought equipment bags containing additional assault gear.

"I wish I could tell you what you can expect," Delaney told them, "but given the temporal instability we've got here, it's liable to be anything. The one thing you've got to do is maintain a secure transition point for bringing in your troops in case it hits the fan."

"This room won't make it," Cooper said. "It's too damn small. Can we use the roof?"

"I don't see why not," Delaney replied. "That's a good idea. I should have thought of that."

"Sounds like you've got enough to worry about," said Cooper. "Tilley, get up to the roof and lock in the transition coordinates, then set up an observation post. If a horse farts out there on the street, I want to know about it. Geordy, I want you to check out the building. I can watch the front from here, but if there's a back entrance, I want it covered."

"Got it."

"What about your other baseops, at the Grand Hotel?" asked Cooper.

"Which one?" Delaney asked, with a sour grimace. "The way the timelines are rippling, I'm not even sure which universe we're in right now. Probably ours, but I wouldn't want to bet the hacienda on it. We don't want to risk covering two different places. Things are uncertain enough as they are. Our chief concern is the stability of this transition point. For all we know, your people could wind up clocking straight into the dead zone."

"Great," said Cooper, dryly. "You got any other good news for me?"

"Just this. If you don't hear from us by sunup, it means we blew it and you're in charge."

"Yeah, but what's my mission?" Cooper asked. "I'm no adjustment specialist, Delaney, I'm a strike force commander. I need a target."

"Drakov, the Network, the S.O.G., anyone who doesn't belong in this time sector," said Delaney. "I know that's not very specific, but it's about the best I can do."

Cooper snorted with disgust. "So how the hell am I supposed to find these people? You gave me a description of Ben Stone and that O'Fallon guy who's calling himself Johnny Ringo, and I can spot Drakov if I see him, but how the fuck am I supposed to identify the others?"

"You'll have to fly this one by the seat of your pants," said Delaney. "With any luck, you won't have to. If we survive the raid on Drakov's base of operations, whether we're able to capture him or not, we'll coordinate the rest of the operation with you. If we don't make it . . . well, whatever you do, it probably won't make much difference. But give it your best shot. Maybe you can do something to minimize the effects of the disruption."

"It's really that bad, huh? Look, maybe we should just start bringing in the troops right now. That way, at least I can give you some cover when you go up against Drakov."

"No way," Delaney said. "Lucas doesn't want to take that chance. This time sector's too unstable. The least little thing is liable to trigger off a timewave or maybe even a timestream split. The only one who knows for sure what's liable to happen is Darkness and he flat out refused to tell us. All we know is that something that's supposed to happen here is going to bring about a terrible temporal disaster in the future unless we can change history and we've only got one shot to make it work. But we don't know when that opportunity is going to come or what it's going to be."

"Shit, I don't envy you," said Cooper. "I don't envy me, either. What you're telling me is that if you don't make it, no matter what I do, I'll be pissing in the wind."

"Probably," Delaney replied. "But look on the bright side. If we don't make it, at least you won't be caught up in whatever's going to happen in the future."

"No, I'll just be caught in whatever's going to happen here and now. I'm not sure which would be worse. Fuck it. It isn't over till it's over. Till then, we just drive on. Good luck, Finn."

"You too, Brian."

Delaney headed for the door, but just then, Tilley called Cooper on his communicator.

"Tilley here. We've got trouble, Colonel," he said.

Delaney paused with his hand on the doorknob.

"What is it?" Cooper asked.

"I've got two men on the roof across the street," said Tilley. "Armed and wearing black commando gear."

"*Damn* it," said Delaney. "It's gotta be the S.O.G."

"They spot you, Tilley?"

"I don't think so," came the reply. "I picked them up on my starlight scope. They're watching the street below and covering the front entrance."

"Geordy, you get that?" Cooper asked.

"I got it," Georgeson said. "I'm downstairs, by the back stairway, covering the back entrance. You want me to check outside?"

"Negative," said Cooper. "Stay put. Tilley—"

"Hold it," Tilley said, "I've got activity. Two men heading this way from the southeast. One of them answers Stone's description, the other one's dressed like a cowboy. Hold on, I'll see if I can . . . there's movement in the alley, heading toward the back! Heads up, Geordy!"

"Shit!" Delaney swore, throwing open the door and drawing his revolver.

"Cover the front!" Cooper shouted to him. Then he spoke quickly into his communicator. "Tilley, watch your back, they may clock up to the roof!"

Cooper drew his disruptor and moved to the window as Delaney ran out into the hall and down the stairs.

"Finn should have been back by now," said Lucas, tensely.

"You think maybe something happened?" Andre asked.

Lucas exhaled heavily. "We're not going to find out waiting around here." He got up, tossed down the whiskey he'd been drinking, picked up his laser rig and strapped it on underneath his coat.

"Be interesting if Wyatt Earp catches you wearing that in town," said Andre.

Lucas grimaced. "I'll tell him it's a fancy Buntline Special," he said. "And then I'll hit him over the head with it."

Andre got up and started heading toward the door. "You're right, we'd better go check on him."

"Aren't you bringing anything?" asked Lucas.

"Hey, you know me, I always pack," she said, lifting her long skirt. Beneath it, she wore high-button shoes and black lycra tights. There was a laser pistol in a holster strapped to her right thigh and a commando bowie in a sheath strapped around her left leg.

"Interesting outfit," Lucas said, with a grin. "What else you got hidden under there?"

"You'll find out on our wedding night," she replied.

"Cute."

"Come on, greenhorn. Let's go find that crazy Irishman."

They went down the stairs and out the front door.

"Here they come," said one of the snipers on the roof of Hafford's Saloon, across the street. He rested his rifle and chambered a round.

"About damn time," one of the others replied. "Let's finish this."

"The girl, too?"

"Yeah, the girl, too. That's what Ringo said, ain't it?"

"I don't like shootin' a woman."

"You want to take it up with Ringo?"

"Hell, no."

"Then let 'em have it!"

As they stepped down off the sidewalk, Andre stumbled.

"Damn heels!" she swore. A shot cracked out and a bullet struck the wood post behind her. More shots followed in rapid succession.

"*Shit!*" cried Lucas. "It's an ambush! Come on!"

They started running.

Up on the roof, the riflemen suddenly stopped shooting.

"What in the hell . . ." one of them said, staring down at the street.

"Where'd they *go*?"

"Shoot, God damn it!"

"At *what*?"

"Son of a bitch! Where in hell did they go?"

"I don't know! One minute there they were, and then they were just . . . gone!"

"Check the street, for God's sake! They gotta be down there somewhere!"

"*Where?* We can see the whole blamed street from here! They plumb vanished!"

"I'm gettin' outta here."

"Wait . . ."

"You wait! I ain't stickin' around for the Earps to come and see what all the shootin' was about."

"Heck, me neither!"

"I just can't understand it. We had 'em right in our sights! *Where the hell did they go?*"

Lucas and Andre suddenly stopped short.

"Holy shit," said Lucas.

One moment, they'd been running down a dark street in the middle of the night, with bullets whistling past them. Suddenly, the shooting had stopped and it was broad daylight, around two or three in the afternoon.

"We've crossed over!" Andre said, looking all around her. They were about half a block away from the Grand Hotel. Nothing looked different, except that in a matter of a few steps, they had moved from night into day, from one timeline into another.

"We've got to go back," said Andre.

"And get our asses shot off?" Lucas said. "Besides, how do we know if we *can* go back?"

"You're hit!" Andre exclaimed, seeing the blood on his shoulder.

Lucas shook his head. "It's just a flesh wound. I'm all right."

"Damn," said Andre. "What happens now?"

"Shit," said Lucas, looking down the street. "I'm afraid I know."

She followed his gaze. Wyatt, Virgil and Morgan Earp, together with Doc Holliday, had just stepped off the sidewalk on Hafford's Corner. Virgil Earp was carrying a cane in his right hand. Doc Holliday held a shotgun in one hand and his nickel-plated Colt in the other. Morgan Earp held a six-gun at his side. They started walking north on Fourth Street, heading across it diagonally toward Fremont Street. And with them was the Montana Kid.

Jenny ran down Fourth Street, past Hafford's Corner and Spangenberg's Gun Shop, heading toward Fremont. The Aztec Rooming House, where Finn Delaney lived, was on the corner of Fremont and Third. She held her skirts up as she ran, past the Post Office and around the corner of the Capitol Saloon, turning left on Fremont. She ran past the Papago Cash Store and Bauer's Meat Market, with the alley between it that led to the back entrance of the O.K. Corral, which fronted on Allen Street. She passed the Assay Office and Fly's Boarding House, past the vacant lot between Fly's Boarding House and Photo Studio and the Harwood house, and she was almost to the corner of Third and Fremont when she heard the shots.

She stopped short, breathing hard. Her heart was hammering in her chest like a wild thing trying to claw its way out. She heard gunfire, but she also saw strange flashes of light, incredibly bright, thin beams lancing out across the street, from one rooftop to the other. Lasers, she thought. Like the weapons that the Master used. She was too late. It had already started. She turned and started running back the other way. All she could think of now was Scott, and Wyatt Earp was on his way to arrest him. Running as fast as she possibly could, she raced back down Fourth Street, heading toward the hotel. Somehow, she had to keep Wyatt from arresting Scott. Scott's friends were in trouble and they needed him.

She stopped as she passed Spangenberg's Gun Store. She ran up onto the sidewalk and snatched up one of the wooden chairs George Spangenberg kept outside the shop, so that he and his customers could sit around and chew tobacco and pass the time of day as they watched the street. She grunted and swung the chair with all her might, smashing through the front display window of the store. She had to pull the chair out and smash it through again to make the hole big enough, then she climbed through, tearing her skirt on the jagged shards of glass and cutting herself in several places. She ignored the pain. She climbed into the store and ran around behind the glass display counters. George had locked them. With a small cry of frustration, she quickly looked around, picked up one of Spangenberg's hardbound account books and used it to break through the glass.

She reached inside the case and took out a Peacemaker with a seven-and-a-half-inch barrel and wood grips. She quickly glanced at the barrel. Engraved on the left side were the words, "Colt Single Action .45." She'd need .45 caliber catridges. She opened up one of the wood cabinets and took out a box of ammunition, opened it and quickly loaded all six chambers. Then she climbed back out through the window, catching her skirt on the broken glass. With a desperate yank, she pulled free, ripping the dress and, carrying the gun in her right hand, ran toward Allen Street, past several astonished cowboys who were coming out of Hafford's Saloon.

They gaped at her open-mouthed as she ran past them, her

hair wild, blood on her arms and cheeks, her dress torn in several places, and a gun in her right hand. Just as she turned the corner, she saw Wyatt and Scott coming out of the hotel, Wyatt with a gun in one hand and Scott's pistols, in their shoulder holster rig, carried in the other. As they stepped down onto the street, Jenny came to a stop and raised the Colt, holding it in both hands.

"Hold it right there, Wyatt!" she shouted.

Scott looked at her, eyes wide. "Jenny!"

Wyatt was equally surprised. "Good Lord," he said. "Jenny, have you lost your head?"

"You let him go!" she shouted. "You give him back his pistols and let him go right now!"

"Jenny, don't—" Scott started, but Wyatt silenced him.

"You keep your mouth shut, Kid," he said, "and don't you move."

"Let him go, Wyatt!" Jenny said, aiming the gun at him.

"I'm afraid I can't do that, Jenny," Earp replied. "Now put down that pistol before somebody gets hurt."

She pulled back the hammer on the Colt. "No, you drop yours, Wyatt! Drop it or I'll shoot, so help me!"

People were peering out through the doors of the saloon and from the hotel windows, ready to duck back quickly if bullets started flying.

"Now be sensible, Jenny. If you don't put down that pistol right now, I'll be forced to shoot the Kid," said Wyatt, aiming his revolver at Scott's back.

"You do that and I'll kill you, Wyatt, I swear to God!"

"You're no shootist, Jenny. You're liable to miss."

"Then I'll just keep shooting till I hit you, Wyatt, and you'll have to kill me, too! I don't care! If Scott dies, I don't want to live!"

"You're talkin' crazy, Jenny. Don't—"

"*Now*, Wyatt! Drop it and let him go right now or I'll shoot, so help me!"

"By God, I think she means it," Wyatt said. "Kid, talk some sense to her. Tell her this is foolish."

"Scott, Finn's in trouble!" she shouted. "He needs you, right now!"

"Better do as she says, Marshal," Scott said, tensing.

Wyatt sighed and shook his head. "You'll both regret this, Kid," he said. He dropped his gun to the street.

"I'll take my guns, Marshal," Scott said, holding out his hand.

Wyatt Earp handed them over. Scott shrugged out of his coat and quickly slipped the rig on. He took out one of the fancy Colts.

"I'm sorry about this, Marshal," he said, "but I haven't got time to explain and I can't have you in the way."

He raised the gun and brought the barrel down on Wyatt's head. Earp collapsed to the street. Scott ran over to Jenny.

"You're amazing, you know that? Where's Finn?"

"At the rooming house," she said. "I heard shots and there were lasers—"

"Shit," said Scott. "Stay here!"

He took off down Fourth Street at a dead run. Jenny hesitated for a moment, then started running after him.

"What the hell is Scott doing with them?" Andre said.

"Maybe that isn't Scott," said Lucas. "At least, not *our* Scott."

"It *has* to be," she said. "We just crossed over. *Scott! Wait!*"

The Kid glanced over his shoulder at them briefly, then turned back and kept on walking.

"It's not him," said Lucas.

Andre shook her head. "But how . . ."

"I don't *know!*" said Lucas. "Maybe we've crossed over again without knowing it. Maybe we're caught in some kind of ripple effect, a timewave. The instability's increasing. Jesus. This is it!"

"How do you know?"

"It's got to be! In this timeline, the Montana Kid was part of the shoot-out at the O.K. Corral. In our timeline, he wasn't even there. Until now. We were right. Scott has to be the key! Come on!"

"What are we going to do?"

"Hell if I know," Lucas said, as they started running after the Earps. "We'll have to wait for Darkness."

"What if he doesn't show?"

"Then we're fucked."

Delaney reached the bottom of the stairs just as Stone and Capiletti came through the front door. Stone leaped to one side as Capiletti went for his sidearm. Finn fired, the loud report of the .45 filling the lobby. The clerk cried out in alarm and dropped down behind his desk as Capiletti fell, a bullet through his chest. Finn ducked back as Stone fired his laser and the beam passed inches from his face. He fired again and missed.

He swore through clenched teeth. A Colt .45 against a laser. Terrific odds. And he only had four bullets left. Two men dressed in black commando gear came diving through the front door. Delaney fired, wounding one of them, then felt a wash of searing heat go past him as the plasma charge narrowly missed him and struck the wall, igniting it. He fired again and missed the third man diving through the door, then darted up the stairs as a second plasma charge was fired, barely missing him and starting another fire as it struck the wall. His clothes were smoldering.

"Get him, dammit!" he heard Stone yell, and then he ducked around the stair post and snapped off another shot, dropping the man who'd fired the first two plasma rounds.

"*They're in, Geordy!*" he shouted. "*Watch it!*"

He started running up the stairs. One bullet left. And no time to reload.

"*Delaney!*"

Cooper was above him on the landing. He tossed down the disruptor. Finn dropped the Colt and caught it, then heard the boom of Cooper's Desert Eagle. He felt something whoosh past his ear and then there was an explosion behind him as the round struck one of the S.O.G. commandos in the chest and ignited, spattering the walls with blood and mangled flesh.

Downstairs, at the back entrance, Georgeson was knocked off his feet as the door exploded inward and the S.O.G. commandos came rushing through. He fired both his lasers from the floor and dropped the first man through the door, then was struck twice by laser fire from the men behind him. He fired again, dropping one more assailant, took another laser hit, but kept on firing, killing the last man through the door. He staggered to his feet, badly wounded, a hole through the side of his face, and several more through his chest and shoulder. He gasped for breath and fell to his knees as one lung collapsed, then looked up and saw Ben Stone coming through the smoke and flames. He raised his lasers, but he wasn't quick enough. Stone fired. The heavy .45 caliber slug smashed into Georgeson's forehead and exited through the other side, taking a bloody lump of bone and brain with it. The Ranger was hurled backwards by the impact, and he was dead before he hit the floor.

Upstairs, Tilley was engaged in a furious crossfire with the men on the roof across the way. He couldn't use his plasma rifle, for fear of setting the building across the street on fire. The desk clerk, oblivious to the laser beams flashing back and forth above him, ran out into the street, screaming, "Fire! Fire! Boarders in the rooming house were dashing down the stairs and out the back, paying no attention to the bodies they tripped over as they stumbled out through the smoke and flames on the first floor. Cooper came out onto the roof just as two of the S.O.G. commandos materialized behind Tilley. He fired twice, the explosive rounds slamming into his targets and making bloody salsa out of them, then dropped to the roof as Tilley spun around and yelled, "*DOWN!*"

Tilley fired over him, taking out one more commando who had clocked in behind Cooper, but not before he took a laser hit in the chest. He cried out and slumped over, grimacing with pain. Cooper started to get up, but a laser beam coming from across the street grazed his temple and he cried out, dropping back down, a smoking furrow in his hair.

"Son of a *bitch*! Tilley, you okay?"

"Don't know . . . damn, it hurts. . . ."

"Hang on, I'll get those bastards!"

Cooper quickly programmed his disc for the leap to the roof across the street. He could only guess wildly at the distance and the height, but there was no other choice. He programmed in his estimate and clocked.

He appeared about three feet above them . . . and five feet over the edge of the roof, with nothing but empty space below him.

"*Aw, fuck!*" he shouted.

As he fell, he fired five times in rapid succession, saw the bullets strike their targets and explode on impact, then the ground came up and he felt the bone-jarring impact and heard a loud snap as he struck.

The stairwell was full of smoke. Ben Stone coughed and squinted, trying to see through it. He heard something and fired at the sound. A man cried out and Stone saw a disruptor come clattering down the stairs. He grinned.

"Got you, you bastard!" he said, triumphantly.

He bent down to pick up the weapon and then suddenly a

figure came flying through the air, directly at him. Delaney hit him and both men tumbled down the stairs. Delaney scrambled to his feet, trying to ignore the pain of the smashed bone in his elbow. He pulled his knife out its sheath and raised it, then saw that Stone was lying motionless on the smoke-filled landing, his neck at a crazy angle. He was dead.

Delaney bent over him and found his warp disc. Coughing from the smoke and grunting with pain, he programmed it for non-specific time and clocked Stone's body to the dead zone. Then he retrieved his disruptor and moved back to the first floor.

Tilley crawled to the edge of the roof and looked over. There was no more laser fire coming from the other side. He heard someone groaning in the street below and looked down to see Cooper lying there, sprawled on his back, his weapon on the ground beside him. He heard movement behind him and spun around—

"Easy, Tilley!" said Delaney.

With a sigh of relief, Tilley lowered his weapon. "We get 'em all?"

"I think so," said Delaney. "I clocked out the bodies. Geordy didn't make it."

"Shit . . ." said Tilley.

"How bad are you hit?"

"Don't know . . ."

"Where's Cooper?"

"Down there," said Tilley, jerking his head toward the street below.

Delaney looked over the side. There was shouting in the street and the distant sound of bells as the fire brigade approached. Cooper was trying to crawl toward where his gun lay in the street.

"Damn," Delaney swore. "Tilley, get out of here. Clock back to Plus Time."

"What about—"

"Forget it. We've lost our transition point. Tell the strike force to stand by. Nobody moves till we send word. Now go!"

"Got it."

Tilley reached for his warp disc and clocked out. Delaney ran back down the stairs and stumbled through the smoke and out the back door. He ran down the alleyway out to the street. People were converging on the rooming house, carrying buckets of water. Delaney ran over to Cooper, who'd just managed to retrieve his gun.

"You okay?"

"Yeah," grimaced Cooper, groaning through his teeth. "Misjudged the distance slightly . . . Peter Pan I ain't. Broke both my damn legs. . . ."

"Come on, we're clocking you out. . . ."

"What about Tilley?"

"He's clocked out already. I think he'll make it."

"Geordy?"

"Dead," said Finn. "But he got 'em all."

"Son of a bitch," said Cooper, gasping.

Delaney fumbled for Cooper's warp disc.

"It's okay, I got it," Cooper said. "The bodies?"

"I clocked 'em out."

"What do you want me to do?"

"Get your legs fixed. Everything's on hold until we get a new transition point. Meanwhile, I've got to find the others. Now get out of here!"

"But we got the bastards, didn't we?"

"Yeah, you got 'em. Now go!"

"Give 'em hell, Delaney. . . ."

Cooper activated his disc and clocked out.

Delaney got his feet and suddenly noticed that it was daylight. Startled, he turned back towards the rooming house. A second earlier, it had been dark and smoke was pouring from the windows. Men were shouting and running in the street, bells were clanging. . . . Now, suddenly, it was broad daylight and the fire had been put out. There were several people standing in the street, looking at the damage. A wagon passed him going one way, two riders walking their horses passed heading in the opposite direction. The sun was high in the sky.

"God damn . . ." Delaney said. "What the hell . . . ?"

Suddenly, it hit him.

"*Timewave!*"

He checked the readout on his warp disc. It was a little after two o'clock. The date was October 26, 1881. And to his right, just turning the corner of Fourth and Fremont Streets, were Virgil, Wyatt and Morgan Earp, together with Doc Holliday.

Nikolai Drakov appeared in the alley between Fly's Boarding House and the Assay Office. He had a small case in his left hand. He turned right down the short passageway leading to the porch between Fly's Photo Studio and the boarding house. So far, everything was going according to plan. From the porch, he could look out into the vacant lot between Fly's establishment and the Harwood house. Standing together in the empty lot were Ike Clanton, his brother, Billy, Tom and Frank McLaury and, slightly behind them, their friend, Billy Claiborne. And, just turning the corner of the boarding house were Virgil and Wyatt Earp, followed by Morgan Earp and Doc Holliday. Virgil was carrying a cane in his right hand. Morgan had his gun out. Holliday was carrying a shotgun in one hand and his pistol in the other.

Drakov opened the case and took out a scoped, stainless steel Colt Python with an eight-inch barrel and black neoprene combat grips. Not as sophisticated as a laser or a plasma gun, but just as effective and, in some ways, more reliable. He kneeled and took a rest position, sighting through the pistol scope. He smiled in anticipation.

Amazing that after everything that happened, it would all come down to just one shot. A mere one hundred and fifty-eight grain, copper-jacketed, hollow-point bullet, no bigger than a dime, would accomplish what even nuclear weapons had failed to do. And he would have his revenge at last.

The future would cease to be. Just one shot, its report masked by the gunfire that would shortly erupt in what was no more than an insignificant blood feud, and everything would change. Universes would shift, setting off a timewave that would travel down the timestream, building in intensity, altering events . . . and in the course of those events that would be altered, Moses Forrester would never be born. He would never live to meet and fall in love with the Russian gypsy girl named Vanna Drakova. She would be spared the torment she had suffered and he, Nikolai Drakov, would never have lived. Sweet oblivion awaited him.

He wondered what would happen the moment he fired the fatal shot. Would he immediately cease to exist? Would there be pain? Or would he suddenly just be gone . . . because from the moment of his action, he would never have existed in the first place?

He would be gone, but his enemies who survived would suffer the knowledge of their failure. They would return to a future that had changed, a time that was unraveling, to find

that their commander, Moses Forrester, had never lived.
Would they remember? Drakov sincerely hoped so. For if they
did, there would be nothing they could do about it. Once the
act was done, any attempt on their part to change it would only
change the future once again, with consequences that could be
even worse in their own time. Further down the timestream,
long after they were dead, the cataclysm would occur. They
wouldn't be around to see it, nor would he. But it didn't really
matter. He would have won. He would have destroyed his
father, beaten his enemies, wiped out his own tortured existence and brought about an end to all of time with no more than
a slight motion of his finger on the trigger. One shot. The
ultimate solution.

He felt an almost sexual thrill of anticipation surge through
him. He took a deep breath, trying to steady his nerves. His
palms were sweating. He wiped them on his trousers. Just one
more moment . . .

Scott came running around the corner of Fourth and Fremont
and came to a dead stop. Suddenly, it was daylight. For a
moment, he was totally disoriented. And then, just ahead of
him, he saw Wyatt Earp, his brothers, Virgil and Morgan, and
Doc Holliday walking down the street, heading for the vacant
lot between Fly's Boarding House and Harwood's place. Just
beyond them, he could see Ike Clanton, Billy Clanton, and
Tom and Frank McLaury lined up in a row and facing them.

The famous shoot-out.

As if mesmerized, he started to move forward.

He heard Virgil Earp call out, "Boys, throw up your hands!
I want your guns!"

The two parties were perhaps six feet apart.

Young Billy Clanton yelled out, "Don't shoot me! I don't
want to fight!"

Tom McLaury said, "I haven't got anything, boys, I am
disarmed." He moved his hands up to his coat and started to
open it.

Virgil called out sharply, "Hold on! I don't mean *that*!"

And as Virgil shouted, Jenny came running around the
corner, saw Scott moving toward the men as if hypnotized
and . . .

Lucas and Andre rounded the corner where the Capitol
Saloon stood and suddenly everything seemed to shift into slow
motion. It felt as if they were moving against some sort of

invisible resistance, the current of the timeflow itself pushing against them. They saw Jenny running just ahead of them and it looked as if she were running underwater, bounding in slow motion, her hair gently rising and falling behind her as she ran toward the men ahead of her, Wyatt, Virgil and Morgan Earp, Doc Holliday and Scott, all standing abreast and facing the Clanton and the McLaury brothers. They heard her call out, as if from the bottom of a well, and her words sounded slow and drawn out, like a record being played at the wrong speed as she shouted, "*Scooottt . . . . . . nooooooooo!*"

With agonizing slowness, Scott and Wyatt both turned around and, at the same time, three shots cracked out, their reports sounding like echoes in a cave. Like feathers floating on the wind, both Wyatt and Scott started to crumple to the ground. . . .

In the next instant, with the suddenness of an earthquake, everything speeded up to normal and Lucas and Andre, straining against the invisible force that seemed to be holding them back, were thrown violently forward, as if shoved hard from behind. They both fell sprawling to the ground, hitting hard. Stunned, Lucas raised his head and saw Jenny running just ahead of them, moving with normal speed, and beyond her, moving toward the Earps and Holliday as if he were spellbound, was Scott. It was almost an exact replay of the scene they had just witnessed a split second earlier. A short distance past the Harwood place, standing in the middle of the street across from the Aztec Rooming House, they saw Finn Delaney. The Earps, Holliday, the Clantons and the McLaurys were already standing in the vacant lot. Scott was a short distance behind them, almost to the corner of Fly's Boarding House and well out of the center of the street. And there was nothing standing in between Jenny, running toward the combatants, and Finn Delaney, standing in the middle of the street, on the far side of Third. And, as he watched, Lucas suddenly saw Dr. Darkness appear out of nowhere, standing at Finn Delaney's side.

Andre started to get up . . . and Lucas saw it all in a flash of realization.

"*No! Stay down!*" He threw himself on top of her.

Delaney watched the men turn into the vacant lot between Fly's and Harwood's and then he saw Scott come running around the corner. As he passed the Capitol Saloon, Scott stopped and simply stood there for a moment, looking disoriented, then he started moving with a sort of odd gait, heading off to the side of the street, past Bauer's Meat Market and the Assay Office, moving toward Fly's Boarding House. . . .

Delaney caught his breath. "Oh, no. . . ." he said. "No, kid, don't do it. . . ."

Jenny came running around the corner, as fast as she could, hard on Scott's heels. Then, just behind her, Lucas and Andre appeared as if out of nowhere, tumbling forward into the street. Christ, this is *it,* thought Delaney, raising his disruptor. He couldn't wait for Darkness. He'd have to kill Neilson before he interfered. . . .

"The girl, Delaney!" said Darkness, suddenly materializing at his side. "*Shoot the girl!*"

Without pausing to think, Finn shifted his aim and fired the disruptor on tight beam. As Jenny opened her mouth to call out, she was suddenly wreathed in the bright blue glow of Cherenkov radiation. An instant later, she was gone, her atoms disintegrated.

And so was Darkness.

Two shots cracked out. And then all hell broke loose.

Simultaneously, Finn Delaney, Lucas Priest, Andre Cross and Scott Neilson all seemed to hear a deafening roaring in their ears, as if an entire ocean were being sucked away, and then there was nothing but the sound of gunfire from the lot, an entire fusillade of shots, one right after the other, and the street became filled with gunsmoke.

Drakov had Finn Delaney square in the crosshairs of his pistol scope. He thumbed back the hammer, put his finger on the trigger and . . . a blackthorn walking stick came down on the gun and knocked it aside. The shot went wild. Startled, Drakov looked up to see a gaunt man in an Inverness tweed coat looming over him, stick raised for another blow. Before he could throw up his arm to ward it off, the stick came down and Drakov collapsed to the floor, unconscious.

Darkness exhaled heavily. "I'll be damned," he said. "It worked."

CONCLUSION ═══════════

They all sat in Moses Forrester's private quarters in the
TAC-HQ building, drinking twelve-year-old Scotch. Andre,
Finn and Lucas sat together on the couch, their drinks on the
coffee table in front of them. Forrester sat across from them, in
his favorite chair, smoking one of his deep-bowled pipes. Scott
Neilson stood by the window, silently staring out at the
glittering lights below.

"We all thought it was Scott," Lucas was saying. "We
believed he was the key. And, in a way, he was. In the other
universe, he . . . or his twin . . . lived about eight hundred
years ago and he really *was* the Montana Kid, a famous
gunfighter. In the other timeline, the Montana Kid was at the
shoot-out at the O.K. Corral, which did not, in fact, take place
at the O.K. Corral, but in the vacant lot a short distance from
the alley that led to its back entrance. I guess 'The Shoot-out
in the Vacant Lot Between Fly's and Harwood's' didn't sound
as glamourous as 'The Shoot-out at the O.K. Corral.' It didn't
really happen there, but it became part of the myth."

"And in the other timeline, both Wyatt Earp and the
Montana Kid died in the shootout?" asked Forrester.

Lucas nodded. "That's what we saw. Jenny had a twin in the
other universe, as well. Actually, there never *was* a Jenny
Reilly in our universe. Not until Drakov put her there, in an
effort to match what happened in the other timeline. What we

first saw, as near as I can figure it, were the events that happened in the parallel timeline, only we'd been caught in a concentrated area of temporal instability, halfway between the two, in the act of crossing over. It was at that exact point that temporal inertia in both timelines reached its strongest surge, creating a sort of temporal whirlpool in which we became caught briefly. What we were seeing were the events that were happening in the other timeline, at the same exact instant as they were happening in *our* timeline, only we were caught in a sort of temporal lag."

"So when you finally broke free and crossed over, you saw those same events replayed an instant later, in our timeline," said Forrester.

"That's right," said Lucas. "In the other timeline, Jenny came running up to Scott and called out his name, because she was afraid he was going to get shot. Both Scott and Wyatt turned around and, in that instant, the shooting started. There were three shots. I'm not sure who fired them——"

"Doc Holliday fired first," said Scott, still standing by the window. He had a faraway look in his eyes. "Virgil didn't want a fight, but Doc wanted it all along. And so did Morgan. There was a lot of bad blood between the two parties and Doc was still angry over the attempt to frame him for that stagecoach robbery and King's escape from jail. Morgan was as hot-blooded as Holliday and they were both close friends. They wanted to finish it right then and there. A lot of people thought that when Virgil yelled out, 'Hold on, I don't mean that!' he was shouting at Billy Clanton and Frank McLaury, who supposedly went for their guns. Only he was really calling out to Doc and Morgan, because he heard them both cocking their weapons. Maybe Tom McLaury opening his coat to show he was unarmed was what set it off. Maybe Doc just had enough and felt like finishing it. Either way, Doc fired first, shooting Frank McLaury in the stomach, and Morgan fired a split second later, at Billy Clanton. But there were only two shots right at the beginning, not three."

"In the other universe, there were three," said Lucas. "There was somebody firing from cover on the porch between Fly's Boarding House and the Photo Studio. It could have been Johnny Behan. But when Jenny called out, Wyatt and the Montana Kid both turned around. Somebody fired first, maybe Holliday, and then the next two bullets got Wyatt and Scott.

So, in the other universe, both Wyatt and the Kid died in the shoot-out."

"Drakov was trying to match the events in our universe to what happened in the parallel timeline," Andre said. "As Darkness explained it to us later, the temporal confluence at that point was so strong that it could have gone one way or the other. The instability had reached the breaking point. If the exact same thing happened in each timeline at the exact same space and time, with the powerful confluence effect focused on that specific point, both timelines would have come together and the force of the temporal inertia in both timelines would have created a massive timewave that would have traveled down the timestream, building in intensity, disrupting history all the way down the line, until . . ."

"Until what?" asked Forrester.

"Who knows?" said Lucas, with a shrug. "Darkness wouldn't tell us. A massive timestream split? A chain reaction? Ultimate entropy?" He sighed. "Frankly, I'm not even sure I want to know."

"So then Jenny Reilly was the key," said Forrester.

"In a way, she was," said Lucas, "but in another way, it was Scott. If she hadn't fallen in love with him . . . but then, that was probably what she'd been programmed to do by Drakov, who kept manipulating her, keeping her off-balance and never letting her know what her real purpose was. He needed her emotions to be in turmoil, so she'd be driven to do what he meant for her to do. After she pulled a gun on Wyatt Earp and rescued Scott, Wyatt had to figure Scott had crossed over the line and had chosen to become an outlaw. When, in *our* timeline, Jenny saw Scott moving toward the scene of the gunfight, she was going to call out his name, just as the other Jenny had in the parallel universe. Wyatt would have heard it and, maybe thinking Scott was about to shoot him, he would have turned around just as Doc and Morgan fired and then Billy Clanton would have shot him in the back."

"And that would have been the third shot," said Forrester.

"No," said Lucas. "The third shot would have been Drakov's. When he shot Finn, to keep him from killing Jenny before she could call out Scott's name."

"Why didn't he just shoot Wyatt Earp?" asked Forrester.

"And lose the chance to kill at least one of us before he ceased to exist?" Delaney said. He shook his head. "He couldn't pass up that opportunity. He knew Billy Clanton was quick with a gun and a good shot. The only reason Wyatt wasn't hit was because he shot Billy in the wrist as he was drawing, a second after Morgan shot him in the chest. And after he shot Delaney, Drakov would still have had the time to make sure of Wyatt with his second shot and Scott with his third, in the event the others missed them."

"Darkness knew about the temporal instability and the surge in temporal inertia that was going to take place right at that point and he wasn't sure if his unstable subatomic structure would maintain its integrity or not," said Andre. "He didn't want to warn us specifically about what was going to happen because he wasn't sure if that would influence our actions and affect the outcome. It all had to be done at the last minute and he had just one shot at it. Even then, it was a gamble. He didn't know if he'd survive it. If he'd been caught in the same temporal vortex as me and Lucas, he may have discorporated."

"He also knew that everything depended on my immediate response," said Delaney, "because he'd essentially have to be in two places at the same time, and even at faster-than-light speed, that's quite a trick. He knew he had a chance to tell me to shoot the girl, to keep her from distracting Wyatt at the last possible instant, and he knew that if I reacted immediately, he could stop Drakov from firing more than one shot. But he *didn't* know if he could stop him from firing that first shot. He was gambling that on seeing me, Drakov would immediately try to shoot me first, instead of Wyatt. He wasn't sure if he'd have a chance to save my life by taching to where Drakov was and deflecting his shot at the last possible second. Even traveling at faster-than-light speed, he had to play it close, so that the temporal inertia in both timestreams would be at its strongest surge . . . and then, when the events in both timelines did *not* match up, the strength of that surge forced them apart, once and for all. Without him, it never would have happened. But thanks to him, the Temporal Crisis is over. Darkness changed the past and saved the future."

"Only Jenny had to die," said Scott.

Delaney looked at him with pain written on his features. "I'm sorry, Scott. I had no other choice."

Neilson nodded. "I understand. And I'm not blaming you. But that still doesn't make her death any easier to bear. I loved her."

"Yeah, kid," said Delaney, softly. "I know."

"So Drakov had it all planned out in advance," said Forrester.

"That's right," said Lucas. "He knew about it because he had done the one thing no one else had ever done before. Not even the Network, because it was so risky. He clocked ahead to the future. He clocked ahead far enough to study the history of the Temporal Crisis and he found out about what happened in the Tombstone scenario. Then he clocked back there, located the crossover points, established the scenario in each timeline and set out to try and make them match exactly, so that the temporal currents would flow together instead of being forced apart. And, apparently, from the standpoint of the future Darkness came from, he succeeded. Darkness had to come back and try to stop him."

"Amazing," Forrester said.

"The one thing Darkness never did explain was how he knew that Drakov would cease to exist if he succeeded," Andre said. "Apparently, somehow, the result of what he did would affect *your* life, sir."

Forrester nodded. "Indeed, it would have," he said. He got up and went to the secret panel that led into his private sanctum. He opened it, went in, and came out a moment later, carrying a framed photograph in his hand.

"Wyatt Earp had a daughter," he said.

"That's impossible," said Scott. "Wyatt and Josie never had any children."

"No, not Wyatt and Josie," Forrester replied. "Wyatt and Nadine McCain. A prostitute he met in Gunnison, Colorado, after he left Arizona. As far as I know, he was only with her once, but he left her pregnant and she gave birth to a daughter that he never knew." He held up the old, faded photograph in the silver frame. "Angie McCain. Who grew up and married a silver miner named Michael Forrester. She was my great, great, great, great, grandmother."

"I'll be damned!" Delaney said.

"Then you *knew* you were descended from Wyatt Earp?" said Andre, stunned. "Why the hell didn't you tell us?"

"For the same reason Darkness didn't," Forrester replied. "I was afraid it would affect your actions. I couldn't afford to take that chance, no matter how things turned out."

"Well, thank God, they turned out all right," said Lucas.

"Cooper's Rangers went in afterward and picked up the Network men. And we were able to bring Drakov back alive for interrogation and he revealed the location of all his clones and hominoids. What's going to happen to them?"

"They won't be harmed," said Forrester. "The mutations, of course, we have no choice but to eliminate. And that will be doing the poor brutes a kindness. As for the others, and my son's own clones, they'll be conditioned, then temporally relocated and allowed to live out normal lives. Most of his clones we were able to pick up while they were still children. A few we got as adults, after they'd already been programmed with his mental engrams. Those will require therapy conditioning. They'll be placed in different modern time sectors, where they'll never run into each other and where their increased lifespan won't make them freaks. As for my son, himself . . ."

"I hear he's going to be all right," said Lucas, gently. "They say that they can rehabilitate him."

Forrester nodded. "The results are already beginning to show," he said. "I went to see him in the hospital this morning. He called me 'Father.' Then he broke down and cried."

Forrester had to turn away for a moment. He cleared his throat.

"Well, it seems as if promotions and decorations are in order," he said. "I thought about making it a formal ceremony, but I know how you feel about such things. . . ." He produced small boxes with new insignia in them and passed them out. "And I thought, Lucas, that you might want to wear your stars at your wedding."

"My *stars*?" said Lucas, staring at the little box with disbelief.

"Congratulations," Forrester said. "Andre, looks like you're going to be marrying a general."

"But . . . but . . ." Lucas stammered.

"I'll need someone to take over for me as Director," Forrester said. "I'm retiring. My son is going to need me when he gets well and I want to spend some time with him. Maybe give him a chance to get back something of the life he never had."

"But . . . *Director*?" Lucas said. "*Me*?"

"I couldn't think of a better man," said Forrester. "Don't you agree, Colonel Delaney?"

"Yes, sir!" Delaney said, with a wide grin.

"Major Cross, congratulations," Forrester said, kissing her on the cheek. "I wish you both all the happiness in the world."

"Thank you, sir."

He turned around. "Lieutenant Neilson?"

He handed him the box with the new insignia, and then took another box out of his pocket.

"The President is supposed to make the formal presentation, so you'll have to give this back to me," he said, "but I thought I'd make sort of an unofficial one myself. On behalf of a grateful government, I'd like to present you with the Medal of Honor."

The others stood up and applauded.

"You'll all be formally decorated with the Medal of Honor by the President," said Forrester, "just don't let him know that I've quietly usurped the privilege. I'm proud of each and every one of you."

Scott stared at the medal and shook his head. "I . . . I don't know what to say." He looked up at Forrester. "Yes, I do. I've got something for you too, sir."

He went over by the door, where he'd put down a small cordura kit bag. He reached inside and took out a twin-shoulder holster rig, holding a matched pair of engraved and silver-plated, pearl-handled Colt Single Action Army .45's.

"For your collection, sir," he said, handing them over. "That is, if you think they're suitable."

Forrester took the guns and smiled. "I will treasure these above all the other artifacts," he said. "Thank you, Lieutenant. Thank you very much."

"I'd like to propose a toast," Delaney said. He held up his glass. "To the soon-to-be General and Mrs. Lucas Priest," he said, turning to Lucas and Andre. "No time like the present!"

They all grinned at the old Temporal Army in-joke. "No time like the present!" they all echoed.

They drank, but one of them was thinking there was no time like the past. Scott Neilson turned and stared out the window at the lights below, but he was seeing another time and another place. He was thinking of a beautiful young girl with long blonde hair and powder blue eyes. And of another life that might have been.

If only they had not run out of time.

AFTERWORD ===========

The incident known as "the gunfight at the O.K. Corral" is one of the most famous and controversial episodes in the history of the American West. In its aftermath, Wyatt Earp and his brothers, Virgil and Morgan, the "fighting Earps," as well as Doc Holliday, became mythic figures in American folklore. (The two remaining Earp brothers, Warren and Jim, who were not involved in the gunfight, have been largely overlooked in the legend of the Old West.)

The story of the shoot-out spawned a number of Hollywood films. (Wyatt Earp was played by Henry Fonda, as well as by Burt Lancaster, among others, and my own favorite portrayal of Doc Holliday was by Kirk Douglas. Douglas, while too physically fit to make a truly convincing Holliday, nevertheless portrayed him in a reasonably authentic manner, tubercular cough, erratic personality and all.) There was also a popular television series of the '50s in which Wyatt Earp was portrayed by Hugh O'Brien. Bat Masterson was also romanticized in a TV series, played as an elegant, cane-carrying dandy by Gene Barry. (Barry used his cane more often than he used his gun, which hardly ever left the holster, whereas the real Bat Masterson knew better.) Years later, even *Star Trek* got into the act, with an episode loosely based on the shoot-out at the O.K. Corral. (Curiously, out of all the cinematic portrayals of the

Earps, the *Star Trek* episode came closest in capturing what the Earps really looked like.)

As a boy, like many of my contemporaries, I was enthralled by the TV westerns of the fifties. Older readers may remember government agent Christopher Colt of *Colt .45*, played by Wade Preston, Clint Walker's *Cheyenne*, John Russell as *Lawman*, Chuck Connors as *The Rifleman*, William Boyd as *Hopalong Cassidy*, Richard Boone as the enigmatic Paladin in *Have Gun, Will Travel*, Jock Mahony as *Yancy Derringer*, Steve McQueen as bounty hunter Josh Randall in *Wanted: Dead or Alive*, Jim Arness as Marshal Matt Dillon of *Gunsmoke*, Gale Davis as *Annie Oakley*, Roy Rogers and Dale Evans, and the immortal Clayton Moore and Jay Silverheels as the *Lone Ranger* and Tonto. Then there was perhaps the most famous TV western series of them all, *Bonanza*.

In the movies, the western has long been a staple. From the silent era of Tom Mix and William S. Hart, to the early "oaters" with stars such as Gene Autry, to all those wonderful John Ford epics starring John Wayne (even the Duke got into the act with a fanciful movie peripherally based on the old Tombstone story, *The Sons of Katie Elder*) and perhaps the most famous western of them all, *The Magnificent Seven*, with Yul Brynner in the role of Chris, a film based on *The Seven Samurai* by Akira Kurosawa. In more recent times, we've had Clint Eastwood's memorable portrayal of "the man with no name" in the Sergio Leone "spaghetti westerns" and later in films produced by his own company, Malpaso Productions. (In some areas of the country, one can still see Eastwood in his first western role, as Rowdy Yates of *Rawhide*.) To give Eastwood credit, his western films have tended to be more accurate than most in terms of historical details, particularly in respect to firearms, and I think his film *The Outlaw Josey Wales* is one of the best westerns ever made. (And Larry McMurty's *Lonesome Dove* is right up there, as well.)

I never outgrew my fascination with westerns. I became a student of western history and I eventually traded in my cap pistols for real guns. (And, in the process, learned what a lot of nonsense the Hollywood image of the Old West gunfighter really was.) To this day, I remain an avid shooter and reloader and while I've fired many different types of weapons, I have remained true to my childhood roots. I don't care for the modern, high-tech semiautomatics. I prefer revolvers and, among revolvers, my favorite remains the Colt Single Action Army.

As many readers doubtless know already, the "fast-draw showdown" is largely a creation of Hollywood screenwriters. Hollywood's version of the Old West had little to do with reality. "Notches" found in old six-guns, for instance, are less likely to be the marks of how many men its owner had killed than they are the result of using the pistol as a hammer on a section of wire fence. (Bat Masterson, in his later years, was once pestered by a collector for one of his "authentic" guns, so he went to a store and bought one, then, as a joke, carved a bunch of notches in the grip and sold it to the gullible collector.) The single-action revolver is a difficult weapon to shoot quickly, and the practice of "fanning," seen so often in the movies and on TV, may look dramatic, but is not very practical. While there were real-life cases where people fanned a six-gun, the fact is that it would be difficult to achieve any kind of accuracy using that technique. It was also hard on the firing mechanism of the weapon, not to mention the heel of the hand!

It is possible that the heel of the hand was used by some shooters merely to cock the pistol as it was brought up, but more likely, if there was a need for rapid fire, a technique known as "slip-shooting" was used. An Old West–style revolver such as the Colt Single Action Army (the legendary Peacemaker) differs from modern double-action revolvers in a number of significant respects, one being that you cannot cock the hammer by squeezing the trigger. It's necessary to cock the hammer manually with the thumb for each shot before the gun will fire. Consequently, "slip-shooting" was a technique in which the gun was held with the trigger fully depressed and the hammer was "slipped" back repeatedly by the thumb. Few people ever fanned a six-gun and the practice is largely a Hollywood exaggeration.

The same can be said for the holsters of most Hollywood cowboys. Hollywood western holsters were specially made to facilitate the largely fictional "fast draw." Usually, they were cut away in the front, had open trigger guards and were often metal-reinforced, attached to the belt through a slot. John Wayne was an exception. His holsters were closer to the authentic holsters of the western era, not attached to his belt, but riding on it by means of a tunnel loop.

Imagine a long piece of leather, laid flat, about twice the length of the holster itself. This is the skirt. The front piece of the holster is stitched to the lower part of the skirt, which forms its back. The upper part of the skirt is slightly wider and has one or two slots cut into it. This part would then be bent back behind the holster and the holster would be inserted through the slots. The belt would then go through the tunnel loop formed by the skirt being bent back behind the holster. These holsters also covered the gun more completely, being higher in the front than those seen in films and television, and usually covering most of the trigger guard.

Hollywood cowboys frequently had leather thongs on their holsters to hook over the hammer, to retain the gun, whereas these "hammer thongs" weren't used on frontier-era holsters. (Even Wyatt Earp was known to have his gun fall out of its holster on occasion. It had to be a bit embarrassing.)

Another Hollywood myth is the "tied-down" gun on the low-slung gunbelt. Supposedly, you could tell a "real" gun-fighter by the fact that he wore his gun tied down to his leg. Few authentic western-era holsters had tie-down thongs and those that did had them not to facilitate a fast draw, but probably to keep the holster from flapping around while riding. As for the low-slung gunbelt, it looks swashbuckling as all hell, but in practice, if you're wearing your gunbelt low and you grab for the gun to go for a fast draw, chances are the entire gunbelt will ride up, holstered gun and all. A tied-down rig might have prevented this to some degree, but in the event of a gunfight, which frequently occurred without warning, no-body would wait around obligingly while you paused to tie down your holster. And if you wore it tied down all the time, tight enough to keep the belt from riding up, it wouldn't have been very comfortable.

The fact is that most people of the frontier era didn't wear their guns tied down and often, they didn't even use holsters, but either stuck their pistols in their belts or in their coat pockets or utilized what was known as a "town carry," simply sticking the gun inside the waistband with the loading gate open, to keep it from sliding down inside the pants. (This is how some of the participants in the O.K. Corral gunfight carried their pistols, including Wyatt Earp. Holliday wore a holster and it appears that Frank McLaury and Billy Clanton did, as well.) Additionally, in the Old West, the word "gun" was generally used to refer to a rifle. A six-shooter was simply called a pistol.

In real life, the winner of a gunfight was usually the guy who had his weapon already out and ready, the one who shot first and most accurately. Allowing the "bad guy" to go for his gun first was a sure-fire ticket to Boot Hill. No matter how fast on the draw a gunfighter was, if he waited until the other guy started his draw first, human reaction time would not allow him to beat his opponent. If the other guy started to draw first, he'd win unless he missed with his first shot. (And there was a good chance of that.) There were very few so-called "gunslingers" who were actually fast on the draw in the Hollywood sense. Two notable exceptions were John Wesley Hardin and Wild Bill Hickok, who was said to be the fastest of them all. Curiously, neither man carried his guns in the traditional Hollywood western style.

Hardin used the crossdraw method and at one time had a special vest made with holsters sewn into each side. (Roughly similar to the way Scott wears his guns in the story.) However, drawing both weapons simultaneously in this manner is almost certain to result in the guns knocking into each other, and it is unlikely that Hardin was able to achieve any speed with this cumbersome method, or that he even used it. (A number of highly skilled, modern firearms experts have tried it and found it incredibly clumsy.) What Hardin probably did was what most shootists did who carried two guns. He drew only one, relying on the second for a backup. The gunfighter with two six-guns blazing is largely a Hollywood myth. The exception, once again, was Hickok, who was observed to be equally adept with either hand. After his vest experiment, Hardin had El Paso Saddlery craft a specially designed shoulder holster for him and, as an added item of interest, that very same type of holster can still be purchased from El Paso Saddlery, which is still in business today. (They can also supply you with authentic western holsters and an exact copy of the rig John Wayne wore in his films. For those western fans who might be interested, their address is P.O. Box 27194, El Paso, Texas, 79926.)

Hickok, contrary to the way he is usually portrayed in films and in the television series starring Guy Madison, did not wear his six-guns in the reverse-draw, butt-forward, hip holster carry. He did, in fact, use a butt-forward carry, but his favorite guns were Navy Colts and he most often wore them tucked into a belt or sash at his waist, angled forward.

The butt-forward technique originally came about as a result of the mounted or cavalry carry. If one was right-handed, the pistol was worn in a holster on the left side, butt facing forward, thereby enabling a crossdraw, which was more easily accomplished while mounted. Additionally, the long, heavy barrels on old percussion Colts rendered this type of carry more convenient. The disadvantage of a crossdraw is that the gun crosses the target as you draw, while in a regular draw, it comes up in line with the target.

I find the crossdraw and reverse draw techniques awkward for a fast draw, but then I'm not a gunfighter and Hickok was reputed to be greased lightning. When he was killed in Deadwood while playing poker, holding a hand consisting of two aces and two eights, in clubs and spades, and a jack of diamonds (thereafter known as the "Dead Man's Hand"), he was shot from behind while seated at the table, in the back of the head. Yet, reportedly, he still managed to draw his gun before he hit the floor. (It was Hickok who gave Wyatt Earp pointers in gun handling when Earp was a young man, and Earp was reputed to have been very fast, as well.)

There was also a technique known as the "border roll" or the "Curly Bill roll" (named after Curly Bill Brocius, who plays a part in the O.K. Corral story), in which the gun was held at the side, upside down, butt forward, with the trigger finger through the trigger guard. It was then quickly spun on the trigger finger and cocked as it was brought up (the probable birth of the spinning one sees in the movies).

The fact is that most shoot-outs in the Old West rarely involved anything like the accuracy depicted in films and on TV. There are numerous documented cases of men blasting away at each other at fairly close range, yet missing with most of their shots. (As appears to have happened at the O.K. Corral gunfight.) There are also numerous stories of innocent bystanders being killed by stray bullets. Curly Bill Brocius once fired his gun off in a bar, only to have the bullet go through the wall and kill his own horse!

Many men who had a reputation as gunfighters had their exploits grossly exaggerated. (As in the case of Bat Masterson, who is only known for a fact to have killed one man in a gunfight, but was credited with over thirty.) So the image of the "deadly Old West gunslinger" is largely an exaggerated one.

Which brings us to the shootout at the O.K. Corral. Wyatt Earp has frequently been portrayed as carrying a "Buntline Special," a Colt six-gun with a very long barrel, somewhere between ten and sixteen inches. This is an example of the type of folklore that has grown up surrounding the story of the Earps. Supposedly, according to the Stuart Lake biography, *Wyatt Earp, Frontier Marshal*, "penny-dreadful" writer Ned Buntline ordered five of these pistols as presents for Wyatt Earp, Bat Masterson, Charlie Basset, Neal Brown and Bill Tilghman, all lawmen in Dodge City. However, there is no evidence to support this contention.

A moment's thought will reveal that a "Buntline-type" revolver, with its extremely long barrel, would have been rather cumbersome to carry and impossible to draw quickly. It is a rather impractical weapon, and Wyatt's wife, Josie, makes no mention of it in her memoirs. In her excellent book, *And Die in the West: The Story of the O.K. Corral Gunfight*, author Paula Mitchell Marks refers to a witness who saw Wyatt carrying "an old pistol, pretty large, fourteen or sixteen inches long. . . ." This sounds like it might have been a "Buntline," however, it sounds like a fish story to me. Marks and other scholars seem to feel that it was more likely a Colt Single Action Army with a seven-and-a-half-inch barrel. Personally, I'm not even sure of that. Wyatt Earp himself mentioned having put this pistol in his overcoat pocket. I think the gun he probably carried was a Colt Single Action Army with a four-and-three-quarter inch barrel, which would have rested reasonably well in a coat pocket. If he had very deep pockets, the barrel might have been seven and a half inches long. But it certainly was not a Buntline Special.

The story of the events leading up to the famous gunfight differs depending on which source one consults, which is why the episode remains controversial to this day. Earp and his brothers are variously portrayed as either noble heroes bent on cleaning up Tombstone or as villains pursuing a personal vendetta. The truth is probably somewhere in between.

Much of the myth surrounding Wyatt Earp owes its existence to the Lake biography, which cannot be considered reliable. According to historian Glenn Boyer, Wyatt Earp's desire to collaborate with Stuart Lake might have come about as a result of his knowledge that Billy Breakenridge was working on his own version of the events in a book called *Helldorado*, in which, he had boasted in advance, he would "really burn the Earps up." However, Wyatt Earp died without ever having read a word of what Lake had written and Lake himself later admitted to fictionalizing much of the story for commercial purposes.

Frank Waters, in his book *The Earps of Tombstone* (subtitled *The Story of Mrs. Virgil Earp*), portrays the Earps as villains, with the obvious intention of debunking the heroic myth set forth by Lake's book. He interviewed Virgil's wife, Allie, in Los Angeles in 1935. According to Glenn Boyer, when she heard about the book, Josie Earp went to Waters' home in Tucson and attempted to interfere with the project. Reportedly, she flew into a rage and Waters' ailing mother had a seizure, which may account for what is obviously a strong bias against Wyatt Earp in the Waters book. Additionally, Boyer tells us, Allie Earp later repudiated the manuscript as "a bunch of lies" and threatened to sue Waters if it was published. And it did not appear until years after she and Josie died.

Thus, the stories in two of the principal sources on the O.K. corral gunfight (*I Married Wyatt Earp*, the memoirs of Josephine Sarah Marcus Earp, collected and edited by Glenn Boyer, and *The Earps of Tombstone* by Frank Waters) both offer much valid research, but they differ widely in their interpretations of events. Waters, in particular, lacks objectivity, as any reader can plainly discern. Allie Earp apparently had an intense personal dislike for her brother-in-law, Wyatt. And while Josie Earp is clearly prejudiced in favor of her husband, editor Boyer supplies us with exhaustive notations of his own, correcting her inaccuracies and/or embellishments and stating the true facts inasmuch as they can be established. So discounting the Lake biography, we're left with two basic versions of the events leading up to the gunfight and it would be interesting to briefly examine each of them in turn. (There have, of course, been other writings, but the work done by Waters and Boyer seem to be the most representative of the two different points of view.)

According to the Waters version, the Earps were rather unsavory characters (Wyatt, in particular) who came to the mining boomtown of Tombstone and in fairly short order established themselves as part of the bad element in town, running afoul of Sheriff Johnny Behan, whose description Waters quotes from "a Tombstone old-timer" as ". . . a polished gentleman who didn't go around loaded down with artillery and swashbuckling about the streets. . . . as the Earps did. His associates were the better class of people."

Leaving aside the seeming folly of a sheriff in a wild boomtown like Tombstone walking about without "artillery," this portrayal of Behan is widely at variance with the way he is depicted by Josie Earp, who lived with him. Josie portrays Behan as an opportunistic and unscrupulous political hack and tells of numerous poker-playing sessions at their home with the Clantons, Johnny Ringo, Curly Bill Brocius and the McLaurys, the rustler element, where Behan was allegedly paid off in his "winnings." Aside from going into considerable detail about the rustlers, Josie also gives us what seems like an astute and factual analysis of the political climate in Tombstone, involving the County Ring and the Townlot Company, details which Waters largely omits.

Though the Clantons and their faction have sometimes been portrayed as honest ranchers ruthlessly gunned down by the Earps, the fact that they were also rustlers is unquestionable. It was common practice in those days for parties from both sides of the border to raid across for cattle and horses (as depicted in Larry McMurtry's wonderful novel, *Lonesome Dove*) and the Clantons were no exception. Since rustled cattle were cheap to buy, the rustlers had considerable support among the locals. Consequently, it is not surprising that there were those in Tombstone who were well-disposed toward the Clanton faction. The rustlers made a point of ingratiating themselves with the local citizens and did not bother the small ranchers, although those with larger spreads were an obvious target.

The County Ring seems to have been a Democratic political organization in Tombstone to which Johnny Behan belonged, in addition to Art Fay, owner of the pro-Democratic paper, the *Tombstone Nugget* (source of much of Waters' anti-Earp material), Harry Woods, the editor of the *Nugget*, John Dunbar, the county treasurer, and Billy Breakenridge, who later claimed to have been Tombstone's deputy but was, according to Josie Earp, only the tax collector and jailer. Josie accuses the County Ring of extensive graft and corruption and Boyer's research seems to support that contention. It certainly appears that they siphoned off taxes for their own personal gain. Boyer mentions evidence of several indictments against members of the Ring, none apparently prosecuted successfully, but Boyer also tells us that the ". . . county treasurer's warrants show that Johnny Behan collected at least four times the fees of any of his next three successors." (As Sheriff, Behan's salary came out of his collections.)

The Townlot Company, otherwise known as the firm of Clark and Gray, was apparently a group of speculators with whom Tombstone's Mayor Alder Randall was involved. There seems to have been a great deal of "lot jumping" in Tombstone, with attempts to occupy lots by force and, to settle such matters, the law had permitted temporary transfer for administration of titling. One version of the story has it that Randall used an extremely liberal interpretation of this law to transfer all titles outright to Clark and Gray, who then demanded large purchase fees from the lot occupants and threatened forcible eviction in the event of failure to comply. Another version has it that Clark and Gray had originally purchased the townsite of Tombstone, but had failed to obtain clear title. Either way, there was a lot of controversy about who owned what and disputes over properties in town frequently escalated into armed conflict (which was not unusual in western boomtowns of the period).

Boyer's research uncovered over a hundred townsite suits against Clark and Gray, with most judgements going against the Townlot Company. The Earps, who had real estate interests in Tombstone, probably became involved in this controversy, which in part would serve to explain the *Nugget*'s opposition to them, since the *Nugget* was controlled by the County Ring. The town's other newspaper, the *Tombstone Epitaph*, was a Republican paper and gave a considerably different accounting of the events of the time. Waters' response to that is to trash the *Epitaph* in his book, making it appear to be a sort of Old West version of modern supermarket tabloids. In any case, there is no question but that both papers were biased in their reporting.

There was also another factor to the bitter rivalry which led to the shootout. Josie Marcus was originally Sheriff Johnny Behan's girl, but she left him for Wyatt Earp (with whom she remained until he died, though there appears to be no evidence that they were ever legally married). So, it would seem that the events leading up to the gunfight stem largely from a political struggle for power and partly from a love triangle, as well. (Allie, Virgil's wife, seems to have been quite hostile to Josie, but this can probably be traced to her close relationship with Wyatt's second wife, Mattie, whom he also never legally married and whom he left for Josie. His first wife had died. Common-law marriages were not unusual at the time. None of the Earps appear to have been legally married.)

In any case, the beginnings of the conflict seem to have been motivated by the aforementioned political struggle involving the County Ring and the Townlot Company, with their connections to the Clanton-McLaury faction, vs. John Clum, founder of the *Epitaph* and later mayor of Tombstone, the Earps and Marshal Fred White, among other local businessmen.

I compressed events considerably and obviously played around with them a lot for the sake of my story. But in real life, the first notable incident occurred in July of 1880, when six mules were stolen from Camp Rucker, the Army camp on the White River, east of Tombstone. Lieutenant J.H. Hurst arrived in Tombstone with a detachment of soldiers and enlisted the aid of Wyatt, Virgil, and Morgan Earp, as well as Wells Fargo agent Marsh Williams. The mules were traced to the McLaury ranch and a brand was allegedly found that had altered the US brand to D8. Apparently, nothing came of the affair. Hurst didn't get his mules back and Frank McLaury wasn't charged, but he vehemently proclaimed his innocence afterward and this seems to have been the beginning of the bad feeling between the Earps and the McLaurys.

The next significant incident occurred on October 27, when Marshal White was killed. A bunch of cowboys started shooting off their guns into the air, on Allen Street. This was against city ordinance and White went out to stop it. The first cowboy he ran across was Curly Bill Brocius. White saw Brocius holding a gun down along his leg. He told him to hand it over.

One version has it that White grabbed the gun and it went off accidentally. Another that White grabbed it just as Curly Bill fired. Still another version describes a brief scuffle, with the Earps involved, during which the gun went off accidentally. In any case, White was mortally wounded. The shooting was found to be accidental and Waters reports it as such, but Josie Earp challenges that finding and believes it to have been premeditated murder.

As she points out in her memories, it's possible that Curly Bill brought his gun up merely to hand it over to White when he demanded its surrender, but if so, then why was it cocked? Curly Bill was later found to have had only one shot fired from his gun, the one that killed Marshal White. This, it was contended, proved that he wasn't part of the shooting White had gone out to stop. He had one empty cartridge and five loaded chambers. However, that meant he had loaded six rounds. Curly Bill was experienced with firearms and, as such, it would seem that he would normally have loaded only *five* chambers. Old-style single actions were normally carried that way, as a safety precaution, since a blow to the hammer (such as might occur if the gun were dropped) could result in the gun going off. The standard practice was to load five, then carry the gun with the hammer down on the empty sixth chamber. Curly Bill had loaded all six, which would seem to suggest that he meant business. According to Josie, it was all a setup by Clark and Gray to murder White and get him out of the way.

Gray later contended that the shooting had been accidental because Curly Bill had "filed off the safety catch" in order to facilitate fanning the gun and it went off as a result. However, this seems improbable. Colt Single Action Army revolvers did not have an external safety lever, such as on modern semiautomatics. What they had was a sort of built-in safety, which I'll describe. There were three hammer positions. Quarter-cock, half-cock and full-cock. In quarter-cock, the first position, the hammer was merely lifted off the primer and the rotating cylinder remained locked. In half-cock, the hammer is locked halfway back and the cylinder is free to rotate, so that the loading gate on the right side of the weapon can be opened and the cylinder manually rotated, the chambers loaded one at a time through the gate. And then there's full-cock, in which the hammer is locked all the way back, with the gun ready to fire when the trigger is squeezed. The clicking one hears when a single-action revolver is cocked is the hammer going past the first two positions and locking all the way back.

If Curly Bill had filed off the safety notches, he would not have been able to lock his hammer back for loading or for cocking. He would have had to hold it back with his thumb while loading or while preparing to fire, which would have been rather awkward. And there would have been absolutely no point to his doing so. If he wanted to fan the gun, he would have simply kept his finger on the trigger while fanning the hammer with the heel of his hand or "slip-shooting" it with his thumb. Filing off the safety notches would have made no difference whatsoever. Since the gun could not have "gone off" unless it had been deliberately cocked, Josie's claim that it was murder seems valid.

Furthermore, we have the evidence that Curly Bill was well known for the "border roll" technique that came to bear his name. Perhaps what happened was that White demanded surrender of the gun, Curly Bill held it out to him, butt first, and then as White reached for it, Curly Bill pulled the roll on him and shot him. If the Earps were already on the scene, and had grabbed Curly Bill from behind, that could explain why it might have looked like an accident.

The next incident leading up to the gunfight was the attempted robbery of a stagecoach that had left Tombstone with some passengers and a shipment of bullion on March 15, 1881. The driver, Bud Philpot, and the shotgun guard, Bob Paul, had changed places. (Which proved fatal for Philpot.) When the outlaws accosted the stage, Paul dropped the reigns to go for his shotgun. One of the outlaws fired, killing Philpot, who pitched forward onto the horses, which then bolted. There was more shooting and one of the passengers was mortally wounded. Paul then regained control of the horses and managed to get the stage to Benson.

A posse was then formed, consisting of men from both factions, among them Bob Paul, Wyatt Earp, Sheriff Behan, Billy Breakenridge, Virgil and Morgan Earp, Bat Masterson and Buckskin Frank Leslie. To this point, most accounts of the incident seem to agree.

Waters reports that disguises were found at the scene of the crime, wigs and fake beards similar to those he alleges Wyatt Earp possessed and used. (He does not say why, though he implies criminal purposes, and other accounts make no mention of any disguises, either found at the scene or in Earp's possession.) The trail led to the Redfield ranch, where a man named Luther King was arrested. Waters reports that he admitted being party to the holdup, but not the shooting, claiming that he only held the horses. Josie Earp gives further details. She claims that King at first protested his innocence and Behan wanted to let him go, but Wyatt Earp and Bob Paul tricked King into confessing by telling him that Kate Elder (also known as Big Nose Kate Fisher), "Doc Holliday's woman," had been on the stage and was killed when the outlaws started shooting. So fearsome was Holliday's reputation as a killer that King immediately confessed, wanting to be certain that Holliday was told he'd only held the horses and was not involved in the shooting. He implicated three men named Harry Head, Bill Leonard and Jim Crane, part of the rustler element. While the rest of the posse continued on their trail, King was taken back to jail, where he conveniently managed to escape by simply stepping out the back door while his horse was being sold.

It was alleged that a confederate had been waiting for him at the back door with a spare horse and that the confederate was Doc Holliday. Holliday was out of town at the time and certain elements seemed anxious to pin the robbery on him (as Waters seems to be, implying that Holliday had borrowed Wyatt's alleged "disguises" to rob the stage). Holliday apparently knew one of the accused holdup men, Bill Leonard, but no one has explained how Holliday happened to know that King would have an opportunity to slip out the back door of the jail while nobody was watching him. Josie Earp contended that the accusation against Holliday was intended to smear Wyatt by association. In either case, it certainly seems highly suspicious that King was able to slip out the back door of the jail with such ease. If, as Josie contends, Behan and his deputies were involved with the rustlers, that would seem to explain it.

Holliday, it should be mentioned, was certainly no choirboy, but every bit the killer he is frequently portrayed to be. He was very close with Wyatt Earp and with his brother, Morgan. (There is a story that Wyatt's friendship with him came about as a result of Holliday saving his life once.) John Henry Holliday was born in Georgia and attended dental school, then headed for the drier climate of the Southwest after he developed tuberculosis. Knowing that he had a fatal illness probably contributed to his wild character and utter fearlessness. (Bat Masterson wrote that he had a ". . . mean disposition and an ungovernable temper and under the influence of liquor was a most dangerous man.")

Following King's escape, accounts again begin to differ. Waters claims it was "The Earp gang" that had attempted to rob the stage, that Wyatt Earp had been involved in similar robberies with the Clantons, as well as with the three named outlaws, and that Wyatt Earp then offered money to Ike Clanton to betray his friends, Head, Leonard and Crane, so that they could be ambushed and killed, thereby making sure they would not be able to identify Wyatt as part of the gang. However, this seems improbable.

Josie Earp writes that Wyatt, in his capacity as a Wells Fargo detective and deputy U.S. Marshal, was looking for an informant and approached Billy Breakenridge in this regard, since he was known to have contact with the rustlers. Breakenridge came up with Ike Clanton. Wyatt then offered Clanton the reward money from Wells Fargo to double-cross his friends and swore to keep secret Clanton's part in the deal. Frank McLaury and Joe Hill, two other rustlers, were allegedly to help Ike Clanton pull off this double-cross in exchange for a thousand dollars apiece, which was a lot of money in those days. Clanton was supposedly anxious to know if this money was offered dead or alive. Obviously, if Leonard, Crane and Head were killed, he and the others could collect their reward and the robbers and their friends would never know who'd set them up. After being assured that it was dead or alive, Clanton allegedly accepted, but the deal fell apart when Head and Leonard were killed in a store robbery attempt in Hachita, New Mexico. Crane was killed shortly thereafter, along with Ike Clanton's father, while rustling cattle. (There have been allegations that the Earps ambushed Old Man Clanton and his party, but evidence points to the killings being executed by Mexican *federales*.)

Subsequently, Marsh Williams, a Wells Fargo agent, (according to Josie) had a few drinks too many in a saloon and told Ike Clanton that he'd never squeal on him about the double cross that Ike had agreed to, or (according to Waters) baited him in public repeatedly about the same subject. Either way, Clanton went into a storm of denial that quickly had the story spread all over town and this, ultimately, was what led to the gunfight. (Significantly, in Clanton's later testimony concerning the events leading up to the shoot-out, he claims that Wyatt invited him to have a drink with him at the bar, during which he asked him to double-cross his friends and Clanton indignantly turned him down. Only Wyatt Earp didn't drink. He detested alcohol and anytime someone asked him to have a drink, he had a cigar, instead.)

Subsequently, there was another stage robbery on September

8, following which Wyatt and Morgan were part of a posse that arrested Pete Spencer and Frank Stilwell, who was one of Behan's deputies. (So much for Behan's associating with the "better class" of people.) The arrest was based on a remark made by one of the outlaws during the robbery, in which money was referred to as "sugar." Stilwell was known to refer to money that way and other evidence pointed to both men. Waters claims that the Earps "enlisted" Stilwell and Spencer as part of the Clanton-McLaury gang and started spreading the news all over town that the Clantons and McLaurys were boasting that they'd kill the Earps for arresting two of their members. Josie Earp tells a different story.

According to Josie, Marietta Spencer (Pete's wife and a close friend of hers from the time they came to Tombstone together on the same train) ran into her house and told her that the rustlers were going to wipe out the Earps, claiming she'd heard it from Pete. (Part of Stilwell and Spencer's bail was put up by Ike Clanton, which seems to establish them as part of Clanton's bunch.) Marietta, who'd been abused by her husband and wanted out, told Josie that the rustlers planned to force Ike Clanton and Frank McLaury to kill the Earps. Apparently, Brocius, Ringo and the other rustlers weren't satisfied with Clanton and McLaury's denials concerning the planned double cross of Head, Leonard and Crane. Clanton and McLaury were told that after they'd called the Earps out, the other rustlers would be on hand to help them finish the job. (Joe Hill seems to have escaped their suspicion.) But the other rustlers never intended to be there and planned to have Clanton and McLaury face the Earps alone. A double cross for a double cross.

Ike Clanton then started boasting about what he was going to do to the Earps, and drinking heavily to get up his nerve. This led to a confrontation with Holliday, who called him out. Clanton claimed to be unarmed. Holliday called him a liar and offered to give him a chance to get a gun and come back. Some accounts report that Wyatt and his brothers separated them, others that they simply looked on with their hands ominously tucked inside their coats. Either way, later on that night, Clanton had apparently acquired a gun (if he hadn't had one all along) and was boasting about being "fixed right" for a showdown in the morning.

On October 26, Ike was in the streets early, armed with a rifle and a six-gun, bragging drunkenly about what he and his friends were going to do to the Earps and Holliday. (He seemed anxious to get Holliday, in particular.) Most accounts agree that Clanton had been up all night, drinking heavily. This would certainly seem odd. The Earps and Holliday had a reputation as gunfighters and if Clanton was planning to take them on, one would think he'd want to be clear-headed and well-rested, instead of staying up all night and getting liquored up. Yet this was what he undoubtedly did. On the other hand, if he believed that the other rustlers would back him up, then he might have felt more confident in the outcome.

When the Earps heard about Clanton going around the streets of Tombstone armed and drunk, boasting he was going to kill them, Virgil and Morgan came and arrested him. Waters writes that Virgil and Morgan came up behind Clanton, disarmed him, and then Virgil clubbed him over the head with his six-gun. Josie writes that Ike threw down on Virgil and Virgil knocked him down with his pistol barrel. Either way, Clanton was fined twenty-five dollars and released. (Most accounts agree on that, at least.) His weapons were confiscated and Virgil asked him where he wanted them left, so he could pick them up as he was leaving town. Clanton asked to have them left at the Grand Hotel, with the barman, which Virgil apparently did.

Again, there are conflicting stories here. Paula Mitchell Marks gives considerably more detail in her recent book than either Josie Earp does in her memoirs or Waters does in his book. And Marks goes out of her way to be as objective as possible. Supposedly, words were exchanged between the Earps and Clanton while he was in custody. Clanton was defiant, the Earps apparently offered him a chance to settle it right then and there, but Clanton, being outnumbered, wisely demurred. In any case, he paid the fine and was released.

Wyatt then ran into Tom McLaury outside the courtroom and "buffaloed" him (knocked him down.) Most accounts agree on that, as well, although there are slightly different versions of what happened. Wyatt either hit him with his fist or belabored him about the head with his pistol (which seems more likely) and left him lying bleeding in the street. McLaury claimed to be unarmed. Wyatt claimed he saw a gun tucked into McLaury's belt, beneath his coat. (But if he did, in fact, see a gun, one wonders why he did not arrest and disarm him.) Either way, Wyatt himself admitted to "buffaloing" Tom McLaury to "take the fight out of him." Within the hour, Frank McLaury and Billy Clanton showed up in town. Both armed. Josie writes that all four of them then started moving around the town, checking the corrals, looking for their reinforcements, which never showed up. Waters writes that Frank McLaury made "several trips by foot to nearby stores."

A significant witness enters the picture here. Railroad engineer H.F. Sills, who knew none of the participants and whose testimony in the subsequent trial was pivotal, had arrived in town only that day. He saw four or five men standing in front of the O.K. Corral and overheard them threatening to kill Virgil Earp and his party. Sills then asked around to find out who Virgil Earp was and warned him. He was also one of the witnesses to the shoot-out.

Josie writes that Virgil was urged by some of the town's citizens to arrest the outlaws immediately, but he replied that he'd simply rather let them "have their mouth" and then leave town. Waters writes that Johnny Behan urged Virgil to disarm the crowd, but that Virgil refused and said he wanted to give them a chance to fight.

Josie writes that Johnny Behan then went to the Clantons and the McLaurys to "get a little publicity, since he knew he had nothing to fear from his friends." According to Behan's statement later, he tried to disarm them, but found that Ike Clanton and Tom McLaury were not armed, whereas Frank McLaury and Billy Clanton refused to give up their guns, for fear of the Earps. (Clanton apparently tried twice to arm himself. Once when he tried to claim his weapons at the Grand Hotel, but the barman, seeing that he was drunk or hungover and still bleeding from being knocked on the head, refused to give them to him. He also went into Spangenberg's gun store, but was unable to obtain a weapon there, either. He seems to have been in pretty bad shape.)

Josie writes that Frank McLaury then told Behan to disarm the Earps. (A request that seems ridiculous, since Wyatt and Virgil were law officers with the power to deputize Morgan and, I suppose, Holliday.) Waters gives Behan's statement that it was his own idea to disarm the Earps. In either case, Behan succeeded in disarming no one. At that point, he stayed well out of it. As a sheriff, he does not seem to have been very effective.

And now comes the famous scene. Wyatt, Virgil, and

Morgan, the three "fighting Earps," along with Doc Holliday, stalking down the street, going to confront the Clantons and the McLaurys at the O.K. Corral. According to some, it was a justifiable shoot-out, with the Earps only defending themselves and ridding Tombstone of some desperate outlaws. According to others, it was cold-blooded murder, with the Earps shooting while the Clanton bunch had their hands in the air.

So what really happened?

As best as it seems possible to reconstruct the incident, Paula Mitchell Marks has done the most thorough job in her outstanding book, *And Die in the West: The Story of the O.K. Corral Gunfight*. Unlike most cinematic depictions, the Earps did not stride down the street all abreast. Virgil and Wyatt walked ahead of Doc and Morgan. Virgil had given Holliday his shotgun and had taken Doc's cane, which he was holding in his gun hand, which would seem to indicate that he was hoping to avoid bloodshed. Wyatt either had his gun out or in his coat pocket. Holliday was carrying Virgil's shotgun and his pistol. Morgan probably had his pistol out. Ike Clanton was apparently still unarmed. Billy Clanton was armed, as was Frank McLaury. Tom McLaury claimed to be unarmed, but might have had a gun concealed on his person.

The shoot-out did not, in fact, occur at the O.K. Corral. The O.K. Corral was actually ninety feet farther down the street, with its entrance fronting on Allen Street. The confrontation actually took place on a vacant lot fronting on Fremont Street, specifically, Lot 2, Block 17, between Fly's Boarding House and Photo Studio and the Harwood house.

The lot was rather small, only fifteen feet wide, and the antagonists were standing anywhere from three to ten feet apart, each side standing abreast in a line at an angle to Fremont Street, near the entrance to the lot. With their backs to Harwood's house and facing the street stood, left to right, Ike Clanton, Billy Clanton, Tom McLaury and Frank McLaury. Frank's horse was a short distance to his left, near the street, as he stood facing the Earps. Billy's horse was behind them and to the right. Behind the Clantons and the McLaurys, near the rear corner of the Harwood house, stood Billy Claiborne, a friend of theirs who was not involved in the shooting. Facing them, left to right, stood Wyatt Earp, Virgil Earp, Morgan Earp and Doc Holliday, the latter standing closest to the street.

Josie Earp claims that there was someone (she alleges it

might have been Johnny Behan) standing on the porch of Fly's Studio, behind the Earps, who fired after the first couple of shots were exchanged, causing the Earps to turn in that direction and, as a result, allowing Tom McLaury to shoot Morgan in the back. Marks goes into some detail as to why this would have been improbable, but she omits the single greatest reason why this probably never happened: It seems highly unlikely, given armed opponents facing them and with shots *already fired,* that the Earps would have turned their backs on them.

One witness reported having overheard Morgan Earp say to Doc Holliday, as they were approaching the lot, "Let 'em have it!" and Doc replying, "All right!" This is generally used as proof by the anti-Earp faction that the Earps intended shooting from the very start. Josie, in fact, confirms this exchange. However, in this case, I am inclined to accept her explanation that while the hot-blooded Holliday and the equally short-tempered Morgan intended to shoot, Virgil was still hoping to avoid bloodshed. Otherwise, he would not have been holding Doc's cane in his gun hand. What Wyatt intended cannot be known for a fact.

Stories differ as to what happened from that point on. One version has it that one or several of the Earps said something to the effect of, "All right, you sons of bitches, you have been looking for a fight and you can have it!" After which Virgil said, "Throw up your hands!" There is, however, some question as to which of the two remarks came first. Other versions have Virgil saying, "I have come to disarm you" or "We have come down here to disarm you and arrest you." Virgil himself later said his words were, "Boys, throw up your hands, I want your guns."

One account has it that Tom McLaury's response to this was to throw open his coat and say he wasn't armed. In this version, Billy Clanton also said, "Don't shoot me, I don't want to fight!" and either threw up his hands or held them out in front of him. (Despite the references to Tom's coat, the coroner testified that he had not been wearing one, as did another witness. He might have thrown open a vest.) Another version has it that on their approach, Frank McLaury and Billy Clanton put their hands on their six-shooters. (Wyatt claimed this was what happened.) Virgil said they drew their pistols and started to cock them after he told them to put their hands up. His response was to raise his own hands (still holding the cane in his right hand) and say, "Hold on! I don't want that!"

Josie tells a slightly different story. She says that Virgil said, "Hold on, I don't mean *that*!" Only she claims he wasn't talking to the Clantons, as everyone believed, but to Doc and Morgan, whom he heard cocking their own weapons. Either way, it seems that Virgil was hoping to avoid any shooting.

Two shots then followed in rapid succession, from two different guns, almost simultaneously. Paula Mitchell Marks carefully examines the different versions of the story. According to Wyatt and Virgil Earp, Billy Clanton fired first and Wyatt second. Billy fired at Wyatt, Wyatt shot at Frank McLaury, whom he judged to be the most dangerous. Frank was hit in the stomach. Wyatt later claimed he never drew or fired until after Billy and Frank had drawn their pistols. As Marks quite correctly points out, this is utter nonsense. Unless Wyatt was capable of exceeding light speed, like Dr. Darkness, his reaction time would never have allowed him to draw and fire if Billy and Frank already had their guns out. And considering how close they all were, he would have been shot for certain.

The other version is that Doc fired first and Morgan second. Josie claims that this was "absolutely true." Marks believes that Wyatt and Virgil were covering up for Doc and Morgan and I'm inclined to agree.

Doc was probably the instigator, which would certainly fit with his personality, and it must have been Doc who fired and shot Frank McLaury in the stomach. Morgan shot Billy Clanton in the chest just as Billy was drawing. Billy's shot went wild. Billy then went down. He was hit in the chest and wrist, but transferred his gun to his left hand and kept on shooting. Ike Clanton ran and was apparently not shot at. (Marks reports another version, that there was a brief scuffle between Ike and Wyatt and that Ike then ran into Fly's Studio.) Tom McLaury ducked behind Billy's horse.

Then, Josie claimed, someone shot from Fly's porch, which was behind the Earps, and they turned around, at which point Tom shot Morgan in the back, shooting across the saddle of Billy's horse. (This part I don't believe, partly for the reason I've already mentioned and partly because no other accounts report gunfire coming from Fly's Studio. I also find it hard to believe that Billy's horse would not have shied at the first sound of gunfire. It's possible the animal was used to the noise, but I have a good deal of experience with both horses and firearms and the two generally don't mix. There is also the question of whether or not Tom McLaury was armed. It's possible he had a pistol concealed on him all along, though one wasn't found on the scene. However, Johnny Behan might have lifted it, to help discredit the Earps. It's also possible that Tom might have used the Winchester in the scabbard on Billy's saddle. Or, in fact, he might have been unarmed, after all. In any case, there is no solid evidence that he was.)

Frank then ducked behind his own horse. Doc had backed away slightly, into the street and out of the smoke. (Unlike modern gunpowder, the black powder of the day gave off a lot of smoke.) Holliday seems to have holstered his pistol and had the shotgun ready. Morgan snapped off a shot at Tom, missed, grazed his horse, which bolted, exposing him, and Doc let him have both barrels. Billy was still in the fight, but couldn't shoot straight anymore. Frank seems to have been trying to lead his horse away, using it for cover. (Considering all the gunfire, which must have had the animal shying, and the fact that he'd been shot in the stomach, Frank must have had his hands full, to say the least.) Billy shot Virgil in the calf. Seriously wounded, Billy was still game, but apparently could no longer shoot with any accuracy.

Tom stumbled a short distance down Fremont Street and fell. Billy remained more or less in his original position. Morgan was hit, probably by Billy, but managed to get back up and continue shooting, concentrating on Frank. Holliday was also concentrating his fire on Frank, while Wyatt and Virgil seem to have been concentrating their fire on Billy. Frank managed to get to the middle of Fremont Street and was apparently staggering from his wound and having trouble controlling his horse, which finally broke and ran. Frank then shouted something at Doc, "I've got you now!" or words to that effect, and shot Doc in the hip, but Doc's holster deflected the bullet and he wasn't wounded except for a bruise, though he believed he had been "shot through."

Morgan and Doc both thought it was their shots that finished Frank. (Although it might have been Wyatt's.) There is some question as to whether Frank was still trying to shoot or was running away. In either case, he caught a bullet in the head and that was that. He died on the sidewalk, even as Doc was running up to him with his revolver out, intent on finishing him. Billy Clanton and Tom McLaury were carried away into a nearby house, where both expired of their wounds soon afterward. Ike Clanton kept on running and was eventually arrested on Tough Nut Street, some distance away, and temporarily taken into custody.

The whole gunfight probably lasted no more than thirty seconds, if that long. Marks reports the total number of shots fired as between twenty-five and thirty, although it's impossible to say for certain. Frank McLaury had two bullets in him. One in the stomach and one through the cranium, beneath the right ear. Tom McLaury had twelve buckshot wounds in his right side, closely grouped, indicating that the range had been very short, since the shot had hardly dispersed. Billy Clanton had been shot three times, once through the wrist (the impact broke his arm), once in the chest and through the lung, and once beneath the twelfth rib on the left side. The latter wound was fatal. Virgil was shot in the calf (the bullet passed clean through) and Morgan was the most seriously wounded of the Earps, shot through the right shoulder at an angle. The bullet chipped one of his vertebrae, barely missing the spinal cord, and exited through the other shoulder. Wyatt and Doc were unhurt, with the exception of the bullet that had harmlessly grazed Holliday's hip. When you compare the number of shots that were reported as being fired to the number of hits, you have some idea of just how "accurate" a frontier gunfight could be. Shooting accurately under stress, as any modern cop who's had the experience can tell you, is extremely difficult and the inherent accuracy of firearms in those days, as well as the quality of the ammunition, was nothing like it is today.

For a full, detailed examination of the story, I highly recommend the Paula Mitchell Marks book as being the most informative. She gives the most complete picture of the events leading up to the shoot-out, the subsequent trial and what happened afterward. Her book is a marvelous piece of scholarship, highly readable and entertaining. The memoirs of Josie Earp, edited by Glenn Boyer, also make wonderful reading and tell much more of Wyatt Earp's story, from after the shoot-out to his death.

To briefly summarize the aftermath, there was a trial and the Earps were acquitted. However, there was divided feeling in the town of Tombstone (and apparently there still is to this day) and there was reportedly some fear about a "cowboy raid" in reprisal, though no such raid ever materialized. Ike Clanton continued trying to get the Earps convicted of murder, but without success. Soon afterward, Virgil was shot by an unknown assailant with a shotgun. He was wounded in the side and in the arm, which necessitated the removal of his elbow joint, leaving him crippled for life. The assailant may have been Ike Clanton. His hat was found at the scene, but Clanton claimed it was a frame, that someone had stolen it and put it there.

Then Morgan was shot through a window while he was playing pool with Robert Hatch, proprietor of the Alhambra saloon. A second shot narrowly missed Wyatt, who was watching the game. The bullet hit Morgan's spinal cord and he died, supposedly telling Wyatt, "They got me, Wyatt. Don't let them get you." The murderers of Morgan appear to have been Frank Stilwell, Pete Spencer, and a half-breed named Florentino Cruz, also known as Indian Charlie. Virgil later left for Colton, California (home of the Earps' parents) with his wife, Allie, and Morgan's body.

At the train depot in Tucson, the Earps spotted Frank Stilwell. Ike Clanton was there, as well, though there is some question as to whether he was actually on the scene or nearby, waiting for Stilwell. It appears to have been another try for the Earps, only Stilwell got more than he bargained for. Wyatt was there with his brother Warren, Doc Holliday, Texas Jack Johnson and Sherm McMasters. There was a lot of shooting, though no one seems to have witnessed it, and Stilwell's body was found on the tracks, riddled with bullets and buckshot. Ike evidently ran again.

Even Josie admits that "This act put Wyatt outside the law." Johnny Behan subsequently organized a posse to go after Wyatt and his bunch. Interestingly, Behan's posse was composed of rustlers, among them Johnny Ringo, one of their leaders. While Behan's posse unsuccessfully chased Wyatt's group, Wyatt and the others rode through the mountains around Tombstone, looking for the other assassins. They got Indian Charlie at a wood camp and shot him dead. Later, they were ambushed at a water hole and Wyatt killed Curly Bill Brocius, though rumors persisted long afterward that Curly Bill was still alive. With a warrant out for him, Wyatt then left Arizona and went to Colorado, along with Doc. The Earps went to

Gunnison, and Doc went to Denver, where he was arrested and turned to Bat Masterson for help. Masterson, a lawman in Trinidad at the time, didn't like Holliday, but out of friendship for Wyatt, he managed to keep Holliday from being extradited to Arizona. Holliday went to Pueblo, then to Leadville for a time, where he gambled and got into more trouble, and eventually wound up in Glenwood Springs, where his tuberculosis finally killed him. He died on November 8, 1887, at the age of thirty-five. His last words were, "This is funny." God knows what he meant, but perhaps he thought that after the kind of life he'd lived, it was ironic that he would die in bed.

Johnny Ringo was found dead, shot through the head, in West Turkey Creek Canyon in the Chiricahua Mountains. It was alleged that Wyatt stole back into Arizona with Doc and killed him, but there is no evidence to support this and it seems improbable. It's not clear if Ringo's death was murder or suicide.

Ike Clanton was shot dead while rustling cattle in Eagle Creek, in June of 1887.

Virgil became a private investigator in Colton and was later elected marshal. He died of pneumonia in Nevada, in 1905.

Johnny Behan went into politics, served in the Spanish American War and the Chinese Boxer Rebellion, then died in Arizona in 1912, of arteriosclerosis and Bright's disease.

Bat Masterson eventually came back east, to New York City, where he became a writer. (A noble profession, indeed.) He wrote some magazine articles based on his experiences on the frontier and then became a sports writer for the *Morning Telegraph*. He died at his desk, of a heart attack, at the age of sixty-seven.

Wyatt and Josie travelled extensively throughout the West. Wyatt apparently did some Wells Fargo detective work and bounty hunting, gambled, went to Alaska during the Klondike gold rush, tried some mining and became very successful as a saloonkeeper. Wyatt and Josie then returned to California, to the small desert town of Vidal, where they kept a modest home and frequently ventured out on mining expeditions, without much success. He had some contact with movie people, whom he found to be a bunch of "damn fool dudes," though he did become good friends with William S. Hart and Tom Mix. On January 12, 1929, he died in bed, with Josie at his side, at the age of eighty-one.

Was Wyatt a hero or a loose cannon? A fearless lawman or a thug with a badge? The answer is that he was probably a bit of all of those. It took hard men to tame the Old West and often those men walked on both sides of the law. Of all the Earps, Virgil seems to have been the one who didn't want the fight to happen. Morgan apparently did, as did Doc. Wyatt? It's impossible to say for certain.

Was it murder? By our modern legal definitions, it most certainly was. I don't believe that any of the Clanton bunch fired first. I think they suddenly realized that they were in over their heads, particularly since Ike (and probably Tom, as well) was unarmed and Ike was not in good shape. I tend to believe the story of the other rustlers double-crossing them. I think they expected help and when it didn't materialize, they realized they were in trouble.

Was what the Earps did justified? By our standards today, the answer has to be no. But this was the Old West, the reality and not the myth, and standards were different. The hero did not wait for the bad guys to draw first. And Doc and Morgan didn't. In fact, it's possible that when Tom McLaury threw open his vest or coat to show he was unarmed, the motion prompted the hair-trigger Holliday to fire. Or maybe Holliday simply didn't want to waste any more time with disarming outlaws and fining them, only to have them come back and make more threats against him, perhaps even carry them out.

In the Old West, the law was most often found at the barrel of a gun. These days, the law shoots blanks and succeeds only in disarming law-abiding citizens. Today, Internal Affairs would have had the Earps for breakfast and they would have wound up in jail. In fact, modern police officers have a term for gung-ho cops—the "Wyatt Earp Syndrome."

Tombstone was certainly a wild town, but was it really any wilder than some of our modern cities? I often wonder what Wyatt Earp would have made of the current crime problem in Washington, D.C., or Miami? I suspect he might have laconically echoed Doc Holliday's last words. . . .

"This is funny."

Simon Hawke
Denver, Colorado

STEVEN BRUST ===========

___JHEREG 0-441-38554-0/$3.95
There are many ways for a young man with quick wits and a quick
sword to advance in the world. Vlad Taltos chose the route of the
assassin and the constant companionship of a young jhereg.

___YENDI 0-441-94460-4/$3.50
Vlad Taltos and his jhereg companion learn how the love of a good
woman can turn a cold-blooded killer into a <u>real</u> mean S.O.B...

___TECKLA 0-441-79977-9/$3.50
The Teckla were revolting. Vlad Taltos always knew they were lazy,
stupid, cowardly peasants...revolting. But now they were revolting
against the empire. No joke.

___TALTOS 0-441-18200/$3.50
Journey to the land of the dead. All expenses paid! Not Vlad Taltos'
idea of an ideal vacation, but this was work. After all, even an
assassin has to earn a living.

___COWBOY FENG'S SPACE BAR AND GRILLE
0-441-11816-X/$3.95
Cowboy Feng's is a great place to visit, but it tends to move around
a bit—from Earth to the Moon to Mars to another solar system—
and always just one step ahead of whatever mysterious conspiracy is
reducing whole worlds to radioactive ash.
